SHERLOCK HOLMES
The Devil's Dust

ALSO AVAILABLE FROM TITAN BOOKS

Sherlock Holmes: The Patchwork Devil
Cavan Scott

Sherlock Holmes: The Labyrinth of Death
James Lovegrove

Sherlock Holmes: The Thinking Engine
James Lovegrove

Sherlock Holmes: Gods of War
James Lovegrove

Sherlock Holmes: The Stuff of Nightmares
James Lovegrove

Sherlock Holmes: The Spirit Box
George Mann

Sherlock Holmes: The Will of the Dead
George Mann

Sherlock Holmes: The Breath of God
Guy Adams

Sherlock Holmes: The Army of Dr Moreau
Guy Adams

Sherlock Holmes: A Betrayal in Blood
Mark A. Latham

Sherlock Holmes: The Legacy of Deeds
Nick Kyme

Sherlock Holmes: The Red Tower
Mark A. Latham

COMING SOON FROM TITAN BOOKS

Sherlock Holmes: The Vanishing Man
Philip Purser-Hallard

SHERLOCK HOLMES
The Devil's Dust

JAMES LOVEGROVE

TITAN BOOKS

Sherlock Holmes: The Devil's Dust
Print edition ISBN: 9781785653612
Electronic edition ISBN: 9781785653629

Published by Titan Books
A division of Titan Publishing Group Ltd
144 Southwark St, London SE1 0UP

First edition: July 2018
2 4 6 8 10 9 7 5 3 1

A CIP catalogue record for this title is available from the British Library.

Printed and bound in the United States.

SHERLOCK HOLMES
The Devil's Dust

FOREWORD

The early portion of my friend Mr Sherlock Holmes's career is to a large extent *terra incognita* as far as these humble memoirs of mine are concerned. In my defence, I am hardly spoiled for choice when it comes to selecting material suitable to present to my readers. The commissions Holmes received were sporadic during the years when he was establishing himself in his unique vocation, for he had yet to garner the reputation – a reputation I have gone some small way towards fostering – that would lead to more extraordinary and compelling cases being brought to his attention.

One episode from this period of his life nevertheless clamours to be recounted. It tells how Holmes crossed paths – and swords – with a certain adventurer whose prowess as a big game hunter was second to none, and whose escapades on the African continent were becoming the stuff of legend, even as the man himself was entering the twilight of old age.

Here, then, is a narrative detailing how Sherlock Holmes, a man of mind, met Allan Quatermain, a man of action, and the dramas that ensued.

John H. Watson, MD, 1904

CHAPTER ONE

A FRAUDULENT CLIENT AND A FAMILIAR ONE

"I assure you, sir," said Sherlock Holmes, "I shall not be taking your case."

The man seated opposite him was agog. I myself was not a little surprised.

"But… But…" Mr Farley Danvers spluttered. "For heaven's sake, why?"

"For these reasons." Holmes ticked them off on his fingers one by one. "First, you are not, as you claim, a concert pianist. Second, you do not have a twin brother, identical or otherwise. Third, you are in the habit of not paying bills promptly. You are, to put it bluntly, a cheat, and I want no truck with you."

Danvers brandished a chequebook. "You would refuse money?"

"You do not deny my accusations?"

"I deny them most vehemently. I have set out the facts of my predicament with all honesty. I am willing to employ you, at the going rate, to conduct an investigation into the theft of my property. Surely you cannot turn me down."

"I can and I shall," said Holmes. "Your game, as I see it, Mr Danvers, is to make me complicit in an insurance swindle. You wish me to prove that certain valuables were stolen from you and pawned, whereas in truth they have not been stolen at all. You would have me write a letter to your insurers, confirming the loss, whereupon they would recompense you. You would then use some of the money to get said precious items out of hock, and keep the remainder as profit. In short, your intention is to use my good name in order to further your immoral ends. Is that not so?"

"Not a bit of it!" the other declared.

"To make matters worse, I foresee that you will dun me at the first opportunity. I would wager that any cheque you write will not be honoured by your bank."

"My credit is as good as any man's."

"I doubt it," said Holmes. "And now, I would be grateful if you would see your way to leaving, this instant. Or will I have to remove you forcibly?"

With many further expostulations of indignation, Farley Danvers stormed out of our rooms.

I shot my friend a searching glance. "Really, Holmes, are you sure he was a crook? He seemed perfectly upright to me."

"Quite sure, Watson. Everything he said was sheer, unadulterated twaddle. Concert pianist? Bah! Did you observe his fingers? Those were not the fingers of a man proficient in that art. The nails were too long, for one thing. A professional pianist trims his short. The tips were not flattened, either, as the fingertips are of somebody who regularly practises at the keyboard for hours. Nor did his hands have the musculature which develops from such activity, particularly in the palms and the wrists."

"I see. So why pretend to be one at all?"

"For effect. Concert pianist, after all, is altogether a more impressive occupation than, say, wine merchant, Danvers's actual livelihood. And in anticipation of your next question, his tie sported the coat of arms of the Worshipful Company of Vintners."

"But how did you know he was not a twin?"

"Danvers referred to his brother by name three times. Twice it was Edward; the third time, Edwin. Who would misremember their own brother's name?"

"It may have been a slip of the tongue."

"Hardly likely, Watson! Have you ever got your late brother's name wrong? Besides, he was wearing a gold signet ring bearing a family crest. The ring had the patina of age, denoting that it must be an heirloom passed down through the generations. Such an item of jewellery traditionally goes to the first-born son, yet Danvers averred that his brother was his senior by some five minutes. Why, then, would Danvers have the ring rather than Edward – or, as it may be, Edwin – unless Edward or Edwin was a fabrication?"

"And his failure to pay bills promptly?"

"As to that, did you not notice how badly the hair at the back of his head was cut, while the rest was comparatively neat?" said Holmes. "It is clear his barber chose to get away with the minimum amount of effort, doing a shoddy job with the parts of hair that Danvers would not himself see. That suggests disgruntlement."

"Or else a slapdash barber."

"I grant you the possibility. However, Danvers's shoes had recently been re-soled, and again, as with the barber, the cobbler was less attentive to his task than he ought to have been. The cutting, gluing and nailing were all of poor quality. One negligent tradesman might be regarded as misfortune. Two begins to look like a pattern. A customer who consistently pays late is a customer who receives poor service."

"So when Danvers said that he suspected his brother of being behind the disappearance of various treasures from his household…?"

"It was the purest hogwash," said Holmes. "I believe he would have had me hunting high and low for the non-existent sibling."

"But why invent a brother at all?"

"What a tragic yarn Danvers spun. All that stuff about this identical twin who had fallen on hard times and whom he had invited under his roof and taken under his wing – this layabout who had then rewarded his kindness by pilfering from him. It is the 'identical' part of the story that counts, for if I had managed to trace the pawnbroker now in possession of the articles and asked for a description of the man who sold them to him…"

I finished the sentence. "The description would have matched that of Danvers himself."

"In short, Farley Danvers was, in a rather clumsy way, covering himself against such a contingency," said Holmes. "He would have signed the pawnbroker's statutory declaration form as 'Edward Danvers' and would swear blind, when pressed, that it was not he who brought the items to the premises but his twin."

"Well," I said, "all in all it's a good thing you saw through him. You might otherwise have wasted a lot of time. Ought we not report him to the authorities?"

"Oh, even the dullest-witted insurance clerk will see through his tissue of lies. No, Watson, we need not detain ourselves over Mr Farley Danvers a moment longer. The impertinent fool will get what he deserves, with or without our involvement."

"What a shame, though, that he was not a genuine paying client. You could do with the money, Holmes, if you don't mind my saying so. Work has been thin on the ground for you lately."

In truth, at that time – the autumn of 1884 – Sherlock

Holmes was anything but overburdened with employment. His career as a consulting detective was, if not in its infancy, then certainly experiencing the pangs of adolescence. It had its peaks and its troughs, but signally more of the latter than the former. Clients were not falling over one another to get to his door. Indeed, the previous year had yielded but one case that I have since considered fit to chronicle – the business with the swamp adder at Stoke Moran – while the few others proved tawdry, uninteresting affairs. The same was true of 1884, save for the events I am setting down in these pages. Holmes had sufficient occupation to generate a modest income, but worldwide renown and financial security still lay some years in the future.

"Something will turn up, Watson," my friend said, reaching for his pipe. "Something always does."

"I do hope so," I said, with feeling.

Moments later, Mrs Hudson entered. "You have another client, Mr Holmes," said she.

"There, Watson," said Holmes with an arch look. "What did I tell you? Show him up, my good woman. Let us see the cut of his jib."

"The client," said Mrs Hudson, "is already here."

"Downstairs, you mean?" Holmes gave vent to a mildly exasperated sigh. "Well then, I repeat, show the gentleman up."

"The client is no gentleman."

"Gentleman, commoner, crossing-sweeper – I don't care a fig about his social standing. As long as his coin is good, I will see him."

"Mr Holmes," said our landlady, folding her arms beneath her bosom, "perhaps I am failing to make myself understood."

"There is no 'perhaps' about it, Mrs Hudson. You are being positively obtuse."

At this point I intervened. "Holmes, can you not tell? Unless I miss my guess entirely, the client to whom Mrs

Hudson is referring is none other than herself."

The lady nodded, declaring, "Thank heavens one of you is not quite so slow on the uptake."

"You, madam," said Holmes, "are presenting yourself before me as a client?"

"Is that a problem, sir?"

He appeared to give the matter some thought, then shrugged his shoulders. "Not in the least. It comes as a surprise, that is all."

"You can make time for me?"

"I believe I can squeeze you into my hectic schedule."

"I shall pay the going rate," Mrs Hudson said as she seated herself in the armchair to which Holmes directed her.

"You will do no such thing," my friend countered sharply. "You are an excellent landlady. You are a cook of no mean ability. And you tolerate my less desirable habits with a forbearance a stoic would envy. I consider those qualities more than adequate recompense for whatever professional services I may now render you."

"I realise that you sometimes have trouble meeting the monthly rent and that on those occasions Dr Watson takes it upon himself to pay the lion's share."

"Tut!" Holmes flapped a dismissive hand. "Let us hear no more of this. Either I work for you *pro bono* or I do not work for you at all. That is the end of the matter."

"Very well." From the pocket of her apron Mrs Hudson drew a folded letter. "It is this that has prompted me to seek your assistance. It came just now by the third post."

She passed the letter to Holmes, who unfolded it with a peremptory shake of the hand and commenced perusal of its contents.

"I see," he said ruminatively. "I see. Hum! And who is this Ada Biddulph? A friend of yours, obviously."

"My oldest friend who, like me, lets rooms in her house in order to make ends meet."

"Yes, I gather as much from her missive. The mention of a lodger is something of a giveaway. What a bind she is in, and no mistake. Neighbours and police all convinced of her culpability! Little wonder her tone is so agitated, not to mention her handwriting. She strives to maintain a neat copperplate throughout, yet her efforts repeatedly degenerate into scrawl and her lines are anything but straight. She is a woman, one may infer, for whom a good appearance is everything, and now her world is crumbling."

"Quite so."

"Holmes," I said. I had discerned – as he had not – a distinct impatience beneath the composure of Mrs Hudson's features. "Perhaps you would see fit to share with me the nature of the predicament in which this Mrs Biddulph finds herself."

"Is this so that you might make notes, Watson, as I have seen you doing of late?"

"I simply would rather not feel excluded from the conversation."

"But you *are* in the habit of making notes about my cases, are you not? I have observed you scribbling away in various journals and loose-leaf pads, during and immediately after the conducting of my investigations. Do not think that I have not. You seem to be treating me much as though I am one of your patients, in need of study and diagnosis. What plans do you have for these 'case histories' you compile? Do you perchance intend to publish them one day?"

"It is a possibility, I suppose. I have not given it a great deal of thought. I just find your methods intriguing and have begun enshrining them on paper for my own satisfaction."

"But maybe also for posterity."

"That remains to be seen. In the meantime, the letter?"

"Yes. Here."

Holmes handed it to me with a wry smile. He was not wrong, in so far as I was indeed considering working up my notes on his cases into narratives. I had long harboured ambitions of pursuing a literary career, as a sideline to my medical practice. Holmes, who by then had been my companion and cohabitee for the best part of four years, fascinated me. His character and his talents were so unusual, so idiosyncratic, that I felt them worthy of analysis. In time, I would indeed settle down to publishing the accounts of his exploits that have since brought me a modicum of acclaim. It would be another three years, however, before the first of these, *A Study in Scarlet*, saw print.

I cast an eye over Mrs Biddulph's letter. Following a brief salutation to Mrs Hudson, addressing her by her Christian name, the text ran thus:

> I write to you in a state of some consternation, my hand trembling such that I can scarcely keep pen to paper. Lord, what torment the past twenty-four hours have been! What alarums and excursions I have had to endure!
>
> It began with my discovery of Mr Niemand, dead in his sitting room. You know Mr Niemand, of course, the fellow to whom I am letting my basement. Lately from India, during the month he has been with me he has been a model tenant – not at all like that disorderly Bohemian whom you house under your roof and about whom you have had cause to grumble more than once.

I chuckled to see Holmes referred to thus, and my friend, fully aware which passage of the letter I had just scanned, shot me a look of reproof mixed with chagrin.

You can well imagine my horror, upon bringing down Mr Niemand's breakfast to him yesterday morning in the basement flat, to find his body sprawled upon the floor. I knew at once, from a single glance, that he was deceased. The utter immobility of a corpse cannot be misidentified. It was the same with my husband. The sight of George sitting there in that armchair, quite dead, is etched in my memory, as fresh as if it were yesterday rather than five years ago. You can just tell, can't you, when the soul has fled the flesh? It brings such a terrible stillness.

I turned tail and ran to summon the nearest constable, and soon my home was overrun with policemen. Amidst all the chaos – the prodding, the nosing, the peering – a consensus seemed to emerge. Mr Niemand had been poisoned. So said the ferrety-looking detective inspector who assumed charge of the case. I never quite caught his name. French-sounding. Lagrange, I think it is.

There was blood around Mr Niemand's nose and mouth, you see, considerable quantities of it. I had not beheld this detail myself, since I had quit the room as soon as I realised he was dead, for fear that I might faint. The inspector told me also that Mr Niemand had egested the contents of his stomach rather violently. This I had been aware of, thanks to the smell in the room.

Imagine my shock when it became apparent that Inspector Lagrange – or whatever his name was – deemed me a likely candidate for being Mr Niemand's poisoner. Although he did not come out and say it in so many words, his insinuations left me in no doubt that, not only had a capital crime been committed, but I was the chief suspect. I, after all, had prepared the meal which Mr Niemand ate the night before and which, by Lagrange's presumption, had been laced with a lethal concoction.

You know as well as I do that I am the last person who could take the life of another. I appreciate that there are some who have cast aspersions upon me after George passed away. Certain of my neighbours hold the opinion that his demise was somehow my doing, for all that the doctor firmly pronounced the cause as a perforated stomach ulcer. Doubtless the inspector had been apprised of those rumours before he arrived at his conclusion. The local gossips would have wasted no time informing his constables, as they pursued their enquiries at other houses along the street. But I was not then a murderess and am not now!

All the same, a cloud of suspicion hangs over me, and Inspector Lagrange has constrained me to remain at home, on my own recognisance, and await further communication from him. Effectively, I am under house-arrest. A constable is stationed outside my door, ostensibly to discourage curiosity-seekers but really to keep an eye on me. I only hope I can prevail upon the fellow to let me take this letter to the postbox on the corner. I am sure, if I invite him to accompany me thither and back, that he will accommodate me.

I implore you, if you can, to help. I am at my wits' end. I did not sleep a wink last night, nor have I eaten a scrap of food since yesterday. A man has died on these premises, in horrible circumstances, and I am innocent of any wrongdoing, and yet I am terrified that I may be held to account.

Yours in desperation,
Ada

"The poor woman," I said, returning the letter to Mrs Hudson, who nodded feelingly.

"You are convinced there is nothing to the neighbours' assertion that Mrs Biddulph killed her husband?" Holmes asked her.

"Pure fiction," Mrs Hudson replied with vehemence. "Baseless and slanderous tittle-tattle. But I know how it arose. George Biddulph was, I regret to say, a drunkard and a beast of a man. He would use Ada cruelly when there was alcohol in him and sometimes when there was not. She put up with it for years, with saintly fortitude, and when he died she shed few tears. For that reason, it was assumed by the locals that she might have had a hand in his demise. She did not mourn as a recently bereaved wife ought – for which, who can blame her? – and even though it was common knowledge that her husband used to beat her, folk still thought the worst of her for not being devastated by his abrupt passing."

"What appalling hypocrisy," I said.

"That is the tenor of the area in which Ada lives. Notting Hill is not what one might call the most salubrious quarter of London. I myself am loath to venture there after dark."

"So Mr Biddulph's death by natural causes was merely that – death by natural causes," said Holmes.

"Not so surprising in a man fond of the bottle," I said.

"And with such a choleric disposition too," said Mrs Hudson. "The doctor was unequivocal in his verdict. Fatal blood poisoning arising from a perforated stomach ulcer, he said, and ruled that there was no suspicion of foul play. That, however, cut no mustard with Ada's neighbours, who reckon she must have slipped George strychnine or some other such poison."

"And now that her lodger, Mr Niemand, has actually died of poisoning," said Holmes, "it would seem to bear out their beliefs about Mrs Biddulph."

"Beliefs which Inspector Lagrange has allowed to infect his own reasoning," I said.

"'Lagrange' sounds remarkably similar to 'Lestrade', don't you think, Watson?"

"You are suggesting they are one and the same person?"

"By her own admission Mrs Biddulph did not apprehend his name clearly. She also describes him as 'ferrety-looking', which Lestrade undoubtedly is. Lagrange would appear to lack investigative rigour, and that too is a Lestradian trait, although one, amidst the plurality of Scotland Yard officials, not confined to him. All in all, the evidence points to the individual in question being our old friend and antagonist."

"Mr Holmes, I need to know," said Mrs Hudson. "Will you take the case?"

"I shall," said Holmes, "unhesitatingly."

"Thank you. That is a weight off my mind. I will write and inform Ada forthwith."

"I think we can do one better than that. Watson? Gather up hat and coat. We are going to pay a call on our not-so-merry widow."

"And I shall accompany you," said Mrs Hudson. "Ada can surely do with seeing a friendly face."

"My dear lady—" Holmes began, but a stern look halted him mid-protest.

"I shall accompany you," Mrs Hudson reiterated in a manner that brooked no further refusal and from Holmes received none.

CHAPTER TWO

INIGO NIEMAND'S LAST SUPPER

Hansoms were in short supply, so we walked the couple of miles to Notting Hill, passing through the canal-threaded quarter of Maida Vale popularly known as "London's Venice" and thence through Portobello and Ladbroke Grove. A late-afternoon fog had descended, dimming the sunlight to a shade of sepia that complemented the bronze and amber hues of the leaves, half of which still clung to the trees, the rest littering the ground. In Notting Hill itself the terraced houses seemed to huddle close together amidst the brumous haze, almost as though they were seeking out one another's company for comfort, or else conspiring.

Ada Biddulph owned a brick-faced three-storey dwelling whose front door was reached by a short flight of steps. A constable stood on the pavement outside, hunched in his cape with the disconsolate air of one who would rather be anywhere else. Holmes showed the fellow his card, which was subjected to a wary, purse-lipped scrutiny.

"Inspector Lestrade can vouch for me," Holmes said.

"I have heard him mention you once or twice, Mr Holmes," said the policeman.

"Then, by your leave, we are permitted to enter?"

"To be honest, sir, I am under no instruction to deter legitimate visitors, only those that have come to gawp."

Without another word Holmes rapped upon the door. Presently it was opened by a woman in middle age who regarded us through a pair of wire-rimmed spectacles with timid caution. Then her gaze fell upon Mrs Hudson, whereupon she at once gave a cry of delight. The two women knotted hands and embraced cordially, and there was much cooing.

Ada Biddulph was in appearance as unlike Mrs Hudson as it is possible to imagine. Where the latter was sturdy and doughty, the former was reed-thin and nervous-looking. It seemed a wonder that the two of them shared commonality, let alone were on closely amiable terms. Yet opposites attract, as the saying goes, and one need look no further than Holmes and me for proof of the adage – two men who were hardly cut from the same cloth but who had, for all our differences, forged a solid bond.

Once Mrs Hudson had made introductions and explained the nature of our errand, Mrs Biddulph invited us in. Soon we were settled in her parlour while she went to prepare a pot of tea, the revivifying qualities of which did much to dispel the chill that the foggy day had instilled within us.

Under interrogation by Holmes, Mrs Biddulph rehearsed the events of the previous morning. She told how she had taken breakfast on a tray down to her lodger, only to discover his body prone upon the sitting-room rug, arms outstretched, legs akimbo. His face was pressed to the floor, but what she could see of it presented a ghastly prospect, for it was reddened and swollen to a considerable degree.

"I set the tray down, somehow managing not to drop it," said she, "and hastened back upstairs. You may think me a coward for that."

"Not at all, madam," said Holmes.

Mrs Hudson, who was sitting beside her friend with a consoling arm about her shoulders, expressed similar sentiments.

"The smell in that room was already turning my stomach and making me lightheaded," Mrs Biddulph continued. "I did not want to pass out. That was my thinking."

"The smell of emesis?"

She nodded. "Horribly pungent, it was. I collared the nearest policeman. After that, everything became a daze, as in a dream. A nightmare, in point of fact, once Inspector Lagrange started levying his none too thinly veiled accusations."

"Lestrade, perhaps? I know almost every detective inspector in London and am unfamiliar with any Lagrange."

"Does his name matter? But yes, come to think of it, it may have been Lestrade. At any rate, I have been trying ever since to maintain equanimity in the face of horrendous circumstances, but it is hard." The pallor of the woman's complexion and the sunkenness of her eyes attested to the truth of her statement.

"You are coping admirably," Holmes assured her, "and it is my intention to dispel any shadow of suspicion that may have attached to you."

"Can you do that?"

"I can make every effort. Would you be so good as to show us to Mr Niemand's lodgings?"

Down a creaky uncarpeted back-staircase we went, the four of us, to enter a flat which consisted of a relatively spacious sitting-room with doors leading off to a small bedroom and tiny bathroom at the rear. The décor was plain and the atmosphere not as dingy as in many basement flats, for this one sat only partially below ground-level and the windows – particularly the large window at the front, which was part of a projecting bay shared with the storey above – let in a goodly amount of light.

Beyond the faint odour of digestive juices that lingered in the air, what was most notable about the place was its state of considerable disarray.

"The mess is the police's doing," Mrs Biddulph said. "Mr Niemand himself liked to keep things neat, but the police, in the course of their examinations, emptied out drawers, ransacked bookshelves, tossed papers around, and then left everything like this, all higgledy-piggledy and topsy-turvy. The only tidying they did was remove the rug upon which the body lay, and the body itself, of course, which they took out through the flat's own front door using the rug as a makeshift stretcher."

"I would rather a horde of rampaging Visigoths had trampled through the place than a cohort of Scotland Yarders," Holmes remarked. "It will be a miracle if any viable clues remain. Yet we should not lose hope. While much has been overturned, much may also have been overlooked."

So saying, he embarked upon one of his thorough and energetic inspections of a crime scene. He darted hither and yon across the flat, now standing on tiptoe, now going down on his knees, now crawling on all fours, and every so often emitting a gasp of exasperation or a murmur of intrigue.

All of this behaviour greatly bewildered Mrs Biddulph, patently enough that Mrs Hudson felt moved to offer her reassurance. "If there is something to be found, Ada, something beneficial to your situation, have no fear that Mr Holmes will find it. For all his eccentricities he is the sharpest man I have known."

I myself was not persuaded that Holmes's efforts would bear fruit. The chaos was simply too extensive. What order could he possibly derive from it?

Finally, after some twenty minutes, my friend stood erect,

quivering somewhat, like a pointer that has caught the scent.

"This is a fascinating state of affairs," he announced. "Fascinating. So much is missing here, so much that might have aided me in my deductions, yet what remains tells a singular story, one fraught with incongruities and inconsistencies. Mr Inigo Niemand was, I would submit, more than he purported to be. Mrs Biddulph, I recall you saying in your letter to Mrs Hudson that your lodger was 'lately from India'. Do I have that right?"

"He told me he had been working in Calcutta as a secretary at the Imperial Legislative Council and had resigned his position in order to return to England. He had grown tired of the tropical climate, he said, and had moreover contracted a couple of diseases which, though not life-threatening, had left him in poor sorts. He hoped that after a few months of recuperation back home he might be well enough again to seek fresh employment. In the meantime he had a small sum in savings upon which to live."

"Calcutta, eh?" said Holmes.

"I had no reason not to take him at his word. He was very tanned, and as for a weakened constitution, he comported himself with a marked fragility, not to say a reticence. He rarely left the house even on fine days, and when he did go out it was seldom for longer than half of an hour. He might manage to walk to the post office or to the newsagent to buy a paper, but that was it. Greater exercise than that seemed beyond him. His appetite was good, mind you, but then I am a dab hand in the kitchen, even if I do say so myself."

"Your culinary accomplishments put mine to shame, Ada," Mrs Hudson said.

"Mr Niemand did once suggest, jokingly, that I might like to use a little more spice in my recipes, but I imagine he had become accustomed to curries while abroad and found English cuisine bland by comparison."

"This India connection is all very well," said Holmes, "but I see no sign of it amongst Niemand's belongings. What I *have* found is this."

He ushered us into the bedroom and drew our attention to a figurine which lay half buried under scattered clothes. It was perhaps nine inches tall, was carved of some dark hardwood, and depicted a warrior-like individual with his head jutting forward and his tongue protruding to its root. Whorls were etched into his scalp, suggestive of curly hair, and in one hand he brandished a crudely rendered representation of a spear.

"Does that look Indian to any of you?" said Holmes. "It does not to me. I am no expert in the anthropological sciences, but I do not believe it to be the handiwork of a Hindu. On the contrary, I would wager good money on it being African in origin."

"Some kind of fetish," I hazarded.

"I would concur. The stance of this little fellow is aggressive, leading one to infer that he is a totem designed to ward off evil – although in that capacity it turns out that he was sadly deficient. Why would the employee of a company working out of India possess an artefact native to an entirely different continent?"

"Perhaps he picked it up on his journey home," I said. "If he travelled by sea all the way, rounding the Horn rather than taking one of the partially overland routes, his ship would have docked at ports in Africa. When I sailed to England from Karachi aboard the troopship *Orontes*, there were stopovers for resupply at Mombasa, Cape Town and Freetown, to name but three."

"For which reason the fetish, in itself, does not make a compelling argument that Niemand was not telling the truth. However, there are also these handkerchiefs to consider." Holmes held up a square of linen. "Here is one. Observe the monogram embroidered in the corner. The initials read 'B.W'. There are three more handkerchiefs identical to this and none of any other nature. Why does a man going by the name of Inigo Niemand have handkerchiefs monogrammed with initials not his own?"

"What if they are heirlooms?" Mrs Hudson said. "They are nice handkerchiefs. They must have cost a pretty penny. Perhaps he inherited them from a cousin, or a grandfather on his mother's side. If they were in my family, I should not want them to go to waste."

"Would one not unpick the stitching of the monogram, though, and have it replaced with one's own initials?"

"Sometimes it is not possible. The unpicking may ruin the integrity of the cloth."

"I bow to your expertise, Mrs Hudson. Nonetheless the anomaly piques my curiosity. For a third and final point of interest, the most significant of them all, let us return to the sitting-room."

As we reassembled in the sitting-room, Holmes bent and extricated a scrap of paper from beneath the writing desk which occupied an alcove by the bay window.

"I spied this earlier. You may recall seeing me stretched out upon my belly, peering under the desk. The police missed it entirely, of course. I should not wonder that it was lying in plain sight when they arrived, until one of them inadvertently kicked it with a clodhopping flat foot and it slid from view. Now, if you turn your gazes to the skirting-board over there below the window, you will see a pen lying on the floor adjacent. You will note that the pen is uncapped and that the cap lies some three yards distant, resting in the crack between two floorboards just there. Mrs Biddulph, the rug upon which Mr Niemand collapsed and which the police removed – it was positioned at the window end of the room?"

"It was."

"I thought as much. One can faintly discern its outline. The rectangular area of bare floor it used to cover is by a tiny margin less darkened and discoloured than the surrounding remainder. And Niemand's body lay pointed which way?"

"That way, his head towards the window."

"And thus also towards the section of skirting board where we see the cap-less pen. He was right-handed?"

"I think so. I am not sure."

"Either way, it does not matter much. The main thing is that he lay prostrate in this direction." Holmes swept a hand towards the bay window. "The piece of paper therefore might well have rested here, just beside him, before it was so carelessly kicked under the desk. The desk is within arm's reach of his position. The pen's cap is also not far. As for the pen itself, it could conceivably have fetched up where it is now after having rolled from his lifeless hand."

"He wrote something down as he lay dying," I said.

"Precisely. There is text upon the paper. See?"

Holmes indicated a row of jagged, uneven characters.

"There are flecks of blood, too," he added. "Along with those, one may descry the impression of the toe end of a boot sole. I would lay good odds on said footwear being the property of a constable."

He retrieved the pen and scribbled a quick line or two with it upon another scrap of paper. He held the two scraps side by side and seemed satisfied with his findings.

"Yes, the ink matches. A slight misalignment between the tines of the nib is discernible in both instances. I would aver that, *in extremis*, Niemand managed to reach up and snatch both pen and paper from the desk, and, even as he gasped his last, jotted down some morsel of information he wished to impart."

"Oh, the poor, brave man," Mrs Biddulph sighed, her eyes brimming with tears. "All this happened right here, just a floor below where I sat, unknowing. How dreadful. It hardly bears thinking about. If only he had cried out. I might have heard. I might have been able to help."

"The poison, if such was the cause of death, was fast-acting," said Holmes. "Niemand must have realised he had little time. His first and only imperative was to write this note, while he still could."

"He wanted to provide some clue as to who killed him," I said. "What does the note say?"

"Ah. There, I am afraid, I draw a blank. Take a look for yourself."

Niemand's message was barely legible, but I managed to make out seven distinct capital letters:

UTHULI L

"'Uthuli L,'" I said. "Could that be someone's name? Someone Indian, perhaps? In Afghanistan I knew a Sepoy with the forename Utphal. 'Utphal red the Unready' we called him, for he was always missing some piece of kit or other. We chevied him about constantly."

"The point of this delightful anecdote being…?"

"Well, the two sound similar – Uthuli and Utphal. And the 'L' could be an abbreviation of a surname."

"That is one possibility. We must also consider the likelihood that the message is not a name at all but the beginning of something longer, a phrase or sentence that Niemand was unable to complete before death overcame him. The progressive faintness and clumsiness of the letters implies a hand rapidly succumbing to enfeeblement."

I returned the scrap of paper to Holmes and he tucked it into a pocket.

"Are you going to share this intelligence with the police?" I enquired.

"At some point I no doubt shall, but for the time being, what they so blunderingly disregarded they do not deserve to know about. That includes the fetish and the handkerchiefs as well. I have a couple more questions for you, Mrs Biddulph, if I may, and then we shall leave you in peace."

"By all means, Mr Holmes. Ask away."

"Inigo Niemand was your lodger for a month, according to your letter to Mrs Hudson."

"That is so. A little under a month."

"You have indicated that he was reclusive."

"Yes. I put it down to his ill health. He preferred to stay indoors. I would go so far as to say he had an antipathy to daylight, for he habitually kept the curtains drawn."

"Interesting. Did he ever have visitors during the time he was renting from you?"

"He did not. No, I tell a lie. Someone did call by. Last Wednesday, I think it was, in the evening."

"You saw the person?"

"No. Since the flat has its own private front door, guests may come and go without entering the main part of the house, as may the lodger himself. That is very convenient for me, you can imagine. Whoever came on Wednesday, I heard him knock and I heard Mr Niemand invite him in, but beyond that I can tell you nothing about him."

"Him. So it was a man."

"It was a man. The sound of their conversation came up through the floorboards, and the voice that was not Mr Niemand's was male."

"Did you hear what either said?"

"I am no eavesdropper, Mr Holmes," Mrs Biddulph replied in a tone of mild affront. "Besides, it was muffled. I heard only the murmur of voices, not individual words."

"Did they argue?"

"Not as far as I could tell. Tone and volume remained at a civil level throughout."

"How long did the visitor stay?"

"An hour or thereabouts."

"Did you see him depart?"

"By then night had fallen and I had drawn the blinds. I heard the flat door open and close, but I did not feel moved to peek out, curious though I was about Mr Niemand's guest. The lodger's business is his own business. That is one of my cardinal rules as a landlady."

"Mine too," said Mrs Hudson. "Believe me," she added with some asperity, "given the queer practices Mr Holmes gets up to, I am glad I keep my nose out of it."

Holmes blithely ignored the jibe. "Has anybody called since?" he asked Mrs Biddulph.

"Not to my knowledge."

"Well, the presence of one anonymous visitor is at least more illuminating than none at all. Now we come to the question of Niemand's last supper. That would seem to lie near the heart of all this, if not right at its epicentre. Over there, at the foot of the stairs, is the breakfast tray, where you deposited it. Over here, upon the table, is the supper tray."

"Just so."

"The contents of the breakfast tray are untouched, of course. Niemand's supper, on the other hand, has been eaten. Not a morsel remains. I see a bowl which contained what appears to have been stew."

"Mutton stew."

"And a plate which, to judge by the crumbs, held bread."

"Two large hunks. The same meal as I myself ate."

"A hearty repast. Niemand used the bread to mop up the

liquid of the stew, down to practically the last drop. The swipe patterns which one can perceive amidst the dried remnants encrusting the bowl denote as much. From the table to the rug is a distance of some four or five paces, in the direction of the window. One may, then, infer that Niemand rose from his chair after he had finished his meal and that he did not get far. The poison struck and he staggered, beginning to feel its effects. He swooned. He fell. Knowing what was happening to him, he seized pen and paper and scribbled his desperate – if enigmatic – message, then expired."

All of the above actions Holmes mimed, reproducing Niemand's dying moments. I had long since apprehended that my friend had a thespian streak, and he would often indulge, as now, his flair for the dramatic.

He returned his attention to the supper tray. "You are in the practice, Mrs Biddulph, of leaving the tray overnight?"

"I pick it up when I bring down breakfast. I consider my daily duties as a landlady discharged with the provision of an evening meal. My work-day resumes at breakfast time."

"It remains here – cutlery, crockery, cruet set and all – until the next morning?"

"I have a second set of china for the exclusive use of my lodger, one I purchased cheap at a bric-a-brac shop on Portobello Road. Plates, bowls, cups, saucers, the lot. That way, should an item get broken, I do not mind so much for it is not my best tableware."

"All of this is good to know," said Holmes. "Would I be permitted to take the empty bowl away with me? I should like to subject it to analysis."

"It is yours."

"Thank you. And one last favour. Might I inspect the exterior of the house, back and front?"

Permission was granted, and Holmes spent some time in the yard, where I heard him rattle the windows at the rear of the flat. He spent some further time in the small light-well area out front, striding to and fro, crouching, squinting. At last he pronounced his survey complete and we took our leave. Holmes saluted the constable on sentry duty, eliciting a disgruntled smile, while Mrs Hudson tendered Mrs Biddulph the promise that she would return on the morrow and see how her friend was faring.

CHAPTER THREE

THE SHADOWER

As we set off down the fog-shrouded street Sherlock Holmes was in a subdued and pensive frame of mind. I knew better than to intrude upon his ruminations, for that was a sure-fire method of earning a caustic rebuke. Instead I busied myself looking out for a passing cab to carry us home.

Mrs Hudson, however, being not quite so intimately experienced in my friend's moods, asked, "Well, Mr Holmes? What conclusions have you arrived at?"

Holmes exhaled testily. "It is too soon to say. The case presents many singular facets. I have done what I can under less than ideal circumstances. This bowl" – he nodded to the item of crockery under his arm – "may yield further gains. Equally, because there is so precious little stew left in it to work with, it may not. That is the best I can offer, for now."

"But you behaved towards Ada as though you are convinced of her innocence."

"I am unconvinced of her guilt, which is not the same thing."

"You surely cannot be of the view that a woman like her

is capable of coldblooded murder."

"I am not prepared to discount any possibility at this juncture," said Holmes. "Not until all the data are in. Facts are the framework upon which to build a case, my dear woman, not fancies or hopes. I realise you wish your friend to be blameless. For what it is worth, I do too. But one must separate desire from duty and opinion from logic. I would be remiss as a detective if I neglected to do so. Head must always rule over heart in these instances, otherwise what is the point?"

Mrs Hudson looked to me for support, but all I could do was give a hapless shrug of the shoulders. I knew better than to appeal to Holmes's finer feelings. Those few he had, he was wont to keep well in check.

We continued along the broad, cobbled thoroughfare but had not gone a dozen more yards when, apparently apropos of nothing, Holmes muttered, "Keep walking."

"What?" I said.

"You heard. Keep walking as though all is as normal. You too, Mrs Hudson. We are merely three confederates strolling along, minding our own business."

"I do not understand," said Mrs Hudson, speaking in a low voice as Holmes had.

"I think I do," I said, likewise softly. "We are being followed. No!" I hissed. "Do not look round, Mrs Hudson. Do exactly as Holmes says. Our shadower must not know that we are on to him."

Mrs Hudson did her utmost to affect a casual air, yet apprehension was all too apparent in her bearing. She moved stiffly, like an automaton. The harder she tried to saunter, the more she looked as though she were marching.

"Oh dear me," she whispered. "I am not as adept as you two at this sort of subterfuge."

"You are doing well," I told her. "Holmes, are you sure

there is someone behind us? The fog is thick and the daylight is waning. It is getting more and more difficult to see. Perhaps you imagined—"

"I imagined nothing," Holmes retorted, cutting me off. "He is a stealthy fellow. He is using not only the billows of fog for cover but any convenient wall or lamppost. His tread is so light as to be effectively silent. If I had not chanced to catch a glimpse of him from the corner of my eye, I would have no inkling he was there at all. But he is most definitely there. Let us turn this next corner, even though it is not the way back to Baker Street."

We did as we were bid, and no sooner were we on the adjoining road than Holmes thrust the bowl into my hands, saying, "Hold on to this. Keep going. Protect Mrs Hudson at all costs, with your life if need be." Then he was off, darting ahead into the fog. In seconds he was lost from view.

I lent Mrs Hudson the crook of my elbow, which she took with some gratitude.

"Doctor, I am frightened," she confided.

"No mischief will befall you, madam, I swear. Any blackguard who so much as raises a hand towards you shall have me to answer to."

Even as I said the words I found myself regretting that I had not had the foresight to bring along my service revolver. I had not anticipated I might need it, but in my defence, neither had Holmes, and it was he I relied upon to stipulate whether the gun's presence was required on a case.

We proceeded side by side, Mrs Hudson and I, wending our way along Notting Hill's mazy streets. My every sense was alert to danger, my body tensed to react at the least provocation. My companion's tension was palpable in her quickened breathing and the pressure applied by the hand clutching my arm, her fingers digging so hard into my flesh that it was almost painful. The sudden rumble of a window sash being lowered startled us both. A cough nearby set my heart racing, until I perceived that it came from a lamplighter who was hoisting his wick on its pole to ignite a gas jet. The folds of the London particular continued to swirl and thicken around us while the twilight shadows deepened.

Then came rapid footfalls, approaching from the rear. Swiftly I disengaged myself from Mrs Hudson and swung round. I raised the bowl without thinking, holding it aloft in both hands. I knew it was evidence, perhaps crucial to the case, but right then it had greater value as a potential weapon, and I did not care if in employing it to defend myself I destroyed it.

A figure loomed from the fog's sulphurous swathes.

"Ho, Watson!" came a familiar voice.

All set to dash the bowl down upon the fellow's head as hard as I could, I stayed the blow.

"Holmes! Is that you?"

"Would you brain me? I am aware that my habits can grate, but not to the extent, surely, that you might wish me bodily harm."

Panting, my friend halted and bent double, hands braced upon knees, to catch his breath.

"How did you get behind us?" I enquired.

"By the simple expedient of diverting down an alleyway between two houses, then taking a circuitous route back the way we came. I planned to catch our shadower unawares. Alas, no such luck. He was wise to my game."

"He has eluded you?"

"With embarrassing ease. I had him in my sights and fully intended to steal up on him and challenge him. He, however, seemed cognisant of my proximity. It was quite uncanny. He did not glance over his shoulder. He did not twitch or give any other hint that he knew I was there, but suddenly he broke into a run, with the head-down determination of one who was clearly fleeing. I gave chase, but he was fast, far faster than I. At a flat-out sprint I could not narrow the gap between us. My quarry soon vanished into the fog, and I could not even track him by ear, for just as he had made no sound when following us at walking pace, so he made no sound when running. It was like trying to keep up with a panther in the jungle."

"Who was he? Any notion?"

"I know little about him save that he was a man of advanced years, to judge by his crop of grizzled white hair, not tall, and thin to the point of emaciation. I would put his weight at no more than nine and a half stone, with nary an ounce of fat on him. His skin was brown, somewhat leathery in appearance, but from the fleeting glimpse I had of his face he is clearly a white man. As he moved he evinced a slight limp, a hitch in one leg suggestive of an old injury, though one not so debilitating that it slowed him any." The last comment was couched in rueful tones. "More than that I cannot attest to with any confidence."

"If you saw him again, you would recognise him?"

"Without a doubt."

"Then that is something. Do you suppose he dogged our footsteps all the way from Mrs Biddulph's house?"

"One cannot help but think so. It is feasible that he might be some roving cutpurse who meant to threaten us and take our money until I scared him off, but I doubt a lone man would be so bold as to target a party of three, especially when two of that party are male."

"He could have assumed you and I were more refined than we really are."

"If so, he would have had a rude awakening. But then there are his extraordinary powers of speed and stealth to consider. Not to mention his tanned appearance."

"You intuit that he has some association with Inigo Niemand, who was tanned too?"

"It seems a remarkable coincidence otherwise. In which case it is probable that our mysterious and wily follower was lying in wait outside Mrs Biddulph's and, when he saw us emerge, felt moved to trail us."

"To what end?"

"Perhaps to listen in on our conversation. Perhaps, if the opportunity had arisen, to make an attempt on our lives. I err towards the former rationale, else he might have tried to kill me when I drew near him, rather than flee."

"Mr Holmes, might you and Dr Watson see fit to continue your discussion at another time?" said Mrs Hudson. "Preferably when we are all safely ensconced in Baker Street once more."

"Of course, my dear lady, of course. I can see that this recent escapade has discomfited you."

"That is putting it mildly."

"Then let us tarry no longer."

With a gallant bow Holmes fell in on Mrs Hudson's right. I did likewise on her left, and, flanking her thus, we escorted her homeward through the fog, without further incident.

CHAPTER FOUR

A DISTAFF BLUEBEARD?

Holmes spent the rest of the evening at his chemistry bench, which was then not yet quite as ridden with acid scars as it would later become. He put the dregs of Niemand's meal to the test, applying various solvents and reagents and studying the reactions. As time went on his manner grew increasingly vexed, until at last he shunted his chair back from the bench, emitting a groan of pure frustration.

"Nothing?" I said.

"A few tantalising hints but none sufficient to confirm beyond doubt the presence of a toxic substance in the stew, and certainly not to identify it. Had I a larger sample to work with than these meagre scrapings, I might achieve a more concrete result."

"I note you did not ask Mrs Biddulph if there was any more of the stew left."

"It would have distressed the woman unduly, implying mistrust of her. Besides, she would not have been so foolish, were she Niemand's poisoner, to adulterate the entire pot. She would have introduced the poison into his helping alone.

Otherwise she would run the risk of diluting the concentration and decreasing the efficacy."

"She did mention that she ate the stew herself," I said. "Was that a lie to throw us off the scent?"

"Or a simple statement of fact. But even if she is Niemand's murderer, we come upon a stumbling block. Why? Why kill him? There appears to be no link between Inigo Niemand and Ada Biddulph beyond their respective statuses as lodger and landlady. What does she stand to gain from his death? I see nothing in it for her. I see only a practical drawback: she loses the income from his rent."

"She could always find another lodger. What if she needed no motive to kill him other than a certain sick, sadistic satisfaction?"

"You think that she is the type who kills for pleasure? A distaff Bluebeard?" Holmes sounded derisive.

"Hear me out. Assume the neighbourhood gossips are correct and Mrs Biddulph did murder her husband. Could it be that she found the deed so darkly gratifying that she wished to repeat it? Having acquired a taste for homicide, she felt a compulsion to do it again, this time her victim being her lodger."

"George Biddulph might be said to have warranted murdering, thanks to his persistent ill-treatment of her, but what could Niemand have done to deserve the same fate?"

"As I said, she simply has a taste for it now. No provocation is necessary. In some twisted part of her mind, she relishes the act of killing."

"She has a taste for it but has not indulged this appetite before now, Watson? Even though it has been five years since her husband perished? I find that hard to stomach – no pun intended."

"Perhaps the opportunity did not present itself until Niemand came along."

"Murder for murder's sake, and damn the consequences."

"Is it not at least worth countenancing as a possibility?"

"I have countenanced it already," Holmes declared, "and while I have not rejected it wholly, it is not my preferred hypothesis. For one thing, if Ada Biddulph was putting on a performance for us this afternoon, if all those tears and tremors were just for show, then she is an actress of consummate skill, easily the rival of Winifred Emery or Ellen Terry. For another thing, there was a set of curious footprints outside the house."

"You did not mention that before."

"I am mentioning it now." Holmes crossed the room to fetch his pipe from its stand and a wad of tobacco from the Persian slipper by the hearth. "Fresh footprints in the yard, discernible in the thin layer of slime upon the flagstones, most prominently visible next to the rear window of the basement flat."

"Mrs Biddulph's?"

"A man's footprints, too large to belong to any woman."

"Niemand's, then."

"Too large to be his, either. I saw shoes of Niemand's, which the police had turfed out of a cupboard. The sizes were no match."

"A policeman's footprints. Is that not the likeliest explanation of all?"

"The soles were not hobnailed as police-issue boots are. They were corrugated, as in a boot designed for hiking or similar."

"Could they have belonged to the man who followed us?"

"Were you not paying attention? That fellow was slight in stature. His shoes would be commensurately small, smaller even than Niemand's. Furthermore, the weight distribution on the footprints was even upon both soles, whereas our pursuer, as I told you, was lame in one leg and had a distinct limp, which would show in any impressions left by his feet. No, Watson, some other person stood recently outside Niemand's bedroom window and perhaps, at some point, opened it from without to let himself in."

"And then poisoned Niemand's meal."

"The one inference does lead enticingly towards the next, although not inevitably. Tell me, what is your impression of Niemand himself? What do you make of his foibles, his proclivities, as described by Mrs Biddulph? Do they not strike you as irregular? The closed curtains, the aversion to daylight…"

"He was recovering from disease. Some tropical fevers are known to cause a sensitivity to light. Infectious jaundice, for one."

"Granted, but he suffered from the lingering effects of such an ailment while retaining a healthy appetite. Is it, in your professional opinion, likely that one so afflicted might still be a trencherman?"

"Not likely but not unheard of either. If I have learned anything in half a decade of medical practice, it is that patients get better in different ways. There are no hard and fast rules. One man may refuel himself copiously in his convalescence, another may find even the thought of food disagreeable."

"Let me put it to you this way." Holmes's pipe was now alight and shedding clouds of smoke that made me think of the fog outdoors, unseen behind the curtains, bumping up against our windowpanes. "Is Mrs Biddulph the impostor in our tale? Or is it perhaps Inigo Niemand? Take that surname: Niemand. What do you make of it?"

"It sounds Germanic in origin."

"It is in no other way suggestive?"

I shrugged my shoulders. "Not to my thinking."

"It is indeed Germanic," Holmes said. "It is, in point of fact, the German word for 'nobody.'"

"Goodness me."

"Yes. Then there is 'Inigo.'"

"What of it? Does it, too, mean something in German?"

"No, but insert two spaces into the word and it becomes 'in I go'. 'In I go, nobody.'"

"Heavens! Do you really think that is the case? The name is some elaborate alias?"

"It might account for the 'B.W.' on the handkerchiefs. Those could be Inigo Niemand's true initials. And as for the dislike of daylight, what if that is not, instead, a dislike of being observed? Niemand chose to keep the curtains closed even during the day. He ventured out of the house seldom, and never for long. This, along with the pseudonym, is the behaviour of somebody in hiding, surely. Somebody who has gone to ground and is keen not to be unearthed."

"But if he did change his identity, as you suggest, why choose a name which practically advertises the fact that he wishes to be anonymous?" I said. "Why not call himself something altogether more ordinary and innocuous? 'John Smith', for example."

"You would have to ask him that."

"But since I cannot…"

"Since you cannot, my best surmise is that Niemand, or whatever his real name was, chose to rechristen himself 'in I go, nobody' without really thinking. It was not a conscious decision, more the first thing that sprang to mind. When one is on the run, keen to evade some pursuer, one does not necessarily plan out one's actions in detail. One operates on instinct as much as anything. In his desperation our man grasped at a pseudonym that seemed to him appropriate. This accords with the impression we are building of someone who was in fear of his life."

"With good cause, as it transpires," I said. "Your construal of the facts, along with the presence of the footprints in the yard, would at least seem to exonerate Mrs Biddulph once and for all."

"It would," said Holmes, "unless she were complicit with the fellow who left them. Rather than our unknown loiterer giving

Inigo Niemand poison himself, he could somehow have coerced her into doing it. It would not have been impossible. Judging by her relationship with her late husband, Mrs Biddulph is the compliant sort, easily cowed."

"What a horrible thought."

"Worse than the thought of a distaff Bluebeard?"

"In some ways, yes. To be forced into murder rather than carry out the deed of your own volition…"

Holmes looked up sharply. His keen grey eyes scintillated in the light of the fire. I thought that he had been struck by some sudden, penetrating insight, a kind of eureka, and that in a moment the full resolution of the case would be laid before me, delivered in tones of measured triumph.

Instead my companion cocked his head, then laid aside his pipe and very slowly and carefully began to rise from his chair. When I opened my mouth to ask what the matter was, he silenced me with an upraised hand.

His movements still precise and unhurried, Holmes reached for the poker that was leaning against one of the andirons in the fireplace. The implement was not quite straight, the kink in it betraying how it had been bent into a curve by the hulking, barbaric Dr Grimesby Roylott the previous year, using main force, and then restored imperfectly to true by Holmes in the same fashion. Holmes now hefted it in his hand, applying the same fencer-like grip he used when conducting practice with his singlestick. Then he padded towards the door that connected the sitting-room to his bedroom.

These actions caused me no small bafflement, and unnerved me too. It appeared there was someone else on the premises, an intruder. I had heard nothing to indicate it, yet I knew Holmes's hearing was more acute than mine, which exposure to gunshots and cannon fire on the battlefield had done much to degrade.

I stood, prepared to give Holmes my full backing in whatever confrontation might ensue. My hands became fists. My jaw was set.

Holmes grasped the door handle, paused to collect himself, then thrust the door wide open.

The bedroom window, which Holmes would never have left open on a night as inclement as this one, gaped open. Wreaths of fog stole in over the sill and the curtains wafted in a chilly breeze. The room itself, though shrouded in darkness, appeared empty.

Holmes did not relax his guard. He eased himself through the doorway like a prowling cat, the poker to the fore. I leaned in after him. We had only the illumination from the sitting-room to see by. There were gloomy corners where someone might be lurking.

What happened next happened fast. Holmes cried, "Aha, you scoundrel! I see you. There you are!" At the same time a figure sprang out from behind the bed. Holmes engaged with him and there was a tremendous struggle. Blows were exchanged. The poker was batted from Holmes's clutches and clattered to the floor, skidding under the chest of drawers. I glimpsed my friend and his opponent lurching to and fro, locked in a fierce embrace like wrestlers grappling. The make-up table at which Holmes donned his disguises was knocked over. Both combatants crashed against a cupboard. The impact made the wall shudder, and a small oil portrait of Holmes's parents by Vernet fell to the floor, the frame breaking.

Then I beheld a sight I had expected never to see. Holmes's prowess in the martial art of *baritsu* was something which he vaunted much and which I had witnessed in action on a couple of occasions and found impressive. I honestly believed there was no man alive who could best him in a fair fight.

How wrong I was, for Holmes's foe had gained the upper hand in the contest. My friend had been brought to his knees and was restrained by an arm around his throat. Holmes resisted, ramming an elbow repeatedly into the man's thigh, but to no avail. It looked as though he was being strangled.

That was when I weighed in. I had held back before, safe in the assumption that victory would inevitably be Holmes's and my assistance was not required. Now, with a guttural snarl, I launched myself at Holmes's assailant, fist raised to deliver a swingeing jab.

To my utter astonishment the man intercepted, catching my wrist with his free hand. Next thing I knew, my arm had been twisted about and yanked up behind my back. I was obliged to bend forward from the waist to relieve the pressure on the limb. I writhed, but the hold on my wrist was irresistibly strong. The harder I fought against it, the further my arm was drawn up, such that my shoulder – the one wounded by a Jezail bullet – began to throb with pain and seemed at risk of dislocation.

All the while, the man retained his dominance over Holmes. I could not help but wonder who this intruder was that had been able to overpower the pair of us with seemingly little difficulty. I could also not help but wonder what were his intentions. He had us at his mercy. Were we to perish by his hand, or would he be content with merely subduing us?

I had my answer as the fellow said, "I mean you gentlemen no harm. I am not here to do battle with you."

"You could have fooled me," I gasped out.

"I was on my mettle. You got the jump on me. I responded instinctively. I am now going to let both of you go. Our hostilities are at an end, but be aware that I will not hesitate to counter, should I sense the least threat from either of you. Do you understand?"

I turned my head to look at Holmes. He, half choked by the arm that encircled his neck like a boa constrictor, nodded.

"We understand," I said.

The stranger let go of Holmes and me simultaneously and stepped away from us with his hands in the air, palms forward, to signify peaceability. I, massaging my shoulder, glared at him, while Holmes rose with alacrity from his semi-recumbent posture and scrutinised the fellow from head to toe.

In the dim light I perceived that our intruder matched in every detail the description Holmes had given of our Notting Hill shadower. Short, sinewy and elderly, he had a face that was as brown as a walnut and as riven with lines, the wrinkles in it so deep they were almost grooves. Beneath a scowling brow his age-paled eyes gleamed like opals. His attire was that of a well-heeled Home Counties squire, but his checked tweed suit hung off him awkwardly, not through any deficiency in the tailoring but simply because he appeared uncomfortable wearing it, as though he were in the habit of going about in something less formal. This impression was reinforced by the leather wristlets which poked out from his shirtcuffs and, visible above his collar, the braided thong from which hung the tooth of some large predator – a crocodile's, I thought. Here was a man who was not at home in the metropolis, nor even in the English countryside, but liked to haunt the wilder regions of the planet.

"Who are you fellows anyway?" said he curtly.

"One might ask the same of you, sir," replied Holmes. "I feel under no compunction to give my name to somebody who has broken into my home. On the contrary, I feel the onus is on you to identify yourself first."

The intruder weighed up the remark, then smiled grimly. "You have an impudence about you that I like, young man. You also acquitted yourself well in our little contretemps just now, which inclines me to look upon you with a modicum of respect. Allan Quatermain is who I am. And you are…?"

CHAPTER FIVE

MACUMAZAHN

Minutes later, Sherlock Holmes, Allan Quatermain and I were ensconced together in the sitting-room as though the brawl in the bedroom had never taken place. I had gone downstairs to placate Mrs Hudson, whom the disturbance overhead had roused from sleep; and now, with a mutual détente having been reached amongst the three of us men, Holmes was offering tobacco to Quatermain.

"Or would you prefer a cigarette?" he said. "No, you lack the distinctive yellowing of the index and middle fingers that is the mark of the cigarette smoker. You are a pipe man."

Quatermain confirmed it by producing a calabash from his jacket pocket. After tamping a pinch of Holmes's rough shag into the bowl and lighting it, he took a few exploratory puffs. "Bitter," he pronounced, "but I have inhaled worse. Indeed, I have several times sampled a native tobacco, *Taduki*, the effects of which are not dissimilar to dakka. You know of dakka? No? Many an African's preferred choice of smoke. Highly intoxicating. But this *Taduki* herb is even more potent and induces visions. Such strange, entrancing visions…"

His voice trailed off, as though he were lost in reverie. His eyes seemed to be peering across a great distance at some vista no one else could see.

"Mostly I have smoked it in the company of the dear departed Lady Ragnall, widow of Ragnall the Egyptologist," he resumed. "A woman who was a great friend of mine and perhaps could have been more, had heart disease not taken her from us just last year. The Honourable Luna Holmes, as she used to be in her maiden days. No relation to you, I suppose?"

Sherlock Holmes shook his head.

"Aunt?" said Quatermain. "Cousin?"

Again Holmes indicated in the negative. "My family tree is not extensive, and no Luna perches on any of its branches, nor indeed any member of the aristocracy."

"Just wondered. But then, Holmes is not an uncommon surname."

"The same cannot be said for Quatermain. You are, of course, the celebrated big game hunter."

"None other."

"I have read of your exploits, in passing. Now and again a report appears in the international columns of the papers. Mention has been made of your involvement in the notorious Battle of Blood River, at which the Boers more or less destroyed the Zulu kingdom, and also in the rise of Cetawayo as ruler of what remained of that people."

"I was present at Cetawayo's death, too," said Quatermain. "I have led a long and storied life."

"The last I heard, you had made yourself fairly wealthy from a diamond-mining venture, somewhere down in southern Africa."

"'Diamond-mining venture'. That is one way of putting it."

"I know, also, that you are popularly known as 'Hunter

Quatermain', and sometimes called 'Macumazahn' by the African natives, a kind of honorific."

"It is my Zulu name and means 'the man who gets up in the middle of the night'. It refers to a certain watchfulness on my part."

"You are sure it does not mean 'the man who gets up *to no good* in the middle of the night'?" I said. "To wit, climbing in through the first-floor window of a private residence and hiding behind a bed."

"Please forgive Watson and his pawky vein of humour, Mr Quatermain," said Holmes. "He makes a valid point all the same. Why resort to such an unusual method of entry when ringing the doorbell would have been more polite and more straightforward and, for that matter, less liable to lead to an altercation?"

"Ah," said Quatermain. "You must appreciate, Mr Holmes, that I am an unorthodox man. Uncivilised, some might say. What I do, I do in my own way."

"That excuses, to some extent, but does not explain. If you wanted a consultation with me, the conventional approach seldom fails." Holmes's eyes narrowed. "Of course, it may be that a consultation is not what you were after."

"Yes, you fancy yourself a private detective, don't you? I recall my good friend Sir Henry Curtis mentioning that some fellow by your name has set himself up in that sort of practice and is making headway. That'd account for you nosing about in Notting Hill and all this hypothecation you've been doing since. But no, I don't need any consultation."

"Indeed," said Holmes, nodding, "you did not come here to talk to me, but rather to hear me talking. How long were you in my bedroom, ear pressed to the door, listening to me 'hypothecate'? Longer, I'll wager, than it took for me to notice how the fire was flaring in a manner that spoke of the presence of an unaccustomed draught."

"I heard not a lot, but enough," said Quatermain. "Enough to know that you have guessed a great deal about this whole affair but are nowhere near close to comprehending the full picture."

"Guessed!" Holmes barked. "I have never guessed in my life, good sir. Schoolboys guess when the Classics master asks them to parse a line of Ovid and they cannot fathom the answer. I deduce."

"Guess, deduce – what's the difference? However you have come by the conclusions you have reached, they remain incomplete, and you are better off that way."

"How so?"

The aged hunter leaned forward in his chair and gestured at Holmes with the stem of his pipe. "These are murky waters you find yourself in, young man. I did not track your spoor halfway across London and shin up a drainpipe in order to deliver a warning, but now that I am here and we are face to face, I feel it would be remiss of me not to do so."

"I am all ears."

"Drop your investigation," Quatermain intoned, fixing Holmes with a grave stare. "Walk away and do not look back. You have no idea the peril in which you are putting yourself and your colleague. I do. I know only too well."

The old man paused there, his face darkening as though a cloud were passing over it. Sombreness deepened every line in that craggy visage, and I was minded to ask whether he had some personal stake in the affair.

Before I could speak, however, Quatermain resumed his thread. "Murky waters, like I said, and there are sharks below, circling. I gave the same advice to that journalist fellow, and I trust you will heed it as he appears to have."

"Journalist?" said Holmes. "You mean the man from *The Times*. What is he called? Ellerthwaite."

"I mean no such person. You are quite wrong."

"Forgive me. I must have been mistaken. Not Ellerthwaite."

"See? You are not half as smart as you think you are, Mr Holmes. But that is fine, as long as you are sufficiently smart to take on board what I have been telling you. I would not want your death on my conscience, least of all when you would seem to have much to give the world. It would be a shame for such a promising career to be nipped in the bud."

"I consider myself duly cautioned."

"Yet you sound as though you have no intention of altering your course."

"I sometimes make a facetious impression," said Holmes.

Quatermain waited for him to expound further, but nothing more was forthcoming. If he was anticipating a guarantee from Holmes to desist from pursuing the case, he was in for a disappointment.

"Well," he said gruffly, "nobody can say I did not try." He rose, tapped out his pipe in the fireplace, and made a half-hearted attempt at straightening out the creases in his trousers. "If you aren't going to do as I ask, then at the very least stay out of my way. I tend to ride roughshod over obstacles, be they human or otherwise. Got that? Good. I shall show myself out."

"Try the stairs," Holmes said. "They tend to be so much less precarious than a drainpipe."

Harrumphing, Quatermain exited the room. Moments later, the front door clunked shut and we heard footfalls in the street below, northward bound.

Holmes leapt to his feet. "Quick, Watson! There is not a second to lose."

He darted to his bedroom and flung open the window, which he had closed after the fight with Quatermain. He swung a leg over the sill and reached for the same drainpipe by which Quatermain had gained ingress.

"Holmes," I demanded, "what in heaven's name are you up to?"

"Is it not obvious? We are giving chase. Quatermain will know if we follow him out the front door. The man has the acute senses of a tiger. But if we can catch up with him by an indirect route and see where he goes, we stand a chance of gleaning not only more about him but more about the case. Now hurry. After me."

CHAPTER SIX

HUNTING HUNTER QUATERMAIN

Holmes scurried agilely down the drainpipe. My own descent was somewhat sedate and more circumspect, for I saw how the drainpipe wobbled beneath my friend's weight and how the bolts affixing it to the brickwork were not the most secure, and I knew myself to be at least a stone heavier than he. Yet I made it to the ground unscathed, and the drainpipe remained where it was, so no damage was done either way.

Then we were off along the backs of the houses on our side of Baker Street, moving in the same direction – north – in which Quatermain had travelled when leaving. We vaulted over walls from yard to yard, until at last we came to a narrow passage affording access to the street itself. Halting at its end, Holmes poked his head round the corner and peered into the fog. Putting a finger to lips, he beckoned me to follow.

We stole along the pavement, keeping to the patches of darkness between the infrequent haloes of gaslight. Distantly ahead I could discern the silhouette of a man whom I took, from the limp evident in his gait, to be Quatermain. The vagaries of the fog lent him an evanescent, phantom-like aspect, for all that he was walking slowly and with an apparent lack of concern. The streets, otherwise, were deserted. On a night such as this, at so late an hour, all sane, sensible Londoners kept themselves indoors; but apparently those adjectives did not apply to Holmes and me.

Quatermain traced a meandering course through Marylebone, still tending northward, until soon we were at Regent's Park.

"Dash it all," Holmes whispered. "Let us pray that he does not enter the park."

For a time it seemed as though my companion's wish was granted, for Quatermain stuck to the road which demarcated the park's perimeter, the Outer Circle, following it clockwise along its south-west stretch. Then, just past the boating lake, as if on a whim, he diverted inward.

We picked up our pace, Holmes almost trembling in his eagerness not to let Quatermain out of our sight. Once we were in the midst of the park's lawned, wooded expanse, the fog crowded around us more densely than ever. That and the paucity of illumination meant we were travelling more or less blind. I was almost certain that we had already lost track of our quarry – and indeed that that had been Quatermain's goal in luring us into the park – but I said nothing. Holmes remained dead set on continuing the pursuit. I heard him mutter to himself, "So you tracked my spoor halfway across London, did you, Quatermain? Well, two can play at that game." As if in proof, he would drop to a crouch every so often and inspect the pathway gravel, a patch of grass or a clump of fallen leaves, before resuming progress.

I reckon it was half an hour before, eventually, Holmes gave it up. He let out a grunt, as of someone stymied, and I could swear I heard him grind his teeth.

"The man is as slippery as the proverbial eel," said he. "He realises full well we are behind him and has been leading us in circles. He sought to hoodwink me by treading in his own footprints, and I will admit that for a while it worked. Now, however, he appears to have vanished into thin air. The trail has gone dead and I am at a loss."

"And that is how it should be, Mr Holmes."

The voice – Quatermain's – echoed towards us through the fog. I could not fathom from which direction it originated, nor from how far away. It was as if Quatermain knew some ventriloquist trick for throwing his voice, so that it seemed to come from everywhere and nowhere at once.

"I really thought you had learned your lesson in Notting Hill," Quatermain continued. "I am a man who was taught bushcraft by a Hottentot and who has been stalked by lions. You cannot sneak up on me. You cannot follow me without my knowledge. Not on city streets and certainly not here, amidst nature, where I am in my element. You, sir, are frankly in danger of becoming a pest. The next time I catch you attempting something like this, it will go hard on you. You have my word on that."

"The next time we meet," Holmes retorted, "if there is a next time, you will not find me unready."

"You will do what, exactly?" said that eerily disembodied voice. "I outmatch you in every respect, you whippersnapper. Even when, while we were fighting, you struck at what you think is my weak point – my bad leg – it availed you naught. I am made of the toughest stuff imaginable. I have been weathered by African sun. I have been seasoned by veldt and desert. I have known starvation and thirst so severe as to bring me to the brink of death, and I have endured. To me, you are a pale, blinkered creature, as soft as a sponge, as clumsy as a sloth. I fear you not."

"In that case you will not be afraid to show yourself. Come

out, Quatermain, from wherever you are skulking. Come out and face me."

The bravado went unanswered. Holmes called Quatermain's name a couple more times into the fog, and received nothing in return save for the chirrup of a blackbird from somewhere in the treetops.

Only reluctantly did he admit defeat, and we trudged homeward in silence. As we neared Baker Street, Holmes roused himself from his gloom to say, "The night has not been a complete waste. If nothing else we have a fresh lead. Quatermain unguardedly mentioned a journalist."

"That he did," I said, "but he did not furnish a name, however slyly you tried to prompt him into doing so."

"He did not furnish a name, no, but he did furnish the name of the newspaper for which the journalist works."

"Did he? I don't recall."

"When he told us about the journalist, how did I frame my subsequent question?"

"You asked if it was somebody-or-other from *The Times*."

"Not so. Think harder. I said, 'You mean the man from *The Times*,' then offered up a bogus name, Ellerthwaite."

"Presumably no such person is employed by that organ."

"Not that I know of. But you are missing the point, Watson. It is the ordering of the sentences that counts. When one is on a 'fishing expedition', trying to elicit a fact from someone which he will not surrender voluntarily, it is important to begin with generalisations before going into specifics. Ergo, I began by naming a newspaper, for there are far fewer of those than there are journalists. I plumped for *The Times*, since the so-called Thunderer is the best-known and the one with the largest circulation, and hey presto, I got a palpable hit. Quatermain is many things but he is no master of deceit. His eyes widened in surprise – not greatly, but appreciably – when he heard me say '*The Times*'. They narrowed again, in superior fashion, when I spoke of an 'Ellerthwaite'. Each of those tiny changes in expression conveyed volumes. The one told me I was right, the other confirmed it by showing how Quatermain looks when he is doing his best to be canny. The face is a terrible unconscious betrayer of truths, if one pays close attention and knows what to look for."

"But how does knowing that Quatermain has met a journalist from *The Times* help us?" I asked.

"It is at least likely that this journalist is the man who visited Inigo Niemand on Wednesday last."

"It stands to reason, I suppose."

"More than that, Watson, it is highly plausible. Now, one may justifiably presume that Quatermain was watching Niemand's flat even then, and this is why he was moved to have words with the journalist as he described, in order to warn him off just as he has striven to with us."

"Yes, very well, I can accept that, but we still have no notion of the journalist's identity."

"But we know which newspaper he writes for, and that is a good place to start."

CHAPTER SEVEN

DARING DAN

Overnight, during the small hours, between our return to Baker Street and the arrival of dawn, the fog receded. When Holmes and I sallied forth the next morning, only a few wispy cobwebs of vapour lingered, hovering in gutters and clinging to the pediments of railings.

Our first port of call was the telegraph office on Thayer Street, where Holmes wired Inspector Lestrade to say that Ada Biddulph should not be considered the prime suspect in Inigo Niemand's murder. It was far from a complete abnegation of guilt, but the hope was it would forestall any move by Lestrade to arrest her, should he get it into his head to do so. Holmes had been loath to send the message, but a campaign of persuasion by me and Mrs Hudson over breakfast had forced him to relent. "The presence of Allan Quatermain has complicated things," he had allowed. "It has made what was a chamber piece a symphony, in which Mrs Biddulph would now seem to be playing a lesser role. She may not even be a part of the orchestra at all."

Our second destination was the offices of *The Times* on

Printing House Square. There, amid the hurly-burly that attends the production of a leading national broadsheet running to three editions a day, we began making enquiries about the unknown journalist. It did not go well. We were passed from desk to desk, editor to editor, and at each stop on our circuitous journey we were treated as a nuisance, an additional burden on already hectic lives. Nobody could spare us more than a minute of his time, and that grudgingly. Nor was anybody able to identify our mystery man based upon the scant information we had to offer, namely that he had visited Notting Hill recently in pursuit of a story. Time after time we were dismissed with a curt "good day", which would very occasionally be prefaced by a semi-sincere "sorry".

Holmes was not downhearted. "To be honest, Watson, I did not have high hopes for that particular approach," he said as we quit the building. "However, I know of a venue where the atmosphere is less formal and the tongues are somewhat looser."

By that he meant a nearby public house on Fleet Street where freelancers were wont to gather at all hours. It was barely eleven o'clock but already the place was thronged with men whose rumpled clothing and haggard demeanour, not to mention ink-stained fingers, betokened their vocation as scriveners. Ale was being supped in copious quantities, and although the prevailing mood was one of jollity and camaraderie, I sensed a tension boiling below. There were deadlines to be met, column inches to be filled, stories to be filed, and drinking was a good way of alleviating those pressures, if not negating them.

Holmes instantly endeared himself to the assembled company by buying a round for everyone. The only person in the pub not delighted by his generosity was me, for he happened to be short of cash just then and it fell to his disgruntled comrade to foot the bill.

With the journalists' sympathies apparently secured, my

friend set about making the same enquiries as he had at *The Times*. For a while it seemed, as at the newspaper offices, that his efforts would not bear fruit. Time and again he was rebuffed, sometimes politely, more often with brusqueness. In a couple of instances I had the impression that his interlocutor did know the subject of Holmes's entreaties but refused to identify him. Some code of honour appeared to be in play – that or an innate suspicion of anyone who was not part of the journalistic fraternity.

Holmes persisted nonetheless. Eventually his eye lit upon a certain fellow whom he felt confident could be prevailed upon to oblige.

"Look at him," he said to me quietly, pointing out the individual, who sat slumped at the bar, on his own, staring into his pint glass. "Have you ever seen such a wreck of a man? Even by the low standards of his peers he cuts a shabby, dissolute figure. Observe the collar of his shirt, which has been laundered so often it has greyed and which no amount of starching can keep upright. Observe, too, the cuffs of his trousers, which have been taken up. Those are second-hand trousers, I'll be bound, and the sewing is not the work of a professional tailor. It is an amateur job, perhaps his own doing. Here is someone who can barely afford to keep the clothes on his back. This makes him, for our purposes, a good target. A half-crown, if you would, Watson. There's a good fellow."

Grudgingly I placed the coin in Holmes's outstretched palm. So far I had sunk practically half a day's wages into this enterprise. I prayed that this would be the last of the expenditure.

Holmes sauntered over to the man and clapped him on the back. "You strike me as in need of company," said he cheerily.

"I am not," came the curt reply. "Go away."

Holmes caught the landlord's eye and raised a finger. "Another pint of porter for my friend here."

"I will not be bribed," the man said. "I have heard you asking after a certain member of our profession who's been following up a lead over Notting Hill way. I am in no mood to help."

"Here is your beer anyway," Holmes said as the glass of thick black liquid arrived. At his invitation, I handed the landlord threepence. "You would not do me the discourtesy of spurning it, would you?"

The man, whose name I regret to say I failed to enshrine in my notes, eyed the drink keenly. Thirst overcoming scruples, he picked it up and took a deep draught.

Wiping foam from his lips with his sleeve, he said, "I am still not prepared to talk. I am not some snitch to be plied with booze until my tongue loosens."

"Quite, quite," said Holmes.

"A stranger comes into this pub, free with his money, wanting to know about a journalist – it does not sit well with some of us. Do you see? It inclines some of us towards distrust."

"I fully understand. You are a betting man, are you not?"

"What's it to you if I am?" His eyes narrowed. "How can you tell, anyway?"

"A fragment of torn-up betting slip poking out from your breast pocket is ample evidence. You have had bad luck at the racetrack lately." Holmes brandished my half-crown. "This might help bring about a reversal of fortune. What do you say?"

The man studied the coin even more thirstily than he had the beer. He cast a glance around him. Then he snatched the half-crown from Holmes's grasp, slipped it into a pocket, and, in a low voice, said, "Dan Greensmith. That's who you're after. Daniel Greensmith is his name, but Dan to all of us. 'Daring Dan' we call him, owing to how intrepid he can be in his reporting – reckless, even."

Holmes said nothing, but there was a glint of satisfaction in his eyes.

"It so happens Dan mentioned something to me just last week relating to Notting Hill," the man went on. "Something about how he was venturing there shortly to meet a contact. Big story, he said. Potentially very big."

"A story of what nature?"

"Ah, there I can't help you. Us journalists, we aren't in the habit of telling one another the details of anything we're working on – especially if it's juicy. We're not exactly the honourable sort. I don't mean me necessarily. I mean journalists as a species. Competitive is putting it mildly. We'd sell our own mothers for a front-page exclusive. If you're on to something and you give a fellow hack even a hint about what it involves, you can bet he'll nip in and steal it from under your nose if he can. It's a basic rule of the job: keep your story *your* story. You learn it as a cub reporter and you don't deviate from it, not if you want to get ahead in this business."

"So Greensmith did not even name the contact?"

"No. All I know is the fellow came to Dan with some kind of exposé, and Dan was after it like a bloodhound."

"Where might one find Greensmith?" Holmes asked. "Would you happen to know where he lives?"

"Southwark, I believe, but I don't have an address for him. Someone official at *The Times* might be more use to you in that regard. What I do know is that he's a regular here." The man's brow furrowed somewhat. "But I haven't seen him for several days. Usually you can rely on him to be around in the saloon, holding court. The sociable type, is Dan Greensmith. Wit and raconteur. If he's away for that long, it can only mean that he's gone deep."

"Deep?"

"When he sinks his teeth into something, professional-wise, Dan won't let go. He loses sight of everything but the story. Doesn't happen every day, but when it does, that's it, Dan's obsessed, to the exclusion of all else. That's what I mean by 'deep'. Immersed, like."

"Remind you of anyone?" I murmured to Holmes, who affected not to hear the barb.

"Absent from the known world until he surfaces again," the journalist continued. "He'll even don disguises if it suits his needs."

"The resemblances mount," I murmured again.

"Disguises?" said Holmes.

The man deliberated. "Well, you've paid for it. Might as well give you your money's worth. I know for a fact that one of Dan's most frequently used aliases is that of a petty crook. He'll dress himself all scruffy, put a patch over one eye, grubby up his face so it looks like he hasn't had a wash for a week, and then he'll amble on over to the seedier parts of town so as to ask questions of the denizens there. Calls himself Black Jack Corcoran when he's out and about like that. Speaks the lingo of the lower orders – policemen are 'bluebottles', handcuffs are 'ruffles', and so on – and passes amongst the felon fraternity like he's one of their own. That's one reason why he's Daring Dan. Imagine if he got caught out. Imagine what those people would do to him if they discovered he'd been shining them on all this time." The journalist shuddered. "Hardly bears thinking about."

"Might Greensmith be availing himself of his Black Jack Corcoran persona right now?"

The man shrugged his shoulders. "Can't say. Maybe. Wouldn't surprise me. On the whole, see, it's your criminal who has his ear to the ground. Dan knows that. We all do. If you want to find out what's really going on, ask a crook. The crook sees more than your average, law-abiding citizen ever will. The crook's antennae are sensitive to comings and goings, things being where they should or shouldn't be, the city's undercurrents, the secrets in the shadows. Most of us are reluctant to get down there in the dirt and scavenge. Reluctant or too scared. Not Dan. He positively relishes it. He's a mudlark of the criminal demimonde. Oh, fancy that. My glass seems to be empty again all of a sudden."

He looked quizzically at Holmes, who in turn looked quizzically at me.

With yet another pint of porter in his hand, the journalist fulfilled Holmes's request for a physical description of Greensmith. By now he was being positively accommodating. Whether it was the drink or something else, I could not tell, but his curmudgeonliness of earlier was gone. I wondered if he was in fact a rather lonely man. Here he was, after all, in a busy pub, surrounded by comrades, but they seemed to shun him, like something tainted. He reeked of failure. Perhaps they did not want to be contaminated by him. And perhaps, in Sherlock Holmes, he was simply glad to have found someone to talk to.

"About your height, maybe an inch or two shy," he said. "In his thirties. Darkish hair. Quite a conk on him, but not sharp like yours. He's fond of a drink – who isn't? – and his nose shows it, all lumpy and red and mottled. What else? I wouldn't call him handsome but he has a certain way about him. Suave. When he's not playing the role of a wrong 'un, that is." The man mused for a moment, then said, "That's the lot. Can't think of anything else."

"You have been more than useful," said Holmes. "My thanks."

"Maybe...?" The man gestured at his glass, and, with a sigh, I yet again fished in my pocket for change.

As Holmes and I left the pub, I could see the cogs whirring away in my friend's brain.

"What are you thinking?" I asked, but really, in the light of what was to come, my interrogative should have been: "What are you planning?"

CHAPTER EIGHT

THE PEREGRINATIONS OF
BLACK JACK CORCORAN

What Holmes was planning was made plain to me that night, when he returned home after being out all afternoon and most of the evening. During that period, I was conducting my rounds and was unaware that Holmes had absented himself from 221B Baker Street until I came in at dusk and spoke to Mrs Hudson. She told me that Holmes had departed sometime between two and two-thirty while she was at the shops. He had left her a note to say she should not expect him back by suppertime but should lay out some cold cuts, which he would consume at whatever late hour saw him grace the house with his presence once more.

Not long after ten, as I was drowsily contemplating turning in, a man with dirt-besmirched face, ragged clothing and a patch over his left eye shambled into our rooms. I could not help but assume that this was none other than Black Jack Corcoran, Daniel Greensmith's down-at-heel alter ego, in the flesh. Who else could it be? He fitted the description we had been given by the journalist at the pub. I imagined Holmes had been searching for him, leaving messages in likely venues. Greensmith had got wind of this, and was now paying a call.

I even addressed the fellow as Greensmith, thinking myself quite clever, whereupon the fellow reached for his bulging, rough-textured nose and tore it away from his face. The action revealed the nose to be an artful confection of theatrical putty which had been hiding the altogether more aquiline proboscis of my friend.

"Holmes!" I cried.

"Of course it is I," said Holmes. "How could you not have realised that? Does Greensmith have a key to the front door? Could he have let himself in?"

"Well, no," I allowed. "I was taken by surprise, that's all. I wasn't thinking straight. The disguise is fairly convincing," I added defensively. "You do not look at all like you."

"So I should hope. Ah! Food. I am famished."

Holmes fell upon the dish of cold cuts, which he washed down with a snifter of brandy.

"I have had a most fascinating time," said he when his hunger was sated. "Would you care to hear about it?"

I made a gesture as though to say, "Be my guest."

"The East End is no place for a gentleman," Holmes began, "but for a ruffian such as Black Jack Corcoran, whose face is known there and who speaks like one to the Cockney manner born, it fits as cosily as a cashmere glove. Someone else's cashmere glove, for Corcoran has a reputation as a notorious pickpocket, so I have learned. A 'mobsman' or 'cly faker', to use the local slang. I say reputation because I find it hard to believe Dan Greensmith genuinely steals."

"Yes, just imagine if he were caught in the act. A police arrest would do little for his professional prospects. Thievery is thievery, whether or not it is in service of a false identity. He would be finished as a journalist."

"Nonetheless somehow he has promulgated rumours that he is a cutpurse, and a superior one. As Dan Greensmith he remains a law-abiding citizen but as Black Jack Corcoran he has residents of the East End convinced he is some sort of master criminal, his skill at 'dipping' second to none."

"He has clearly spent some while cultivating this persona."

"And done it well. Reportedly he is, too, rather free with his 'uxter' – that's money, Watson – which inclines the locals to look favourably on him."

"Better to be free with one's own money than with someone else's," I said under my breath.

"What's that, old fellow?"

"Nothing. Pray, carry on."

Holmes resumed his account. "It was no mean feat pretending to be someone I have never met. I trusted that Black Jack's distinctive appearance – the eyepatch in particular – would be so recognisable in itself that people would overlook any differences between my impersonation and Greensmith's own. I was disabused of that notion fairly rapidly. I received numerous looks askance when I introduced myself. Anyone who knew Black Jack seemed uncertain that this was the same man."

"Which of course it was not."

"I was even challenged once or twice. Some wary individual would proclaim that my voice had changed or that I did not seem as stooped as normal. I would supply some excuse to account for the discrepancy, then make myself scarce. It was a process of trial and error. With each of these encounters I learned a little more about how Black Jack comported himself and I would adapt my performance accordingly. Soon enough I had it down pat. The voice, the mannerisms, the slope-shouldered shuffle with which he walked – to all intents and purposes I was Black Jack."

"But why?" I asked. "What did you hope to accomplish?"

"Any titbits of data I could acquire about Black Jack, and hence about Greensmith, would have been welcome," said Holmes. "To that end I frequented many a tavern and bought many a drink for a stranger. Black Jack, as I have said, is renowned as a 'soft touch'. He can always be relied upon to reach a hand into his pocket at the bar. He is also happy to lend a sixpence here or there to those who claim to be in need, and never calls in the debt."

"Thus does Greensmith gain the confidence of the underclass with whom he mingles."

"And in return is rewarded with useful information."

"And were you?"

"I am now somewhat wiser about a number of misdemeanours that have aroused my interest of late. The matter of the Bermondsey costermonger, for instance, who appears to have two right hands, and the macabre business of the Limehouse undertaker, the cat fancier's wife and the missing gold teeth. When I have more time, I shall follow up on the revelations that have been vouchsafed to me and convey my findings to the authorities. My principal aim, however, was to see whether I could establish the whereabouts of the other Black Jack Corcoran."

"The real one," I said, adding, "If a sham identity may be described as real."

"Through various conversations I was able to piece together a chronicle of Black Jack's recent activities. Greensmith, it seems, has indeed been parading around the East End in that guise over the past couple of days. His itinerary has been wayward, taking in countless ports of call along the way. He has been a veritable Henry Mayhew in his peregrinations amongst the London poor, interviewing all and sundry. And then…"

"And then?"

Holmes rubbed his chin ruminatively. "Then, as of yesterday afternoon, nothing. No sign of him. No reports. Only rumours."

"Rumours?"

"Troubling ones. Intimations that Black Jack is in dire straits. I met more than one person in the borough of Shoreditch, particularly, who was disconcerted to see me. To see Black Jack, that is. 'I 'eard you was not at liberty,' said a young wipe-hauler with whom I chatted briefly. A wipe-hauler, Watson, is a pickpocket who specialises in stealing handkerchiefs."

"How fortunate I am to have you to translate criminal parlance into plain English for me, Holmes."

"I pressed the youngster for more detail, asking him where he had come by that intelligence. 'Just the word as is goin' about,' said he. His tone was harsh and he seemed to want to have nothing to do with me, as if merely by being seen with Black Jack Corcoran he might invite trouble down on his own head. I could not understand why he was so hostile, at least not until I met another youngster, this one a girl about whom the best one can say is that she was experienced beyond her tender years. She was a little more generous with her time, and a little more forthcoming, if no less chary. 'Ain't Mr Starkey got 'is 'ooks into you?' said she. 'So folks round 'ere is sayin'. If he ain't yet, I'd do a scoot if I was you, mister, and sharpish. I've 'eard tell you're a blower and Mr Starkey knows it and is gunnin' for you.'"

"A blower?"

"Forgive me, Watson. I thought you had had your fill of my translations. A blower is an informant, someone who 'peaches' on his criminal brethren to the police."

"My goodness. If Black Jack – or rather, Greensmith – has gained that status somehow…"

"Then one does not rate his chances of survival, not in that particular milieu. I could not establish beyond doubt whether the accusations against Black Jack were official or merely speculation. Either way, I thought it prudent, at that point, to hasten out of the East End, lest I fall foul of them."

"A wise precaution," I said. "Who is this Starkey of whom the girl spoke? Do you know?"

"I am afraid I do," said Holmes. "He is a notorious gang leader who presides over a tenement full of cutthroats and thugs in Shoreditch. It is called the Hive, and Starkey is its queen bee, sitting pretty at the centre whilst his workers and drones go out and do his bidding. There is not a citizen within the vicinity who does not live in terror of him and his henchmen. Even the police are afraid to confront him."

"Then we can only pray to God that Daniel Greensmith has not wound up in his clutches."

"We can do that," said Holmes, "but we can also do something more practical."

"I dread what you are to say next."

"If Starkey has indeed 'got 'is 'ooks' into Greensmith, then it is beholden upon us to rescue him."

I sighed. "That is exactly what I dreaded. And no doubt we must do it sooner rather than later."

"No time like the present. I shall unburden myself of this disguise, which has outlived its usefulness. And while I am about that, perhaps you should fetch your—"

But I was already up and on my way to my bedroom to retrieve my service revolver from its berth in my chest of drawers.

CHAPTER NINE

ENCOUNTERS IN THE EAST END

I had been tired before Holmes returned home, but now I was awake and alert, with apprehension prickling in my belly.

We journeyed eastward from Baker Street, exchanging our safe, civilised corner of London for the capital's least desirable region. The haunt of crooks, drunks, vagabonds, outcasts and other elements of the lapsed masses, along with the honest poor, the East End was a place so lawless and wild that somewhere like Notting Hill seemed an oasis of decency by comparison. Anyone with a modicum of respectability, let alone a modicum of common sense, avoided it. Even the police patrolled there in pairs, never singly, and were still not immune from harm. In short, this present venture of ours struck me as foolhardy indeed.

As if to illustrate the point, our cabman was willing to take us as far as Aldgate Pump but no further. "Even in broad daylight, driving through the East End is more than my life's worth," he said. "But at this late hour? You're on your own, gents. May God go with you."

On foot, Holmes and I entered this city within a city. As we forged deeper into its labyrinth, I found my hand straying to my pocket to clasp the butt of my gun. Around us the buildings seemed to glower. The very brickwork exuded menace, like a sweat. Figures darted furtively across our path. At any moment I expected we would be accosted or assaulted. Then there were the bodies which lay sprawled in the gutter. Whether they were insensible or dead, it was hard to tell, but they were obstacles one trod around with distaste, regardless.

"I would rather take my chances in the Ghazi-infested crags of the Khyber Pass than here," I remarked to Holmes.

"Do turn back, then," my companion offered. "I should think none the less of you for it."

"I should think the less of myself if I did."

I spoke with more courage than I felt, and indeed mere moments later my nerve was tested when a gruff voice addressed us, unbidden, from the shadows of an alley.

"You two toffs look like a pair of sheep what has gone sorely astray," it said. "How about I do you a good turn and escort you back where you came from? For a fee, of course."

"How about I put a bullet in your head?" I replied, drawing my revolver. It was obvious, from the man's tone, that money would have to change hands even if we did not accept the service being tendered. The offer was as much extortion as commerce.

The villain, whoever he was, said no more. His hurried departing footfalls were his answer.

A little further on, we fell foul of a trio of toughs armed with bludgeons. Two approached from the front while the third stole up from the rear, all holding their knobbed wooden clubs aloft. They stalked towards us with the poise of predators who are certain their prey will not resist. The area they had chosen for their ambush was unusually well illuminated, attesting to their self-confidence. Their grins glinted in the lamplight like the blades of knives.

I tensed, ready to draw my gun again.

Holmes, however, having sized up all three men, spoke to them thus.

"You would do well to disregard my friend and me, and look to your own affairs. I refer to this fellow here." He indicated the man nearest us, a leering bravo with a battered bowler perched at an angle on his head. "And to his relations with your sister, sir." This comment Holmes addressed over his shoulder to the man behind us. "I believe you are unaware of the attentions he has been paying her, and how she has reciprocated them."

"That ain't true," the man behind us said, addressing his cohort. "Is it, Albie? Tell me it ain't. You and Becky?"

"No, no, it ain't," said the one called Albie. "Not a bit of it, Luther, I swear."

"Is that so?" Luther snarled. "Then how comes you're tremblin' all of a sudden, Albie? How comes your voice has gone all high and quivery? Answer me that."

"Well, you see, all right, I was going to tell you. When the moment was right, like. I have squired Becky, but only once or twice. God's honest truth. All polite and proper. It ain't no more than that."

"Oh, I think it is," Holmes interjected. "That single hair protruding from beneath your lapel tells another story – a hair which happens to be of the exact same flaxen shade as friend Luther's, yet longer, curlier and altogether more feminine. Becky has lain her head against your chest, Albie, during what one can only assume to be a romantic tryst."

Albie, peering down at his lapel, hurriedly extricated the hair from its berth and tossed it aside. His expression was panicked.

"What have I told you about Becky, Albie?" Luther said. "You know full well what that girl means to me. Apple of our mother's eye, she always was, and Mum made me swear, on her deathbed, I'd see to it that no man touched her as wasn't right for her."

"Well, ain't I right for her?" Albie retorted with indignation. "I'm not good enough to be Becky's beau, that's what you're saying. You swine! I'm easily your equal, if not your better. She could do far worse."

"Only if she was seduced by the Devil himself."

"The Devil?" Albie exclaimed hotly. "*You're* the Devil, Luther!"

Albie threw himself at the other man, and a vicious altercation ensued. Bludgeon blows were exchanged, accompanied by animalistic grunts and growls. The third ruffian attempted in vain to break up the brawl and received a hit to the jaw that had not been intended for him. Dazed, he reeled away, losing his balance and toppling to the ground.

In all the fuss, Holmes and I were forgotten. We took the opportunity to make a hasty departure.

"It was long odds but I thought it worth a shot," my friend admitted, once we had put the scene of the incident well behind us. "When I spied the hair sticking out from behind Albie's lapel, its similarity to the hair on Luther's head was too close to ignore. I inferred the existence of a sister. I posited a brotherly over-protectiveness. Human nature, in its worst aspect, did the rest."

"So much for honour amongst thieves," I said. "But what if your ploy had not worked?"

"Well then, it would have been a matter of us battling our way out of our predicament. How much more satisfying, though, to have prevailed by using our wits rather than firearms and fisticuffs!"

"Not to mention less potentially injurious to our health. Now that I think about it, Holmes, oughtn't we to have donned disguises before we went out? Made ourselves look more like East Enders, in the hopes of passing unnoticed?" With hindsight this seemed to me the most judicious of measures, and I wished it had occurred to me earlier.

"I did entertain the notion briefly," Holmes replied. "I rejected it. I myself may be proficient at such impersonations, but you, Watson, with the best will in the world, are not. However you dress, even if it were in rags, you would invariably project the air of an Englishman of quality. Disguise is not merely about clothing or make-up. It is about posture, gait, one's general bearing. You have not studied the art of dissembling, as I have, and without that there is not even the remotest possibility of you being able to pull off the deceit. People around here would spot you for a fake as soon as they saw you, and then it would have gone hard for both of us – harder than if we present ourselves as just what we are."

"Very well, but at least we could have invited a constable to accompany us, as an added precaution."

"A policeman would draw greater attention to us, not less. We do not want to stand out. Above all we do not want to be directly associated with the law. I think you will see, once we reach our destination, how dangerous that might be."

CHAPTER TEN

INTO THE HIVE

We continued on our way without any further encounters of note, until at last, in the very heart of Shoreditch, we stood outside the aforementioned destination: a building which even by the modest standards of the East End was ramshackle and unkempt. It was part of a terrace of tall, thin houses each of which teetered drunkenly against the next. The entire area was one of those rookeries into which were crammed far more people than there was space to reasonably accommodate them with any degree of sanitariness.

The house in question was the so-called Hive to which Holmes had made reference earlier. It boasted walls caked with filth and windows that were broken and patched with whatever materials came to hand, mainly rags and newspaper. Refuse littered the pavement before it, and a host of rats made merry amidst the detritus.

In these respects the Hive was little different from its neighbours. What set it apart was the din that emanated from within. Sounds of revelry poured forth onto the street, but it was revelry of a savage, raucous sort, more like the braying of donkeys or the howling of wolves than anything human. Guttural oaths rent the air, along with snatches of songs whose lyrics were coarser than any I had heard even in the army. Several times these ditties were counterpointed by the *crack* of glass shattering, as though a bottle had been dropped or more likely thrown. The Hive was, not to put too fine a point on it, abuzz.

"You want us," I said to Holmes, "to go in *there*?"

"'Want' is not the word," replied he. "It is a necessity. If Greensmith is somewhere on the premises, we cannot just leave him to languish. It would be unconscionable."

"And if he is not?"

"Then we will have had a wasted journey. We will, nonetheless, have been exposed to a stratum of society well outside our usual ambit, which should at least be instructive."

"'Destructive' seems nearer the mark."

"Come, come, my friend. Such querulousness does not befit you. You are a soldier and a doctor, neither of which occupations attracts the faint of heart."

"Nor does either attract the suicidal," I said.

"Should we run into trouble, I am confident we can reason our way out of it, much as we did with those three louts."

"Three louts are one thing, but a house full of them?"

"You seem to fail to appreciate the urgency here, Watson," Holmes said. "We need to find Greensmith. This is the most expedient means of achieving that end. Heaven only knows what Starkey might be doing to him right now. The sooner we can prise him from the fellow's grasp, the better."

I was not so confident. All the same, I followed Holmes as he climbed the front steps, both of us navigating around the ordure accumulated thereon, and rapped at the door.

To those who have read others of my literary works, Holmes's behaviour here may seem at odds with the characterisation that has become so familiar. What of the cool, detached logician who broods over a problem, sometimes for days? What of the imperturbable intellectual who considers his every move beforehand? What of him?

All I can say is that Holmes, at the time of this adventure, was still a young man, barely out of his twenties. The impetuousness of youth had yet to ebb in him altogether. The Sherlock Holmes who first enjoined me to share rooms with him after we had known each other for less than ten minutes, who killed a terrier to prove the effectiveness of a poison pill, and who stood up to the bullying of Dr Grimesby Roylott with laughing contempt, was the same Sherlock Holmes whom I depict in this narrative. Where a maturer, wiser Holmes might have feared to tread, that younger, hot-tempered fellow rushed in; and I, often against my better judgement, was drawn along in his wake.

The door was opened, after some interval, by a hulking great ape in an ill-fitting houndstooth check suit.

"What do you want?" he demanded, eyeing us much as he might have an earthworm upon which he had accidentally trodden.

With almost comical politesse Holmes presented his card. The giant took it in one paw and scowled at the text as though it were written in Chinese. Then he crushed the card and tossed it at my companion's feet.

"Even if I could read," he said, "I don't give a damn who you are. You've come to the wrong place. Now scram!"

"The name Sherlock Holmes, I suppose, means nothing to you."

"You could be the Duke of ruddy Wellington for all I care. You don't belong 'ere, you ain't welcome, and if you don't skedaddle right this instant, that massive great 'ooter of yours will be plastered sideways across your fizzog." He brandished a fist to illustrate his point, and it was a vivid illustration indeed, for his hand was practically the size of my head, with knuckles so thickly callused they resembled golf balls.

"I believe you are threatening me," said Holmes calmly.

"Why, how very perspicacious of you, sir," said the ape, mimicking the fruity tones of the high-born.

"Were you to attempt to lay a finger on me, it would not end well for you."

The man scanned Holmes from head to toe, then barked a scornful laugh. "Really? A piece of string like you couldn't beat me even on your best day. I could take on the both of you together, you and old muttonchops there, and win without even breakin' a sweat."

"Is that so?"

"I've been a prizefighter, I'll 'ave you know. Bare-knuckle stuff. None of your Queensberry Rules. I've put down blokes twice your size and thrice as ugly."

I felt moved to intervene before Holmes could antagonise the fellow any further. "We apologise for bothering you," I said. "We shall be going now."

"No, Watson," said Holmes, and my spirits sank. "The gauntlet has been thrown. Only a coward would not pick it up."

The ape squinted at him. "You actually want to do this? You're volunteerin' to mix it up with me? Me, Ned Maynard, 'eavyweight champion, what never lost a bout in twelve years and sent three of 'is opponents to the 'ospital and one to the morgue?"

"Are you going to brag all night or are we going to fight?"

A punch was thrown. A minute later, it was over.

In a way, I pitied Ned Maynard. He could not have known what he was getting into. The skills which had brought him success as a pugilist – mighty jabs, barrelling roundhouses, piston-powerful uppercuts – were of little use against the nimbler, subtler techniques of *baritsu*. Compared with Holmes he was a lumbering rhino. Not one of his blows found its mark.

The scuffle started on the steps and ended in the roadway with Maynard down on one knee, his right arm hanging limp and useless by his side. His eyes had taken on a giddy, unfocused look, as though he did not quite know where he was, and a peculiar whimpering issued from his throat, like that of a perplexed puppy.

Holmes, standing over him, was poised to deliver the *coup de grâce*. He refrained, however, and instead extended a hand towards Maynard and helped the dazed giant to his feet.

"My friend and I," said he, "are desirous of a meeting with your boss, Mr Starkey. Would you be so kind as to take us to him?"

Maynard nodded in a baffled manner and tottered back towards the Hive, massaging his benumbed arm. Holmes and I fell in behind him.

"No tricks now," Holmes warned Maynard. "Take us direct to Starkey. Don't try and lead us into an ambush, or there'll be more of the treatment you just received."

The big man, cowed by his humiliation at Holmes's hands, merely nodded. I think he was too addled even to think of double-crossing us.

What scenes the interior of the house presented! No novel by Rabelais could do it justice, nor any etching by Hogarth. Everywhere one looked there was licentiousness and degradation. Cheap alcohol flowed like water. Upon the stairs what appeared to be a bundle of soiled laundry turned out to be a sot so inebriated that he had passed out face down while ascending. Through an open doorway on the first floor I saw a pair of delinquents in the throes of argument. What the bone of contention was, I cannot be sure; it may have been the bottle of gin one of them clasped to his breast, or it may have been the weary-looking female who sat in the corner of the room in a state of some disrobement. As they staggered to and fro, exchanging spittle-flecked insults and tripping over their own feet, the two men resembled nothing so much as clowns at a circus, albeit a circus of a profane variety.

The stench which permeated the building was so noisome it made one choke. It was like an open sewer, with yeasty top-notes of stale beer. There was no item of furniture that was not battered, woodworm-riddled and on its last legs. Kapok and horsehair bulged out through threadbare upholstery. My eye fell upon a book, a startling sight amidst all the orgiastic carnage, lying open on the floor of a landing. I was oddly touched by its presence, thinking it evidence that at least someone on the premises had finer sensibilities; someone aspired to more than being a mindless brute. That was until I realised that the book was situated outside a water closet and that all of its pages had been torn out.

Our cumbersome guide led us to the topmost floor and knocked at a door into which the word PRYVIT had been carved with a knife. From within came a growled "Who is it?"

"Me, Mr Starkey. Ned."

"What do you want?"

"I've brought up a couple of gents."

"Couple of gents? What do *they* want?"

"I don't know, boss. One of 'em, I do know, fights like a ballerina and a viper put together. Stitched me up good and proper, even though 'e's 'alf my weight and skinny as a rake."

"How the devil is that possible?"

"Can't say. Why don't you ask 'im yourself?"

The door was opened by a man who was much shorter than the gravelly deepness of his voice had led me to expect. He stood barely five feet tall, squat and broad, with a near-spherical head from which his ears protruded like amphora handles. His hair was so close-cropped that he was nearly bald, while his unshaven chin sported black bristles with streaks of silver. His clothing was finery gone to seed, the seams of his velvet smoking jacket coming apart, a pocket of his brocade waistcoat missing, his silk cravat moth-eaten, as though he had once had pretensions to sartorial elegance but had found sustaining it too much like hard work.

"Mr Starkey," said Holmes, holding out a hand. "Sherlock Holmes. Pleased to make your acquaintance."

"Likewise I'm sure," said Starkey, bemusedly shaking it.

"My colleague, Dr John Watson."

Taking my cue from Holmes, I too shared a handshake with Starkey. His grip was damp and I had to resist the temptation to wipe my palm on my trousers afterwards.

"They're a rum pair, all right, as you can see," said Maynard, quirking the corner of his mouth. "I reckoned there wasn't no 'arm in bringin' 'em up 'ere. Thought they'd more or less earnt it, on account of 'ow this 'Olmes fellow got the better of me. And of course, you like a bit of novelty, don't you, boss? You're always sayin' 'ow distraction from the 'umdrum never 'urts. But if you want 'em shown out," he added, "I can arrange it. I'll rally the lads and we'll evict 'em together, nice and forceful-like. Nifty footwork or not, they won't stand a chance against us mob-'anded."

Starkey glanced from Maynard to Holmes to me and back again.

"Sherlock Holmes, Sherlock Holmes..." he mused. "Now where do I know that name from? It's ringing a bell. Wait. You're that detective, aren't you?"

"Your servant, sir," said Holmes with a bow.

"You help the Peelers, right?"

"From time to time I have afforded some modest assistance to Her Majesty's Constabulary, yes."

"And you've put several poor souls in the jug."

"I can be said to have been instrumental in the jailing of certain malefactors."

"Yes, it's coming to me now," said Starkey, and he produced a pistol from his pocket. "So give me one good reason why I should not shoot you where you stand."

CHAPTER ELEVEN

THE KING OF SHOREDITCH

Starkey cocked the hammer of the gun. Holmes stayed my hand before it could dive to my pocket. His grip on my wrist, unobserved by Starkey, was brief but sent a clear instruction. I should wait. Better to keep the presence of my revolver a secret for now, since it might be advantageous to us later.

"Mr Starkey," my friend said, seemingly unperturbed by the firearm that was levelled at his chest. "I grant you that by your lights my death might seem warranted. I will not plead for my life. It would, I appreciate, be a futile exercise. What I crave, if I may, is an audience. Ten minutes of your time, that is all, no more."

Starkey frowned. "An audience? You make it sound like I'm royalty or something. What do you want to talk about?"

"A man called Daniel Greensmith. You might know him better as Black Jack Corcoran."

Starkey's expression soured and his grip on the pistol tightened. "That lying scoundrel. That wretched two-faced impostor. What about him? I don't think there's anything to discuss."

"You are under the impression that he is a police informant."

"I know full well he is!" Starkey snapped. "What else could he be?"

"How have you arrived at that conclusion?"

The gang boss bent his head to one side and scratched one protuberant ear. "I've got my reasons."

"What if I told you that you were labouring under a misapprehension?"

"What if I told *you* that all this fancy talk of yours is making me want to put a bullet in you, simply so as you'll shut up?"

"Then we would seem to be at stalemate," said Holmes. "But as I look into the room behind you, which appears to be your study or office, I note that atop the desk there sits a bottle of Tokay. I am rather partial to Tokay, and yours gives the impression of being a good one. A seventy-two Ausbruch Essence, is it not?"

Starkey was thoroughly wrong-footed. "I have you at gunpoint, I've told you I'm going to shoot you – and you wish to share a drink with me?"

"Are you not thirsty? I am. Positively parched, as a matter of fact."

The gang boss looked at Holmes as though unsure as to his sanity. "Either you have one hell of a nerve, Mr Holmes, or you're as barmy as they come." A smile that was half smirk crept across his face. "In either case I find that intriguing. Very well. Come on through and let us have a drink."

Much to my relief Starkey stowed away the pistol and ushered us into the room. The closing of the door shut out most of the rumpus below, which was also to my relief. We took our seat upon chairs that had seen better days but were not wrecks of the kind found elsewhere in the house. Starkey used his shirtcuff to wipe clean some grimy glasses, which he then charged to the brim with Tokay. The topaz-coloured sweet Hungarian wine has never been to my liking, nor to Holmes's as far as I am aware, despite his avowals a few moments earlier. Even the few sips I took of it were so sickly that they turned my stomach. Starkey, however, emptied his glass at a gulp, and Holmes duly did the same. Then Starkey helped the two of them to a refill, and these second servings went the way of the first, no less swiftly.

Around us the room was packed with valuables: porcelain ornaments, fob watches, ormolu clocks, portraits, cameos, carved ivory statuettes, elephant's-foot umbrella stands, chinoiserie and more. They were piled to the rafters, all in a jumble, as though this were some bric-a-brac shop whose owner had abandoned any attempt at organisation. Whether the items were stolen goods or offerings paid in tribute to Starkey by the locals over whom he held sway, I could not adjudge. What was certain was that none of these possessions were his by right, else he would surely have displayed them with greater care and less haphazardly. We were in some sort of Aladdin's Cave of loot, a treasure trove of ill-gotten gains.

"So, Mr Sherlock Holmes," said Starkey, "what's all this about Corcoran not being a blower?"

"I might counter that with a query of my own. What has led you to presume that he is?"

"Ah well, you see, I've had my suspicions about the fellow for some while. Couldn't put my finger on what was bothering me about him, but something just didn't sit right. Bloke wanders about the East End all amiable and – what's the word? Gregarious. Fond of a chat. Free with his cash. It isn't natural. Nobody's that nice, not unless he's after something in return. I'd got to wondering whether he might be a missionary or the like. Gains your trust, then next thing you know, it's all hallelujahs and 'Have you been saved?' But there seemed to be none of that with Black Jack Corcoran. Besides, he's a dipper, right? No soldier of Christ is going to make a living from the wallet-lifting game, or even pretend to. So I started asking myself, what *is* he up to? Because there he is, coming the Rothschild with everyone he meets. It's got to be a put-on, no?"

"An understandable conclusion."

"Absolutely, sir. Absolutely. Corcoran just wasn't kosher. So what I did, see, was next time he turned up in Shoreditch, I had one of my lads tail him. 'Go where he goes,' I said to the fellow. Phantom Phillips, that's his moniker. Famously good at not being seen, is Phillips. Moves about like a ghost, hence the 'Phantom' part. 'Find out what he does when he's not playing Lady Bountiful,' I said to him. So, come the end of the day, Black Jack Corcoran heads off west, and Phantom Phillips is with him, and at first he reckons Corcoran is going to Kensington or Covent Garden, somewhere where there's crowds of toffs and rich pickings. But no, it's to Southwark that he travels, and what does he do when he gets there but go into a house. It's a fairly nice gaff, so says Phillips, small but well-appointed, and Corcoran saunters right in through the front door. Doesn't go round the back and break a window or anything. So Phillips decides it must be Corcoran's own house, and he hangs about outside for a time because he's curious, and then what happens?"

"Do tell."

"Phillips spies Corcoran in an upstairs window," said Starkey, "only he's all cleaned up now and he's put on smartish clothes. And here's the clincher: he's not got that eyepatch on any more, and underneath there's a perfectly good eye. Phillips swears to it. It's not blank like a pearl. It's not all red and oozing. It's certainly not missing. It's a match for its mate across the other side of his snout. Now who does that? Who dresses up in tatty *schmatte* and puts an eyepatch on and professes to be a pickpocket and gets people to open up to him? I'm no detective, Mr Holmes, but even I can put two and two together."

"The product of your arithmetic being that Corcoran must be reporting back to the police and getting paid for his tip-offs."

Starkey spread out his hands. "What else? In my world, everybody has some sort of fiddle going. Corcoran's is snitching."

"So you acted."

"Of course I acted. I gathered my lads and I said, 'You ever see that Black Jack Corcoran, you nab him. Next time he shows his face round these parts,' I told them, 'you bring him to me.'"

"Why not simply instruct them to kidnap Corcoran from his house in Southwark? Surely that would be just as easy, if not easier."

"Ah well, you see, I have my turf, and there's other gangs have their turf, and it doesn't do for us to cross borders. That's how trouble starts, isn't it? Phillips on his own, nobody would notice, sly monkey that he is – but a handful of my men in Southwark? Even just two or three? That'd be considered an incursion, and there's fellows down there who would definitely take it amiss. Besides, I knew Corcoran would be back round these parts eventually. Like the spider in its web, you wait long enough and you're patient enough, and the fly will always come your way in the end. It helped that I put a bounty on his head, a whole sovereign for the bloke who spotted him and dragged him back to the Hive. I told my boys I wanted him in one piece but he didn't have to be in pristine condition, if you know what I'm saying."

I shot a sidelong glance at Holmes. He had been very lucky not to have run into any of Starkey's mob when posing as Corcoran earlier. By the just perceptible pursing of his lips, I sensed he realised this.

"Lo and behold," Starkey continued, "not a day later, who should put in an appearance?"

"So now Corcoran is your captive," Holmes said.

"He may be."

"There is no 'may' about it, unless you have already killed him."

"What do you take me for?" Starkey looked offended. "The type who'd just casually bump off a man, easy as that?" He snapped his fingers. "You do me a disservice."

"No, I imagine that, like a cat, you like to play with your food before dispatching it."

"There you might have something."

"Is he here? In this building?"

"What does it matter to you? Why are you so interested in the fellow? Have the coppers sent you to negotiate his release? Is that it? Wouldn't dare come to fetch their pet themselves so they get a civilian to be their proxy."

"I am an independent contractor in this particular affair," said Holmes. "You have my word on that."

Starkey studied him keenly. "A man's word isn't worth a breath of wind, not where I'm from."

"Where I am from, it is his bond."

"I know that, which is what inclines me to believe you. I consider myself a shrewd judge of character, Mr Holmes; and for all that we sit on opposite sides of the fence, morally-wise, I can't help but think that you're honest. What do you want Corcoran for anyway?"

"Let me lay my cards on the table. Corcoran's real name is Daniel Greensmith and he is instrumental in a case I am presently investigating. When he is not masquerading as Black Jack, he is a journalist. He has never, to the best of my knowledge, colluded with the police. His safe return would very likely enable me to unravel a baffling mystery and clear a woman's name from suspicion."

"You're asking me to hand him over to you."

"In a nutshell, yes."

"And what's in it for me?"

That, I thought, was Starkey's personal ethos summed up in a single sentence: *what's in it for me?*

"The opportunity to prove that you can be magnanimous," said Holmes. "Starkey of the Hive lets a man go free after being persuaded that he has had him apprehended in error."

"That'd be admitting I'd made a mistake. Wouldn't reflect well upon me. A man in my position has got a certain reputation to uphold."

"You do not rule this borough by fear alone, do you?"

"Some would say I do."

"I have a feeling that you command a degree of respect amongst the locals. What is this hoard of items around us if not a sign that you are held in some esteem? Here are heirlooms. Here are cherished belongings. Some of them may not have come into the donors' hands by reputable means, but still they were passed on to you."

"Given to me by folk when asking a favour or just hoping to curry favour. I prefer cash but will take valuables in lieu."

"You could sell them on but you have chosen not to. You surround yourself with them. They are mementoes. They serve as a daily reminder that you are the king of Shoreditch, with loyal subjects in whose admiration you are happy to bask."

"The king of Shoreditch." Starkey rolled the phrase around his tongue. I could see he liked the sound of it. "Your point being that every once in a while I should prove myself deserving of my crown."

"By showing wisdom and clemency," said Holmes. "No monarch should be Herod all the time. A little Solomon now and then does not go amiss."

"Oh, Mr Holmes." His Royal Highness shook his head, amused. "Don't think I don't know a soft-soap job when I see one. You hope that if you keep this up, I'm going to roll over and let you tickle my belly. That's not my style."

"Very well. How about a more tangible incentive then?"

"Money? You'd buy Corcoran's life?"

"Name your price."

Starkey weighed the prospect up and rejected it. "I'm not short of money. I have all I could want and more."

"Then I can offer a quid pro quo."

"I said I'm not short of money."

"It is not that kind of quid. Think how I bested your man Maynard."

"It is remarkable that you took on an ox like him and triumphed. I'd like to have seen it."

"Those fighting skills of mine that he found so confounding," said Holmes, "I would be willing to pass on to him and the rest of your gang."

Starkey inclined his head from side to side in a manner that made me think of a magpie whose eye has been caught by some sparkly object. "Now then, sir. That is a most intriguing proposition. Most intriguing. My boys are a pretty effective lot, as is. Brute force yields results. It's never a bad thing to have an edge, though. Sometimes we get into clashes with other mobs. Can't help it, even though we try to respect the boundaries, like I said. We've got the Stratford Angels over to the east and the Hackney Butchers up north, both trying to make inroads into our territory. We can see them off, but they outnumber us and they keep coming." He paused for a moment. "All right then, Mr Holmes. Teach the lads a few of your tricks, and Corcoran – or Greensleeves, or whatever his real name is – is yours."

"I have your word on that?" said Holmes.

"You do."

"Yet you have just told us that round here a man's word is valueless."

"Others' maybe. Not mine."

Holmes weighed it up. "Very well. Just know this. Watson and I are both of the sort whose absence would be noted, were we to go missing for some mysterious reason."

"I'll keep that under consideration," said Starkey.

"Also," said Holmes, "there is one condition."

"You're haggling with me?"

"Simply negotiating the terms of the deal."

"Which is another way of saying haggling."

"If that is how you care to look at it. I want to see Greensmith first. I want to be sure that you do have him and that he is still alive."

"Bless me!" Starkey clapped hand to breast in mock-offence. "It's as though you do not trust me, even still."

"I never purchase goods sight unseen."

Starkey chuckled. "That is a sensible philosophy and does you credit. In some respects you are a man after my own heart. Yes, I think I can see my way to doing as you require, but I need a guarantee from you in return that you will honour your side of the bargain."

"I promise I shall. A lesson on the finer points of *baritsu* will be given to any of your men who care to attend."

"I'm after a little more than just a promise. Let me put it plainly. Fail to deliver, and the life of your friend here is forfeit."

"Unacceptable," stated Holmes flatly. "My life perhaps, but not Watson's."

"I don't think you're the sort who's too bothered about putting his own neck on the line. The neck of a friend, on the other hand…"

Holmes looked at me. "Watson, I realise it is asking a lot, but would you be agreeable?"

"To serve as collateral?" I said. "You can understand I am none too eager."

"You will be in no danger. Mr Starkey's men will have their *baritsu* lesson; we will gain custody of Greensmith. What can possibly go awry?"

CHAPTER TWELVE

THE MAN IN THE CHAIR

Out of the Hive we trooped, Holmes, Starkey and I, as the chimes of midnight struck.

We three were attended by a contingent of Starkey's men, some dozen of them, all told, marching in two groups to the fore and at the rear. These were the least drunk in Starkey's household, the ones whom their leader could count on to do as ordered without delay or demurral. We must have looked a motley procession to those passers-by who chanced to see us straggling through the night-time streets, and I did my best to maintain a dignified bearing so that, although I was clearly in the company of Starkey and his troops, no one would mistake me for their peer.

Starkey felt confident enough in his ascendancy over us that he had returned his pistol to his pocket. My service revolver sat snug in mine, nudging against my hip. Starkey remained ignorant of the fact that I was armed, which gave me an ace up my sleeve. I hoped I would not have cause to play it, yet I was all too mindful of the fact that should the situation develop in a way that was to our detriment, I would be first in the firing line.

Our journey's end was a warehouse not far from the Hive. Admission was obtained by dint of Starkey letting out a distinctive pattern of knocks which prompted the opening of a door from within by yet another of his men.

The interior of the building was dusty, draughty and virtually empty, with here and there a lantern affording fitful illumination. I could only infer that Starkey did not use the warehouse for the purposes of storage – at least not the storage of goods and chattels.

We filed through the building until we came to a kind of cabin at its centre, a crude subsidiary structure thrown together from timber offcuts. It had no windows and was accessible via a door with a lintel so low that out of the three of us who passed through it – Holmes and I, followed by Starkey – only Starkey was not obliged to stoop.

The cabin's purpose, as I soon discovered, was to provide additional privacy and sound-proofing, for inside we found a man who was tied to a chair and had been very badly treated. I could only assume this was Daring Dan Greensmith, and he did not look too intrepid just then. His head sagged, and were it not for the ropes binding him he would surely have slumped to the ground in a heap. Bloodstains spattered the floorboards all around him, some old, some fresh, and from what I could see of his face it was a mass of bruises.

"I thought your instructions were that he was to be brought to you in one piece," said Holmes to Starkey.

"That is true," came the reply, "and he was. Can I help it if a couple of my lads have been a little enthusiastic in their dealings with him since he got here?"

"Enthusiastic?" I said. "This is barbarism. I must examine the fellow straight away. He looks half dead. I can scarcely make out whether he is breathing or not."

"All in good time," Starkey said.

"Greensmith, I presume, was given the opportunity to object to such molestation," said Holmes. "Specifically I mean that he was able to protest his innocence of the crime of which he stands accused by you."

"He did say one or two things while the boys were busy softening him up," Starkey said. "'You've got the wrong man. I've done nothing.' I took it that he was just trying to save his own skin. You can never rely on anything a bloke tells you while he's on the receiving end of a drubbing. It's only after he's gone the distance that you'll start getting the truth out of him, and your Mr Greensmith looks ready for that now, if you ask me."

"I still insist upon examining him," I said.

"And I insist," said Starkey, with stern emphasis, "that you stay exactly where you are, Doctor, unless you wish to take his place in that chair. Your continued good health rests entirely on my goodwill, remember."

The sound of our voices stirred Greensmith out of his beaten stupor. He raised his head and looked at us blearily through eyelids so fatly swollen they were almost shut. A frothy mixture of blood and spittle leaked from his slack lips. He was at death's door, I could tell. Without urgent medical attention he might not last the night. He might not even last the next hour.

I did not need to impart my diagnosis to Holmes. His sombre expression told me he had arrived at the same conclusion.

"Mr Greensmith?" said he. "Daniel Greensmith?"

The man in the chair mumbled a few words. Barely intelligible, they seemed to constitute an acknowledgement that that was his name, along with a plea for mercy.

"Mr Greensmith, I am Sherlock Holmes. I have been seeking you on a matter of some urgency. I am going to help you, and I trust that you can help me. I need to know about Notting Hill and about Inigo Niemand. Anything you have, any scraps of data, may be crucial."

Greensmith merely moaned. He was too far gone to make any sense. He barely seemed to understand what was being asked of him.

Holmes turned to Starkey. "You have sold me a pup," he said with some asperity. "Our deal is off. Watson and I are going to leave now, and we shall be taking Greensmith with us."

"Really, Mr Holmes?" said Starkey, eyebrows arching. "You are welching on a bargain, and to cap it all you have the temerity to say you are making off with my property?"

"This man is not property, yours or anyone's. He is a victim of the foulest injustice, and there will be consequences."

"And now you're threatening me. Hear that, lads?" Starkey addressed this remark to his men, who had remained outside the cabin. "Somehow Mr Holmes has got it into his head that we should be scared of him."

A collective low chortling conveyed what the assembled thugs thought of that.

"I promised your men a *baritsu* lesson," said Holmes. "I am going to give them that very thing, although it may not be in a manner quite to their liking."

He stepped smartly out of the cabin, and as I peered past Starkey through the doorway, I saw him immediately adopt one of the attacking postures of his martial art. His hands orbited each other, half-clenched like talons, and he rested his weight upon his back foot while lifting his front foot so that it was almost *en pointe*.

Starkey's men fanned out in a semicircle around him. One of them smacked fist into palm. Another licked his lips with relish.

Before battle could commence, Starkey produced his pistol.

"Mr Holmes," said he, aiming at my friend through the doorway.

Holmes glanced round. "You said you would like to have seen *baritsu* in action, Starkey. Here is your chance. Why pass it up?"

"I'm not risking you winning your way to freedom."

"And I," said I, drawing my revolver and pointing it at Starkey, "am not risking you taking Sherlock Holmes's life."

"You have a gun too." Starkey sounded crestfallen but phlegmatic. "Why did I not anticipate that? Well, this is a pretty pass. What now, eh?"

I cocked the hammer. "Now you tell your men to untie Greensmith, and Holmes and I shall help him out of here."

"Or..." Starkey pivoted abruptly, so that his pistol was pointing at Greensmith. "How about I put a bullet in him instead? He's the trophy here. Without him, you have nothing. It's no skin off my nose if he dies, whereas you will lose out."

"If I see your finger so much as tense on that trigger," I said, "I will shoot. I will not hesitate."

"Are you a killer, Dr Watson?" said Starkey. "Do you have what it takes to murder a man?"

"Try me." I firmed my grip on the revolver.

Starkey looked into my eyes. What he saw there was what I meant him to see – grim fixity of purpose – for he appeared to have second thoughts. Then, all at once, he lowered his weapon.

"If he means that much to you," he said, motioning at Greensmith, "take him. I've no need of the wretch. I've had my fun with him. Hopefully he'll have learned his lesson and won't come round Shoreditch bothering anyone again."

"Empty it," I said, nodding at the weapon.

Grudgingly Starkey thumbed the release catch on the barrel and tipped the cartridges out onto the floor.

"Toss the gun into the corner."

He did that too. "But I'm not telling my men to untie him."

"Fine. Then you do it."

"I am no one's lackey. I'd rather die."

In the fact of such mulish obstinacy I had no alternative. Keeping my revolver trained upon Starkey, I set about undoing the knots on Greensmith's ropes myself. With only one hand it took a while.

In the meantime Holmes guarded the doorway of the cabin. "Don't be tempted to rush at me," he warned Starkey's men. "I will be able to hold you off long enough to give my friend plenty of time to shoot. You wouldn't want your boss's death on your heads, would you? Without his leadership where would you be? And of course, it only takes one bullet to kill a man. That leaves Watson with four in the cylinder to distribute amongst the rest of you."

Their meaty faces registered comprehension and compliance. Holmes's logic seemed unassailable.

At last the ropes tumbled free. I propped a shoulder beneath Greensmith's armpit and hoisted him to his feet. He sagged against me, just so much dead weight.

I walked him past Starkey and through the doorway. Holmes fell in step beside me, putting his own shoulder under Greensmith and sharing the burden.

Starkey's men remained in their semicircle, a barricade of sizeable bodies and sullen expressions.

"Let them pass," said Starkey, trying to sound munificent but unable to keep a note of bitterness from his voice.

The barricade parted. We strode through.

"Don't think I won't forget this," Starkey called out after us. "I am a man who knows how to bear a grudge. There will come a time when you both shall pay for what has happened here, and it'll be sooner than you think. You mark my words."

"We stand ready," Holmes called back, without looking round.

We continued to walk, all but dragging Greensmith between us. I could hardly believe that we had done it. We had bearded a brash, mercurial gang boss in his den, we had rescued Greensmith from his clutches, and we were going to get away scot-free.

That was when Allan Quatermain appeared and everything went to pot.

CHAPTER THIRTEEN

THE CHOICE OF TARGET

We heard a sudden commotion behind us. A gunshot rang out. A round ricocheted off a wooden support pillar just beside us, showering us with splinters.

We turned to find Quatermain wrestling with one of Starkey's men, having manifested seemingly from nowhere. The thug had a pistol which he had been keeping concealed until, doubtless at a silent gesture of command from Starkey, he had taken it out with the intention of shooting us from behind as we departed. That was why Starkey had averred so confidently that our comeuppance would arrive sooner than we thought. He too had had an ace up his sleeve.

Quatermain wrenched the man's gun arm up, so that the second round he loosed off at us also went wide, disappearing amongst the roof beams.

Another of Starkey's men threw himself at Quatermain. Then the rest of them piled in. Quatermain was buried under a scrum of burly bodies. I saw him flailing, lashing out at his attackers with one hand while still vying for control of the gun with the other.

"Holmes," I said, "against those odds I don't think even Quatermain can prevail."

"I concur, Watson."

Leaving me to support Greensmith on my own, Holmes launched himself into the fray.

My friend delivered a flurry of blows which sent two of Starkey's men reeling, one clutching a shattered nose, the other a dislocated wrist. A third thug lashed out at Holmes with a pocketknife, the blade missing his throat by a whisker. Holmes retaliated by swatting the knife out of the man's hand and at the same time driving a fist hard into his solar plexus. The breath left the fellow's lungs at the kind of speed and pressure of a gust of air from a set of bellows. Holmes bowled him over, and he lay on the floor clutching his belly and gasping.

The intervention by Holmes gave Quatermain sufficient respite to ward off his remaining assailants. He now had possession of the gun belonging to Starkey's man. For a moment I dared to think that matters were now firmly in hand once more. Between them, Holmes and Quatermain had succeeded in undoing our reversal of fortune.

Then Starkey emerged from the cabin, and his pistol was back in his possession. He had had sufficient time to reload it. He took aim.

I, hampered by Greensmith's bulk, failed to raise my own pistol in time. Starkey got off a shot, at close range. I heard a roar of pain and saw Quatermain recoil, clutching one arm. He staggered and fell to his knees, face contorted in agony. Blood poured down his sleeve.

Starkey traversed the few paces between them and pressed the barrel of the gun to Quatermain's temple.

"Mr Holmes!" he bellowed. "Stand down, this instant, unless you wish to see your saviour's brains plastered all over the floor.

You too, Dr Watson. Drop your firearm. It's your turn to be the one who capitulates. Do it!"

With the utmost reluctance I laid my revolver down on the ground. Despair and resentment churned in my gut. Holmes, meanwhile, allowed himself to be seized roughly by two of Starkey's mob. His arms were pinioned behind his back.

"Now then, what's all this malarkey?" the gang boss said, jabbing his gun hard against Quatermain's head. "Some old coot comes blazing in like a firework, waving his fists about, starting a ruckus. Where are you from, eh? What's your connection to Mr Holmes? Are you his father or something?"

"Hardly," Quatermain replied through gritted teeth. "I am someone who could not stand idly by while one of your men aimed a gun at Holmes and his ally."

"Yes, and very heroic of you it was too."

"And very cowardly it was of you to authorise shooting someone in the back."

"You have fire," said Starkey, grinding the gun into Quatermain's skull. "I like that. It'll be a shame to snuff it out."

"He has nothing to do with any of this," said Holmes to the gang boss. "I do not even know why he is here. I have no meaningful association with the fellow, and therefore you should feel free to release him."

"I think that is up to me to decide, not you."

"Nonetheless, holding him hostage is in no way advantageous to you where I am concerned."

"And yet you surrendered, meek as a lamb, when you saw he was at my mercy. Does that not somewhat contradict your assertion?"

"I am here," Quatermain declared, "because I happen to have been keeping a weather eye on Daniel Greensmith. I learned that, in his guise as Black Jack Corcoran, he had got into difficulties.

Feeling a perhaps unwarranted sense of responsibility for the fellow, I went looking for him."

"And found Watson and me in a fine predicament," said Holmes. "You realise, Quatermain, that I was attempting to distance myself from you just now? Denying any link between us was all for your benefit, and you have unpicked my efforts."

Quatermain grunted.

"Quatermain," said Starkey. "Is that your name? Come on, answer me. Yes? No?" The gang boss prodded him with the pistol yet again.

"Yes, that is I. Allan Quatermain. And if you jab me with that gun one more time, you rascal—"

"You'll what?" Starkey sneered. "You're in a great deal of pain, Mr Quatermain. It's written all over your face. There's a bullet lodged in the meat of your arm and it's hurting like the devil. I doubt you could even stand, never mind attack."

"You might be surprised."

A thought appeared to strike Starkey. "Wait. Allan Quatermain… You're the explorer, aren't you? The fellow who travels to the African wilderness all the time and tames the natives and depletes the wildlife."

"A most inexact summation of my accomplishments."

"But you are he? That same Quatermain? You must be."

"Close enough."

"Well, well, well." A gleam had entered Starkey's eye. I could see him calculating inwardly. "This is a turn-up for the books. One of the things people say about you, Mr Quatermain, is that you're a terrific shot. A veritable deadeye. You can bring down an elephant at a thousand paces."

"With the appropriate gun, yes. A double-eight breech-loading rifle, for instance. Although a thousand paces, even with an eleven-drachms black powder charge, would be pushing it."

"Details, details. My point is that you never miss. That's what I've heard tell about you."

"I never miss when it counts."

"Then let's see if you live up to your reputation. Up you get."

With some effort and many a grimace of discomfort, Quatermain rose from the floor.

"Jem," Starkey said to one of his men, "bring me Dr Watson's revolver, would you? Good lad. Now hand it to Mr Quatermain. Easy there, Quatermain. Don't go having any funny ideas. I'm keeping pressure on this trigger. I'm just a twitch away from firing. All I'm proposing is that I give you a little target practice. A challenge to your hallowed sharpshooting skills. But you need something to aim at and some sort of incentive to convince you to play along. What'll it be?" He pretended to ponder. "I have it! A capital idea!"

He swivelled to look at Holmes.

"You," he said. "You can be the target, and the prize will be freedom for all four of you."

CHAPTER FOURTEEN

V.R.

Over my vociferous protestations, Holmes was frogmarched to a wall and made to stand there, facing outward. Quatermain, in turn, was instructed to position himself some thirty yards from my friend. Starkey remained directly behind Quatermain, gun directed unwaveringly at the back of his skull.

Quatermain took a moment to familiarise himself with my revolver. "Webley Bull Dog," he said. "Nickel-plated. Ivory grip. Top-break loading. Kept in excellent condition, for which my compliments, Doctor. Eley's No. 2 smokeless cartridges, by the looks of things. A good choice, although I might have gone for a .450 calibre round myself rather than a .442. Higher grain count, greater stopping power."

"Eley's has served me well thus far," I said, marvelling that Quatermain should be considering a handgun's stopping power when he was about to fire it at a man he knew to be my close friend.

"The Webley is not renowned for its accuracy at a range above twenty-five yards," he added, "but I shall make allowances. It will not hinder me."

"See that it does not," said Holmes. He sounded unduly upbeat. Indeed, he evinced no concern at all to be participating in this sinister, deadly game that Starkey had organised. His courage was remarkable. I doubted I could have been so sanguine were I in his shoes, although I must admit to wondering whether the three glasses of Tokay he had drunk not long earlier might have played a part.

"As near as you can to Mr Holmes's head," Starkey told Quatermain. "I don't want you to kill him. I don't even want you to clip him. I just want to see how close you can get without actually hitting him, and once that is achieved, you may all go free."

"Yes, I am clear on the rules, Starkey," said Quatermain tersely. "Holmes? I must implore you to remain quite still. I assure you that you are in no danger. All the same, any sudden movement by you may have regrettable consequences."

"I shall be as still as a statue," said Holmes. "You need have no worries on that account. Just prove to me that everything they say about your marksmanship is true."

"I shall endeavour to."

Quatermain raised the revolver in his right hand. His injured arm – the left – was still bleeding profusely, and I could only imagine how greatly he was suffering from the bullet wound. I prayed that the pain would not distract him from the proficient completion of his task.

Meanwhile Greensmith, whom I had laid out upon the floor, was going into rapid decline. I could all but see the life ebbing from his supine frame. Save for offering him the occasional encouraging exhortation, however, there was little I could do in that moment. I could only hope that the ghastly scenario playing out in front of me would be over with soon, so that I could find him the help he needed before it was too late.

"Come along, Mr Quatermain," Starkey chided. "Hop to it. We haven't got all night."

Quatermain sighted down the barrel, closing one eye.

Holmes squared his shoulders and held his head erect, chin out. "Any time you are ready," said he. "Please, if you can, leave my brain intact. I am rather fond of it the way it is, likewise the casing that surrounds it."

Suddenly, swiftly, Quatermain opened fire. Shot after shot left the revolver in rapid succession, each thudding into the wall adjacent to Holmes's head. He emptied the cylinder in under four seconds, during which time my heart skipped several beats. At any moment I expected the worst: a cry from Holmes, a spurt of blood, the sight of my friend's body convulsing and collapsing.

When it was finished, however, Holmes remained upright and unharmed. I think I may have glimpsed his spine sagging somewhat, as though in relief, but if so it was the tiniest of movements, barely discernible.

"Now, look at that," said a patently delighted Starkey. "You have grouped all five shots very closely together, just to the left of Mr Holmes. Excellent. And not a scratch on the man himself, either."

"I have not merely grouped them," said Quatermain.

"No indeed. You have made a pattern. A V-shape."

"To stand for 'victory'. We have gone through with this little charade of yours, Starkey. We have done as requested. We have succeeded. I believe we are due our reward."

"Very much so."

"But," said Holmes, "you are not going to give it to us, are you, Starkey? Not yet. There is more."

"You read me like a book, sir. It has been highly entertaining watching Mr Quatermain shoot, hasn't it, lads?"

Starkey's thugs nodded in avid agreement.

"It would be even more entertaining," their leader continued, "to watch it done again, don't you think?"

The men lowed, cattle-like, in the affirmative.

"Let us get our money's worth," said Starkey. "One further display of your prowess, if you please, Mr Quatermain. How about an 'R' to go with the 'V'? Put it to the right of Mr Holmes's head. Then we shall have a tribute to our glorious monarch – long may she reign – etched in bullet holes."

I objected in the strongest terms. "This is monstrous, Starkey. You have no intention of ending it there. You will have Quatermain keep at it all night, until eventually he slips up and Holmes is wounded or worse."

"Not at all, Doctor. This second bout will be the last, trust me."

"You'll forgive me if I say I doubt it."

"Honestly, once I have an 'R' to accompany the 'V', my patriotic soul will be content."

"It is fine, Watson," said Holmes. "Let Starkey have his fun. Quatermain will be as reliable with a second salvo as he was with the first. I am sure of it."

"So am I," said Quatermain.

"So am I," Starkey chimed in, "which is why this time things will be a mite different. Mr Quatermain will use his left arm."

"What!" I expostulated. "There is a bullet deep in his biceps. He can scarcely be expected to lift the arm, let alone keep it steady."

"Nonetheless those are the conditions. Oh, and your gun, Doctor, seems altogether too dependable a weapon. You can have it back. Jem, would you do the honours? There. I think Mr Quatermain will be availing himself of Charlie's pistol this time around."

Charlie, it transpired, was the one who had been on the point of shooting Holmes and me when Quatermain intercepted him. As he passed his firearm to Quatermain, the latter's moue of disgust spoke volumes.

"A Beaumont–Adams," he said. "Could you not find something less antiquated? A blunderbuss, perhaps? It even still uses the old rimfire cap-and-ball rounds. It has not been adapted to take centrefire cartridges like most of its brethren. Nor has it been cleaned in years, to judge by the copious corrosion stains."

"Make do, Mr Quatermain, make do," said Starkey.

"I am more at risk from this gun than is Mr Holmes. There is every chance it might blow up in my face."

"Well, we'll see, shan't we?"

Quatermain transferred the revolver to his left hand. He winced as he raised that arm. It dropped, and he raised it anew, this time hissing through his teeth. Blood dripped from his trembling hand as he curled his forefinger around the trigger.

"Remember to ensure that the 'R' looks like an 'R'," said Starkey, sounding not unlike a schoolmaster cajoling a pupil into improving his calligraphy. "I'd hate for you to have to start over from scratch."

The second series of shots was far slower than the previous. In between each, Quatermain was obliged to lower the pistol and relax his arm for several seconds – to allow the pain from his biceps to subside – before elevating it again. There was a kind of horror in his expression, alongside a fierce determination.

As the echoes of the gun reports faded away, Starkey surveyed Quatermain's handiwork. "Oh no," he said, lips pursed. "Dear me, no. That won't do. That won't do at all. Call that an 'R'? It is barely even a 'K'."

"What do you expect?" said Quatermain. "The Beaumont-Adams holds only five rounds, same as the Webley, and an 'R' is altogether a more complicated letter than a 'V'."

"Then Charlie will reload it with another five rounds. That

should enable you to fill in the gaps and complete the letter."

Hence the agony was prolonged – literally, in Quatermain's case – as Holmes was obliged to act as a human target for a third time. Quatermain, again left-handed, took aim and fired. The duration of the intervals between shots lengthened exponentially. Just maintaining a grip on the pistol seemed to demand everything he had, let alone raising it aloft. Perspiration broke out upon his brow, while his lips were drawn back in a snarl of concentration.

Still he persevered, and it was then that I felt the first stirrings of an admiration. Allan Quatermain had struck me as a throwback, someone who had turned away from the privileges and comforts of modernity in favour of a more primitive lifestyle. The wild called, and he heeded its summons and followed. His sojourns in the veldt had moulded him into a lean, brown snake of a man, content with the bare essentials, lacking in the graces. He looked civilised and was anything but.

For all that, he possessed a grit and tenacity far exceeding the average. Not even the hardiest outdoorsman could have rivalled the resilience, both physical and mental, that he exhibited.

Holmes must have sensed these qualities in Quatermain long before I did, else he would not have felt safe being subjected to this trial. He did not so much as flinch as the further five rounds whacked into the wall beside his head, a couple of them mere inches from his cheek.

Once this third volley was done, Holmes turned to examine the pattern made by the bullet holes.

"If that is not an 'R,'" he asseverated, "I don't know what is."

"Agreed," said Starkey. He offered Quatermain a slow handclap, his men joining in. "My congratulations, sir. You have earned your liberty, and that of these others, fair and square. You too, Mr Holmes, deserve a round of applause. Such backbone.

How were you not tempted at least to close your eyes?"

"It is better to know one's fate than blinker oneself to it."

"Most profound. Most profound. I shall bid you gents adieu now. This has been an enlightening and diverting evening. Lads?"

As Starkey sauntered out of the warehouse with his retinue of thugs, I found it hard to believe that he was leaving us to our own devices like this. In the manner of a child with a toy, he had picked us up, amused himself with us, then put us back down and walked away without a second thought.

Feeling both belittled and relieved, I bent to give Greensmith my full attention once more. The journalist was barely alive. I tapped his contusion-distended face a couple of times.

"Stay with us, Greensmith," I said. "Do not succumb."

Holmes knelt beside me, frowning in concern. "What is the prognosis?" he murmured.

"Time is short," I confided. "I fear there is nothing to be done."

"Listen to me," he said more loudly, addressing the dying man. "Focus upon my voice. You have an opportunity to file one last article, Greensmith. The scoop of a lifetime. What do you know about Inigo Niemand? Who is he really? What information did he divulge to you? Did you find out anything more about him during your enquiries in the East End?"

Consciousness glimmered faintly in Greensmith's features. His swollen, blood-smeared mouth moved.

"Ffffan..." he said.

"Fan?" said Holmes.

"Fanthorpe."

"Fanthorpe? Is that Niemand's real name? Greensmith, tell us more. Is Inigo Niemand Fanthorpe?"

Again the mouth moved, but all that emerged was a rasping hiss.

"Greensmith," Holmes persisted. "Greensmith. Who is Fanthorpe?"

"Holmes," I said.

"What is Fanthorpe's connection to Niemand?"

"Holmes," I said again.

"Just one moment, Watson."

"No, Holmes. There is no moment. He is gone. Look."

Greensmith lay motionless upon the warehouse floor. His chest betrayed not the slightest rise and fall. Soul had fled body, forsaking that deep dark valley of pain for, I hoped, a sunnier, happier clime.

CHAPTER FIFTEEN

GONE TO GROUND

"Dash it all!" Holmes exclaimed hotly. "A lead, lost."

"And a man's life," I pointed out.

"Yes, yes. That too. If only Greensmith had given us more than a mere name before he perished."

With an intemperate curse, my friend straightened up. His eye fell briefly upon the "V.R." which Quatermain had drilled into the wall. Anyone who has read my tale "The Adventure of the Musgrave Ritual" will know that Holmes himself later inscribed the same two letters, using the same medium, in the wall of our sitting-room while indulging in one of his queer humours. The forebear of that act of patriotic vandalism, an acknowledgement of his esteem for our nation's beloved Victoria Regina, may be found here in these very pages; but perhaps, too, Holmes pocked the sitting-room wall with Boxer rounds in such a formulation as a tribute to his own mettle in the face of a considerable ordeal. Should his courage ever falter, that "V.R." at Baker Street was a permanent reminder of the heights to which it might soar.

"Quatermain," he said, casting his gaze about. "Where is Quatermain?"

While Holmes and I had been busy with Greensmith, it seemed Quatermain had taken advantage of our preoccupation and quietly absconded.

"I am not letting him get away from me!" Holmes declared. "Not again!"

"But how, after our lack of success when tailing him last time, can we hope to do better this time?" I said.

"Easily. This time he has left a trail even a blind man could follow. Behold."

Droplets of blood were visible upon the floorboards, leading out of the warehouse. Holmes snatched up one of the lanterns, and the chase was on.

The trail was not perhaps as manifestly obvious as Holmes had stated. Indeed, on a number of occasions it seemed as though we had lost it. However, after some searching about, my friend would turn up a fresh patch of spilled blood upon a pavement corner or upon some railings and our mission would resume. Throughout, his eyes never lost their steely glitter, nor did the taut sinews in his thin neck slacken. For those who think of Sherlock Holmes solely as the cerebral sage of Baker Street, sunk in sedentary, brooding deliberation upon a problem, I present an image of him as a darting, questing figure on an errand of pure physicality, dependent upon the keenness of his senses alone.

We wound our way through darkened East London until we ended up in Victoria Park.

"Quatermain has led us a merry dance again, it seems," I said, "just as he did at Regent's Park."

"I beg to differ," said Holmes. "I think he is in too much pain and has lost too much blood to act with such a level of cunning. By the same token, if he were intending to cover his tracks he would have stemmed the blood flow by now. What this is, Watson, is desperation. This is an injured beast going to ground."

"But where?"

"We shall learn that soon enough."

The blood trail led us to a cluster of trees that stood footed in dense shrubbery. The leaves of the bushes formed a seemingly impenetrable thicket to a height of some ten feet. Holmes signalled that we should advance with caution. It struck me as absurd that Quatermain might be hiding within the thicket; yet, knowing what I did of the man, it did not seem beyond the bounds of possibility either.

Holmes was almost at the thicket when, from amongst the leaves, an iron blade abruptly protruded. It was large and wedge-shaped, and its cutting edge halted mere inches from Holmes's nose.

As Holmes reared back, so more of the blade emerged. It remained within close proximity of his face, changing angle to match his movements. When he bent left, the blade followed; right, likewise. Visible now was the thick wooden shaft to which it was attached, and I perceived that the whole thing constituted a battle-axe of some sort.

"Quatermain," said Holmes, "there is no need for such a show of intimidation. It is only I, Sherlock Holmes."

The unseen wielder of the axe said nothing.

"We have come to help," I said. "You have a bullet in you. It must be removed. I can perform the surgery if you let me."

Again, answer came there none from the dark depths of the thicket. The axe, however, gave a quiver, as though it were a living thing registering surprise.

"You shall not get a better offer than that, Quatermain," said Holmes. "Watson's skills as a battlefield surgeon are without compare." My friend had no first-hand evidence to back up this assertion, but I appreciated the remark nonetheless and hoped that Quatermain would too.

The axe now wavered and drooped somewhat.

"Will you allow us in?" Holmes said. "You know that we are not your foe. Our encounter with Starkey has proven that, if nothing else. We are on the same side."

Moments passed, and then the axe was retracted, withdrawing into the thicket like the stinger of a wasp returning to its sheath in the insect's abdomen.

Then, shortly after that, a hand parted the leaves of the bushes not far along from where we stood.

"This way," said a voice.

Neither voice nor hand belonged to Quatermain. The former was deeper than his and bore a thick accent, while the latter was notably darker in complexion and equipped with gaunt fingers that ended in broad, spatulate tips.

The owner of both proved to be a large African man of venerable age, sporting a high, noble brow and sharp brown eyes that glittered in a lively fashion in the lantern light. Flecks of white salted the black of his scrubby beard and close-cropped hair, and I observed that there was a deep triangular depression in his forehead, the imprint of some old, imperfectly healed wound. He wore a collarless shirt and a pair of baggy flannel trousers, neither of which appeared to have been tailored for him but rather must have been begged or borrowed. His hand grasped the rugged handle of the axe, which, in its entirety, was a truly fearsome-looking implement.

"You say you are friends of Macumazahn?" The African pronounced Quatermain's Zulu name peculiarly, accompanying the "c" with a click in the back of his throat that sounded like a drop of water falling into a subterranean pool.

"I might not go that far," said Holmes, "but we are certainly not hostile to his interests."

"He has lately mentioned a Mr Sherlock Holmes. He has

been none too complimentary, but I have sensed a portion of respect all the same. Come further in. He is here."

The African ushered us into the heart of the thicket, axe still in hand. We went as he did, crawling on hands and knees through a low tunnel that snaked between trunks and boughs. It disgorged onto a small clearing whose area could not have been more than a dozen square yards in total.

There, a crude camp had been made. A rectangle of tarpaulin was stretched over the top to keep out the worst of the elements, while bedrolls were laid across the bare earth floor. Some basic cooking and eating utensils and a couple of rifles were the sole other accoutrements.

Upon one of the bedrolls lay Quatermain, on his back. He was sound asleep, but not at peace. His body spasmed and jerked and his face was glazed with sweat, as though he was in the grip of a fever. A bandage had been applied to his arm but it was a dressing of the most rudimentary sort, just a torn strip of cloth, and blood from the bullet wound had soaked it to saturation.

"I have done what I can for him," said the African, "but I am no doctor and I have no medicines. If you truly can bring him succour, I beseech you to do so."

I knelt by Quatermain and felt his brow. It was hot.

"Did he pass out when he got here?" I asked.

"No, but he was weak and in much pain. He desired the oblivion of *Taduki*, so that he might rest."

"*Taduki*?"

"The drug," said Holmes. "Remember, Watson? The tobacco-like herb about which Quatermain told us. The one which induces 'such strange, entrancing visions."

"I helped him partake of it." The African gestured at a pipe which lay by Quatermain's side, the same calabash he had smoked at Baker Street.

"Sleep cannot extract a bullet," I said, "nor stave off infection. Listen, my good man…" I realised I needed to know the African's name. I could not keep addressing him as "my good man" if I were to have his cooperation when tending to Quatermain. "What may I call you?"

"Umslopogaas," said he. "You stand face to face with Umslopogaas, of the blood of Chaka, of the people of the Amazulu, a captain in the regiment of the Nkomabakosi, and long-time comrade of Macumazahn, he who is the slayer of elephants, eater up of lions, clever one, watchful one, brave one, quick one, whose shot never misses, who strikes straight home, who grasps a hand and holds it to the death as a true friend should. And what may I call you, *koos*?"

I took it that "*koos*" was a term of endearment or deference. "Watson," I said.

Umslopogaas seemed to expect more from me than that, as though I should reel off a litany of descriptors as he had.

"John H. Watson, M.D.," I said, "graduate of the University of London and Netley Hospital, late of the Army Medical Service, my regiment being the Fifth Northumberland Fusiliers, a veteran of the Second Afghan War, now a general practitioner and… and companion of Mr Sherlock Holmes, consulting detective of Baker Street, he whose business is to know what other people do not know and who uses the knowledge which he possesses in order to ensure that justice be done."

The Zulu gave a quick, gratified grin. "Now we know each other better, as men should who are strangers."

"Umslopogaas, I am going to have to remove the bullet from Quatermain's arm," I said. "It cannot be left there to fester. Ideally this should take place at a hospital or in my consulting rooms, but he has already lost a lot of blood and moving him from here would only cause him to lose more."

"Agreed. You must make do."

"It is handy that Quatermain has anaesthetised himself, as that renders the job somewhat more straightforward. However, the pain of the operation may yet rouse him from his state of stupefaction. If he begins to become agitated and to writhe, I shall require you, as his friend, to soothe him and if necessary to hold him down. Can you manage that?"

"Of course, *koos*."

I produced the portable medical kit I was wont to carry with me in case of emergency. Not much larger than a cigarette case, it contained scalpel, tweezers, needle, scissors, a loop of surgical thread and a small phial of rubbing alcohol for disinfecting. Then I unwound the bandage from Quatermain's arm and inspected the injury.

The bullet had gone deep. My probing little finger sank in up to the second knuckle before its tip touched metal. Quatermain, in his drug-fuelled slumber, softly moaned.

"This will not be pretty," I predicted, and it was not. I had to dig around with the tweezers for nearly quarter of an hour, taking the utmost care to preserve the integrity of the surrounding flesh, before I felt the bullet start to come loose. Prying it out from its berth took another ten minutes, during which time Quatermain's eyelids began fluttering and he let out increasingly voluble noises of complaint. Towards the end of the procedure he was almost fully awake and Umslopogaas was obliged to secure his shoulders with both hands and bear down so that he did not thrash about too much. All the while the Zulu murmured to the patient in his own tongue, which rippled across its soft consonants with the rising-and-falling cadences of a song.

At last I levered the little flattened nugget of lead free. I swabbed off the blood that coated my hands and set to work with the needle and thread. It was not the neatest specimen of suturing that I have ever done, but under the circumstances it could have been worse. Quatermain would have an ugly scar upon his arm for the rest of his days and perhaps some slight stiffness in the limb, although somehow I could not foresee either troubling him greatly.

I sat back, exhausted after concentrating so hard for so long. Quatermain was gradually lapsing back into unconsciousness. His features looked more composed than before, and already less heat was radiating from his brow.

"A miracle worker!" Umslopogaas declared, clapping me on the back. "A true healer! Dr John H. Watson, M.D., graduate of the University of London and Netley Hospital, I commend you on your medical magnificence. You are mighty with knife and with thread. You are a prince of cuts and stitches. Forever now shall I hail you as a remover of bullets and a sealer-up of wounds without rival, and more importantly as he who saved the life of Macumazahn. I shall dare to call you friend, you who have kept the spirit of *my* friend safely tethered to his body."

"It was nothing really."

"It was everything," Umslopogaas contradicted.

"Umslopogaas," Quatermain piped up in a faint, feeble voice. His eyes were half opened. "You are embarrassing the man. He is unfamiliar with the Zulu practice of bongering. He thinks, as a true-born Englishman, that you are going overboard with all this praise."

Nodding, Umslopogaas fell silent.

"More *Taduki*," Quatermain said. It was barely a croak.

The Zulu fell to preparing a pipe full of the herb, which came in a leather pouch and looked not unlike ordinary tobacco, albeit with a greenish tinge. When lit, the smell of it was sweet, floral, but also ever so slightly rotten, reminiscent of tropical plants in a hot-house.

"Hate the stuff as a rule," Quatermain confided, "but it has its uses."

A few puffs of *Taduki* smoke, and he began to drift off again.

"Before you forsake us altogether for the Land of Nod, Quatermain," said Holmes, "there are things we must discuss."

"I would counsel letting him sleep," I said. "He has been through an ordeal. Later, when he has rested, he should be clearer-headed and perhaps more amenable."

"At the very least tell me about Fanthorpe," Holmes said to Quatermain. "Who is he?"

Quatermain shook his head slowly, although whether in refusal or perplexity, it was difficult to tell. His hand went to his pocket, whence he fetched out a small chased-silver locket. His thumb triggered the clasp, and the locket sprang open to reveal two tiny photographs within, one of a woman, the other of a young man. Quatermain studied both with a rueful air, before his eyelids closed firmly and his breathing deepened to that of someone sunk in the profoundest of slumbers.

"Damn him, the fellow is elusive even when stationary," said Holmes. He turned to Umslopogaas. "Well then, sir, it falls to you to help us fill in the blanks here."

"I do not feel at liberty to do so," said the Zulu, with a wary glance at Quatermain.

"We might start with why you and Quatermain have established yourselves in a little camp in the park rather than, say, at a hotel."

"Oh, as to that, the answer is easy. It is to 'keep a low profile', as Macumazahn says. He does not wish it known that he is at large in London, and because I am with him he would be more conspicuous than usual. There are black-skinned men like me in this city, I know, but not many, and each of us is readily noticed.

Besides, Macumazahn is more comfortable in conditions such as this, on a hard bed under a soft roof, than on a soft bed under a hard roof. He has lately bought a house in a part of England called Yorkshire. I assume you have heard of it."

"Yorkshire?" said Holmes with a twinkle in his eye. "Yes. A wild land where the indigenous tribesmen are not always friendly and speak a dialect of their own which few outsiders understand."

"You are mocking. I have been there myself and it is not at all as you say. Macumazahn himself speaks fondly of the region's hills and of 'the Moors' and 'the Dales'. However, for him nothing can compare with the bush of the Okavango or the elephant-hunting grounds beyond Bamangwato. In those places and their ilk does he find his true self, more so than he ever could in a big Yorkshire house or in any building. In wide-open spaces, under the sky, is where Macumazahn thrives. Especially when he is stalking prey."

"And who is his prey in London?"

Again, Umslopogaas made a show of reticence.

"In that case, let me tell you what I think," said Holmes. "The locket which Quatermain took out just now, the one still in his hand, seems more than germane. The two subjects depicted therein are of importance to him. That much is obvious, else why would they be memorialised in the locket and why would he choose to gaze upon them so, the last thing he sees as his consciousness fades? One of the photographs, that of the woman, is of considerably greater vintage than the other, being a daguerreotype. Furthermore, the woman's hairstyle dates back some two or three decades. I am no expert in feminine fashions, that most mutable and ineffable of phenomena, but the centre parting and the 'wings' over the ears are suggestive of that era. Given Quatermain's age, the logical inference is that the lady is his wife."

Umslopogaas canted his head to one side, a gesture which

could as well have signified denial as acknowledgement. He was more than shrewd, this Zulu.

"Another logical inference," Holmes continued, "is that the lady herself is long dead. Otherwise Quatermain would in the intervening years have replaced the picture with another more up-to-date. Here in the locket his wife is as she was and always will be in his memory. Am I correct so far?"

Umslopogaas paused, then said, "Stella. Her name was Stella, and she was Macumazahn's second wife and mother of his only son. She perished giving birth to the boy."

"Said son being the occupant of the other half of the locket, for his physiognomic resemblances to both the woman adjacent and to Quatermain himself are marked. I am going to chance my arm and state that he too is dead. My reasons for making the deduction are as follows. The picture of him is recent, showing clear evidence of the advance in photographic techniques since the other was taken.

"In addition," Holmes continued, "the picture has been clipped out from a larger print and inserted into the locket, and the clipping was not done competently. Scissor marks can be discerned around its perimeter, and those marks, in their visible roughness, tell a story not of the steady hand of a professional photographer but the unsteady hand of an amateur. Not only that but the picture has been inserted into the locket atop another picture, whose edges show through from behind.

"Now, why would Quatermain cut out a picture of his son to supplant another picture in the locket unless he sought a handy souvenir of how the lad looked in near-adulthood? I would wager that the picture beneath it is of the same young man as a child, but I shall not be so impertinent as to disentangle the locket from Quatermain's grasp in order to verify that theory."

"Harry," said Umslopogaas. "His name was Harry."

"'Was'. So I am right and he is deceased. Recently deceased, moreover."

Umslopogaas bowed his head.

"Yes, I thought as much," my friend said, pleased with himself. "Hence the clumsiness of the cutting-out, indicative of a state of some mental upheaval."

"Holmes," I said, "a little tact would not go amiss. Can you not see that the subject is upsetting to Umslopogaas?"

"I apologise, Umslopogaas," said Holmes. "I get carried away sometimes. You knew Harry Quatermain, I take it."

"Not intimately but well enough," came the reply, "and because I am Macumazahn's brother-in-battle, I share with him in all things, including grief. Also, I am the one whom he charged with safeguarding the young man from harm, and wretched soul that I am, I failed in that duty. Failed dismally!"

Tears sprang to the Zulu's eyes, and I was moved to place an arm around his shoulders as he cried.

At last he was able to speak again. "I am resolved to tell you as much as I know. Macumazahn might not desire me to, but you have shown yourselves – you especially, Dr John H. Watson – to be men of good standing. I am going to unburden myself of a story, but take note: it is a solemn and tragic one."

CHAPTER SIXTEEN

THE SIREN CALL OF
EXCITEMENT AND DERRING-DO

The Zulu commenced his tale.

"Macumazahn's son aspired to become a doctor, like you, Dr John H. Watson," said he. "There can be few nobler callings than the curing of the sick."

I shrugged as if to say he would get no disagreement from me on that front.

"He was studying here in London, as did you, perhaps at the selfsame place of education as you," Umslopogaas continued. "However, Harry wished to take what he learned and apply it amongst the peoples of Africa. For he shared Macumazahn's love for the continent and perhaps felt it all the more strongly than his father for having been born there. Hot sun and dry plains and the roar of the lion and the whisper of the tall *tambookie* grass – you might say these were in Harry's blood, and no amount of time spent in England might erase them. He would return to Africa when he could, not least on that occasion some years ago when, as a boy on the cusp of manhood, he accompanied Macumazahn prospecting for gold in the Transvaal, at a place called Pilgrim's Rest.

"This summer just past, when Harry was a year away from gaining his qualification, the lure of Africa once again proved too strong and he took a temporary leave of absence and boarded a ship bound for Durban. His plan was to visit remote villages and outposts, bringing what aid he could to those there who were ailing.

"It so happened that a disease had lately broken out in the region. Amongst us Zulus it is known as the plague of blisters and also, more often, the lizard sickness, for the bodies of any who contract it become covered in bubbling, weeping sores, their skin looking like that of a reptile. Many it kills. Those who survive are scarred for life and may be left blind."

"Sounds to me like smallpox," I said.

"Such is the white man's name for it," said Umslopogaas. "When Harry learned that an epidemic of the lizard sickness had struck, up near Vryheid, just north of Natal, he did not hesitate. He put together a caravan of four wagons and some twenty men with a view to travelling thither.

"I did my best to stop him. Before Harry's arrival in Africa, Macumazahn had sent word to me that I was to greet the lad when his ship put in and look after him from thereon until his return to England. In the discharging of that duty I accompanied him wherever he went. I had Groan-Maker ready." He indicated the fearsome axe. "It was with me at all times, so that I might defend him from danger. I would willingly have given my life to protect the life of Macumazahn's son and thought it a small price to pay.

"So when Harry told me of his intentions, I spoke to him strongly and sternly, much as his own father might. I said he was making a grave error of judgement. What could he do for those afflicted with the lizard sickness? He could at best offer them solace as they died, and perhaps ease their suffering somewhat, but he could not prevent the disease running its course. Their lives were in the gods' hands, not any man's.

"But Harry Quatermain was not to be deterred. He wished to do good. I believe him to have been spurred, too, by the same restless urge to journey into the unknown and to seek adventure that drives his father. Not for Harry the quiet life, tending flowers in a garden, making polite conversation over teacups. For him there was only the siren call of excitement and derring-do, which was his destiny."

I must confess that I had never heard "derring-do" used in conversation before. It had always seemed to me a word reserved for prose only, especially the prose of a certain kind of lowbrow novel. I was, nonetheless, finding Umslopogaas's florid, literate English quite enchanting and could have listened to him talk all day long.

"My protests," Umslopogaas continued, "fell upon deaf ears, so I had no alternative but to go with Harry on his foray northward. My vow to Macumazahn could not be forsworn. I would have died of shame had I not honoured it. I insisted to Harry that I would be coming along and that I would impale myself upon Groan-Maker's blade there and then if he refused. He saw then how adamant I was, and could not deny me. He even pronounced himself glad that he would have my company upon the journey.

"We trekked for some fifteen days. Our caravan was well provisioned, our horses steady as we rode them, our oxen strong as they pulled the wagons. Naught could have waylaid us, or so I thought. Ha! How the gods laugh at him who grows complacent! How they love to cut the legs out from under him!

"We were in the foothills of the mountains called by white men the Drakensberg Range and, by us Zulus, uKhahlamba, and we were making good headway, until came rain. Such rain. You English may not comprehend what real rainfall is, here in a country where a few meagre droplets scatter down from time to time like a sprinkling of blossom loosened by the breeze. Rain where I am from is a monster. It rages for days on end. It batters one's head like a mallet and turns slow rivers to foaming torrents and solid ground to liquid. It descends from clouds that tower higher than mountains and is the laughter of demons.

"What choice had we when the rain started but to halt our caravan, erect shelter and wait? To carry on would have been foolishness. The tracks we were following were turning to deep mud, and there was a danger of rockslides in the mountain passes.

"We abided under canvas for a week, and a miserable time we had of it. The rain did not once let up. Water seeped into our beds. It extinguished our cooking fires. It made our feet go grey. Harry Quatermain did his utmost to remain resolute. Again and again he proclaimed that the rain would not dissuade him from his objective. As soon as it ceased, he would move on.

"And then it did cease, and the sun showed his bright face once more, and the land steamed and dried and hardened. But alas! Such woe! For I had taken ill. I, who have survived so much in my long life. I, who know hardship as well as I know my own shadow. I, who bear the cicatrices of countless battles, here upon my body..."

Umslopogaas tugged open his shirt to reveal an expanse of chest, criss-crossed with scar tissue, the legacy of laceration by knife, sword, arrow and who knows what else.

"And here too upon my head."

Now he pointed to the triangular depression upon his brow.

"A nasty injury," I said.

"Oh, yes indeed, Doctor! Brains flowed out when I was struck there by my foe. Believe you me, grey matter gushed, and I swooned and became like as to one dead. Yet, even as I slipped into insensibility, I had at least the satisfaction of knowing that he who had smote me thus – Faku, the captain of King Dingaan's army – was dead too, for I had already dealt him a mortal blow with Groan-Maker. Faku's retaliation – hurling his own axe at me with the last of his strength – was the final low act of a thoroughgoing villain. This happened during the war between Zulu and Boer, and this was also the time I lost forever my love Nada, she who was known as Nada the Lily and was the most beauteous of all Zulu women. I have not been the same since. The scar, in its way, reminds me of her. It is a physical manifestation of the absence she left in my soul.

"But back to my story. Illness had seized me. It held me in its remorseless claws. An enfeeblement of the lungs, brought on by the bad weather, and its name was pneumonia. I was laid low. I, Umslopogaas, the great Slaughterer; I who have made one hundred and three kills as a warrior and put a notch for each in the rhinoceros-horn handle of my axe – I was reduced to a quivering, cough-wracked wretch by an enemy I could neither see nor fight. But then I am old, I know it, and with age comes vulnerability to such maladies.

"Harry Quatermain did minister to me as I lay upon my sickbed. Never let it be said that he was not diligent or failed to heed his vocation as a physician. He stayed by my side while the illness assailed me, ever with a cold damp cloth to mop my brow and a draught of soothing nostrum from his collection of medical supplies to quell my pangs, even as my breath became short and my chest ached like fire and I tossed and turned like a whirlwind. Were it not for him I might well have expired and now be dwelling amongst the spirits of my ancestors, including King Chaka, who was secretly my father.

"As soon as I began to recover, however, and show signs that I would not die, Harry did a wrong thing. The headstrongness of youth was upon him, and I cannot fault him for that, for we have each of us been young and bereft of continence; and yet I regret it all the same. He left. He took half the caravan, with its drivers and bearers and outriders, and continued onward without me. He told me, full of apology, that he could bear to tarry no longer. He had lost enough time as it was. He ordered those men who stayed with me to look after me as though I were his father, and that was no mean edict, for Macumazahn is revered throughout the region and his name carries as much heft as any chieftain's.

"Naturally I was angry that Harry had deserted me, because it rendered my vow to Macumazahn obsolete. Yet I was still too frail of health to hinder him or give chase. Merely to stand upright left me trembling like a newborn springbok calf. All I could do was fume helplessly and pray to the gods that Harry would come to no harm. But the gods..."

"They did not listen," I said.

"Or they did, but in their capriciousness chose to spurn my entreaties. Harry was gone for many days, and as soon as I was well enough, I commanded the half of the caravan that had remained behind at our encampment to be on the move again. We rolled north, and at every town and village we enquired after the young white man Quatermain. At some such places we did not dare risk lingering, since smallpox had visited there and left its heinous mark in graves that were freshly dug and in the ravaged skin and ulcer-whitened eyes of the afflicted still living. Reports nonetheless were given of Harry, whose doctoring had eased the passing of many and was credited even with saving a few. O, rash, brave youngster, to expose yourself to such risks in the service of others – of strangers, moreover – without seeming concern for your own wellbeing!

"Eventually we found ourselves in mining country, where Boers and Britishers have set aside their differences in the name of commerce, and together, in relative harmony, draw diamonds, copper, gold, silver and more from the soil, enriching themselves greatly from the proceeds as they gouge deep gashes in the earth. It was here that the trail dwindled. Confirmed sightings of Harry's caravan were few and far between. The smallpox was less prevalent amongst the communities of white men that had sprung up around the deposits of jewels and precious metals. Perhaps they had better cleanliness there, and a better diet, and that helped keep the disease at bay."

"There are certain strains of smallpox to which those of European extraction have built up an immunity," I said, "but to which other races, not least Africans, are highly susceptible. I have read about it in *The Lancet*."

"You would know more about it than I, *koos*. I bow before your expertise." Umslopogaas literally bowed. "I assumed, at any rate, that Harry had been unable to find any occupation there for himself and had gone on to seek the sick elsewhere.

"Then came the news. The dire news. A Hottentot cattle herder, at whose kraal we fetched up one evening, said in response to my enquiries that a young Englishman named Harry lay dead at a town half a day's journey west. Such was the rumour he had heard, at any rate.

"I refused to believe him. I accused the man of being a liar. Yet I did not hesitate to set out for the town. All alone, I rode through the night, pushing myself and my horse to the brink of exhaustion. My heart pounded within my breast. My head swam. The dead man was not Harry Quatermain, I told myself. He could not be. Nothing could be more awful than if the son of Macumazahn had died.

"Under a pitiless cold moon I rode, and at dawn reached my destination, which was one of those settlements I described earlier, a community of miners. Its name was Silasville, and it was a sprawling expanse of huts and cabins large enough to be called a town, nestling beside a small lake and a line of low hills, and I will tell you, sirs, I was joyous when I saw it. I was joyous because I presumed that plenty of white men must live there, and that meant that if someone was deceased, there was every chance it was not Harry Quatermain. I know 'Harry' is a name bestowed upon many an Englishman. I entered Silasville full of hope.

"My hope crumbled when I was hailed by someone I knew, one of the bearers who had been in the half of the caravan which Harry had taken with him. His face was heavy. His demeanour spoke of sorrow and defeat.

"In that instant, I understood beyond all doubt that my worst fears were well-founded."

CHAPTER SEVENTEEN

SILASVILLE

Umslopogaas's composure disintegrated. He buried his face in his hands, his shoulders heaved, and great agonised sobs issued forth from his throat.

Crouching there in that confined space within the thicket, Holmes and I exchanged looks. I could see that my friend, while not unsympathetic to Umslopogaas's remorse, was growing impatient. He was obviously wishing that Umslopogaas would confine himself to the meat of his narrative and not indulge in digressions or emotional outbursts.

For my part, I was content to let the story unfold at whatever pace its teller liked. However, mindful of Holmes's short temper and keen to avert some expression of exasperation which might offend Umslopogaas, I decided to cajole the African into resuming his monologue.

"Your English is excellent, Umslopogaas," I said. "You speak it better than many for whom it is their mother tongue."

"I thank you, Dr John H. Watson," Umslopogaas said with a tearful sniff. "I came by it courtesy of Macumazahn. Over the

years he has taught me both how to speak your language and
how to read it. He has given me books by your nation's most
celebrated writers. I admire greatly the works of Mr Dickens,
Miss Austen and Mrs Gaskell. Sir Walter Scott, too, with his fine
romances of Scotland."

"Then you are a man of taste. Those are all authors whom I
admire as well and, what is more, in whose footsteps I one day
hope to follow."

"You write novels?"

"I fully intend to, if suitable subject matter presents itself."
I darted a glance at Holmes. "But you were saying about
Harry Quatermain...?"

"Yes." Umslopogaas collected himself. "With an icy feeling
in my belly, a dread so all-consuming it left me benumbed, I
let the bearer direct me to Silasville's hospital. I call it hospital
but it was barely that. It was a shed where a man whom I shall
not dignify with the title 'doctor' treated miners who were sick
or injured. He was a drunkard, this fellow. With the sweat that
oozed from his pores came the reek of alcohol, and he seemed
incapable of speaking in any way but thickly, as though his
mouth were crammed with sand. In a back room, which one
might laughingly term a surgery, lay a body. He took me through
to see it, but only after I had convinced him that it was in his best
interests to do so. A shaken fist, a glare of the eyes – that was all
it took to overcome his initial stubborn refusal.

"Upon a wooden trestle table, beneath a sheet, I found
Harry. He had been dead long enough that he needed urgent
burying, for his flesh had begun to resemble marble and flies
were becoming interested. It was unmistakably he. That thatch
of short, upward-sticking hair, those features so much like
Macumazahn's own... Indeed, to look at Harry Quatermain
was akin to looking at his father in his younger days, when

Macumazahn and I first became acquainted. And now here the lad was, so still, so empty, a shell, a husk...

"I was broken. I could not countenance the thought of this thing that had happened. It was too heavy to bear, like a boulder inside me. I raged. I howled. I beat my breast and clawed at my scalp.

"When I had calmed, I made demands. 'How did he die?' I asked the so-called doctor. 'What killed him?'

"The man had no plain answer. 'I do not know,' said he. 'He was brought to me yesterday morning, already far too gone to be saved. He breathed his last upon this very table, just minutes after I began tending to him. Some disease perhaps?'

"'Disease? Which one? Tell me, you booze-befuddled nitwit. Which disease carried him off?'

"'I cannot say. Tropical diseases are not my forte. I am told that he had been visiting places where smallpox is rife. Perhaps it was that.'

"'Smallpox!' I exclaimed. 'Even I can tell he did not contract smallpox. Where are the blisters? I see not one. You are an idiot and a charlatan. You are a disgrace to your profession.'

"The man was of no help to me. Before my fury he quailed and retreated, and I subsequently found him suckling from a hipflask, as though from his mother's teat.

"My imperative was to get Harry Quatermain's mortal remains out of that town. It was not a good place. I had sensed that upon arrival – a distinct tension in the air, a dark undercurrent that blew like a wind between its meagre dwellings – and my instinctive impression was confirmed the moment I set foot outside the hospital, which I exited in order to find somewhere where I might purchase a bolt of cloth. My plan was to wrap Harry in bindings and transport him out into the wilderness to some fitting burial spot. I had not gone far down Silasville's main street, however, when I was accosted by a large Boer with a beard red as fire, who positioned himself in front of me, arms folded. At his side were a half-dozen other white men, all equally large.

"The red-bearded Boer introduced himself as Marius van Hoek and said he was site foreman at the gold mine nearby. He asked me to state my business in Silasville, using certain Afrikaans epithets for one of my race which are far from complimentary. I struggled to maintain a cool head. I did not want any trouble, for all that Marius van Hoek and his entourage seemed eager to provide it. I explained that I was there to collect the body of Harry Quatermain and take it to be interred. Such was my one and only desire, and if Mr Van Hoek and his associates would allow me to be on my way, I would be very grateful."

"You were most diplomatic," I said.

"Believe me, I would have liked nothing more than to give those men the fight they were looking for. They would have learned that a lone Zulu was more than a match for them. Had they numbered ten, twenty, even thirty, it would have made no difference. I could have unstrapped Groan-Maker from my back, cast it aside and dealt with them with my bare hands, and still won.

"But there is a time and a place for brawling, and this was not it. For a long while we eyed each other, Marius van Hoek and I, and then he said, 'Take the damned corpse and leave. As fast as you can. If you are still here at midday, you will have me to answer to.' He uttered a few further derogatory names, spat at my feet, and strode off.

"I have been insulted by far better men than him, and so dismissed his hostility as one might swat away a mosquito. My anger still bubbled but I did not let it boil over. Quietly I bought the cloth, I swathed Harry in it from head to toe, and I rode out of Silasville with the cadaver draped athwart my horse's flanks.

"In the shade of a rocky hillock, that feature of the landscape which the Boers call a *kopje*, I dug a trench. I hewed it from the earth with Groan-Maker, and in it I laid Harry Quatermain. I covered the body in soil and stones, and wailed and chanted over the grave, singing songs of heroism and valour and commending Harry to his god.

"Then I began a long, unhappy journey that took me to Cape Town, where I stowed away aboard a freighter of the Union Steamship Company line, bound for Southampton. I shall not detain you with an account of that sea voyage."

"No, there is no need," said Holmes.

"It was long, that I will say, and uneventful up until the point when one of the crewmen discovered my hiding place in the cargo hold, a nest I had made for myself amidst the packing crates where I was subsisting upon my supplies of beans, dried termites and strips of salted beef, along with such drinkable water as I could obtain from the bilges. I was hauled before the captain, who was minded to throw me off at the next port, but I pleaded to be allowed to earn my passage. I was not familiar with the operation of a ship, I told him, but I was strong and hardworking. 'See these muscles?' I said." Umslopogaas flexed his arms and puffed out his chest. "'Are these the muscles of a weakling?'

"I was, moreover, on an errand of mercy, I said. I explained about Harry Quatermain and his father, and the captain believed my tale and was moved to take pity on me. He set me to work on menial tasks, such as swabbing the decks and shovelling coal, and even gave me clothing from his own wardrobe – these garments I am clad in now – so that I did not have to go about 'like a half-naked savage', as he put it.

"In the six weeks it took us to steam from Cape Town to England I learned much about shipboard life and was soon welcomed by the crew as one of their own, for I proved my worth in every role I was given. Being a mixed lot – Portuguese, Malays, Irishmen, Lascars – they were not the sort to close ranks against a foreigner, as a group of men of one single race might."

"Can I ask why you simply did not send Quatermain a telegram about Harry?" said Holmes. "You would have saved yourself an arduous expedition."

"Some news cannot be delivered save in person," replied Umslopogaas. "It would not have been right for Macumazahn to have learned of his son's death from words on paper. It should come from a friend, man to man."

"A sentiment that does you credit, Umslopogaas," I said.

"When at last we docked at Southampton, I had endeared myself to my crewmates to such an extent that they clubbed together and gave me money for a train ticket to Yorkshire. There were tears in my eyes, sirs, when they did that. I am not ashamed to admit it. I bawled like a baby in the face of such generosity. We Zulus have a word: *ubuntu*. It is the idea that people should all recognise one another as human beings, equals under the sun. We should treat one another as members of one great tribe, regardless of racial origin, and take care of one another accordingly, like family. I had not expected to find *ubuntu* amongst those sailors, but there it was, large as life. Their kindness will be forever enshrined in my memory.

"Northward I went through England, an alien country about which I had heard so much from Macumazahn that I felt I knew it. Still, the paleness of the blue sky was a source of astonishment to me, nor had I realised that sunshine could ever be chilly. People in the train carriage around me were fanning themselves and joking about how hot the weather was for early autumn, saying it was as though summer had neglected to consult the calendar, while I shivered and hugged myself to keep warm. One man even jested to me that I had brought a heatwave with me from my homeland.

"Then I came to Yorkshire, a rugged, rolling green place parcelled up into small pieces by dark stone walls. Distant sheep moved like maggots across the hillsides, and cloud shadows rippled over shallow valleys.

"It was after nightfall as I approached Macumazahn's house, which looked to me the size of a palace. Lights shone in many windows, and from outside I spied my old friend seated in his library with two companions. One was a giant of a man, grey-eyed and noble-looking, with a chest as broad as a baobab trunk and hair as yellow as the savannah. The other was a smaller, darker-haired fellow with a round belly and a glass lens over one eye. This threesome seemed convivial together, smoking cigars and drinking wine with not a care in the world, and I regretted all the more the terrible nature of my mission.

"Such a startlement was there upon Macumazahn's face when he answered my knock at the front door, and then he swept me up in a crushing embrace, with a cry of unalloyed delight. In short order he was introducing me to his companions. The grey-eyed giant was Sir Henry Curtis, gentleman of leisure, and the portly fellow Captain John Good, formerly an officer in Her Majesty's Navy. 'This is Umslopogaas,' said Macumazahn, 'whom I have not seen in some twelve years but about whom you have frequently heard me speak, and never without admiration and approbation.' Both men said it was a pleasure to meet me, and I basked in the sincere warmth of their greetings, even as my heart felt leaden in my breast.

"'But what brings you here, Umslopogaas?' Macumazahn asked. 'Not that this isn't the pleasantest of surprises, but why have you come all this way to see me? What could possibly have prompted you to undertake a journey of several thousand miles? This cannot be simply a social call.' His smile lessened somewhat. 'Is it about Harry?'

"I did not need to reply. My sombre silence said it all.

"'My God,' said Macumazahn. 'Quick. Tell me. What has happened? Out with it, man!'

"My voice faltered as I gave him the news, which he had half guessed already. When I was done, he – mighty Macumazahn, peerless hunter, scourge of lions, who has never shied from battle no matter how high the odds stacked against him – all but collapsed. Sir Henry and Captain Good hastened to his side and supported him, helping him to a chair and plying him with whisky.

"When he had recovered somewhat from the shock, I prostrated myself before him and begged his forgiveness. I had let him down, I said. I was an unworthy wretch. He had every right to slay me on the spot, and I would not resist. I would welcome death by his hand as just punishment for my sins.

"Though his spirit was broken, Macumazahn brushed aside my remonstrations. 'You have done nothing wrong, Umslopogaas,' said he with solemn dignity. 'You have no reason to feel guilty. Harry is – was – an impulsive lad. I could not curb that tendency in him any more than I could command the Nile not to flood; nor would I have wanted to, for no offspring of mine could ever grow up timid and lily-livered. Ah, if only I had gone with him to Africa! But I thought him mature enough to make the trip on his own, and besides, I was too busy. I was too bound up in financial matters. The wealth to which we three – Sir Henry, Captain Good and I – can now lay claim after our discovery of King Solomon's diamond mines has brought with it copious demands upon our time. I seem to spend the better part of each day in correspondence with accountants, stockbrokers, lawyers and the like. No, if anyone is to blame for Harry's sad fate, Umslopogaas, it is not you, but I.'

"For several days thereafter, Macumazahn brooded and pined. I remained his house guest, as did Sir Henry and Captain

Good, and together we did our best to ease his troubled soul and keep him from falling into despondency. More than once he partook of *Taduki*, so as to lose himself for a while in hallucinatory dreams, about which I was none too happy. Misery is better confronted than avoided. Yet a man must mourn as a man must mourn, each in his own way. He must be permitted to deal with his grief however he wishes, whether by indulging in solitary rumination or in public lamentation or indeed in the torpor of drugs. No one else may dictate for him his course through the dark forest to the brighter uplands beyond. Thus it had been for me when my Nada died, and thus it was for Macumazahn now.

"Then one morning Macumazahn came to me and asked me to tell him again all I knew about how Harry had met his end. He said to spare no detail. I did as I was bid, and Macumazahn listened, and his next enquiry was, 'The town was Silasville, is that correct?' I replied that that was the very name of the place.

"'Silasville,' said he, 'exists only to house those who work at the gold mine beside which it has arisen.'

"For a moment I wondered whether Macumazahn was making some declaration of intent. Would he wreak vengeance against an entire town? Raze it to the ground in a fit of fury? I would not have put it past him.

"'I have read about it in the newspapers,' he said. 'I get copies of *The Natal Witness* sent to me regularly from Pietermaritzburg, so that I may keep abreast of current events in the continent I consider my spiritual home. Silasville is infamous for the level of strife and discontent amongst the miners there, which exceeds that to be found at almost any other mine. I understand that the management have instigated a crackdown on the workforce several times, in response to protests about working conditions and safety concerns. On occasion, the crackdowns have been fairly brutal. There have even been reports of miners being killed during these violent suppressions. The workforce is predominantly black, while those charged with overseeing them and keeping them in line are exclusively white.'

"'So it goes, Macumazahn,' said I. 'All across Africa, that is the pattern. The white man regards the black man as slave. Sometimes the black man *is* slave. In either case, the black man's life is considered secondary to the white man's, as a thing that may be disposed of without regret or consequence.'

"'That I denounce as one of the true evils of colonialism,' said Macumazahn. 'I could not defend it even if I wanted to. At Silasville, however, the level of disregard for the black man's welfare is egregious even by African standards. What can you tell me of the circumstances by which Harry came to be there?'

"I was unclear on those. All I knew was what I had learned from the bearer whom I had encountered in the town. Three days before I arrived there myself, Harry with his half of the caravan had pitched camp on Silasville's outskirts. Harry then went into the town to buy victuals and other necessities. When, after a night and a day had passed, he failed to return, some members of the caravan went in search of him. It was then that they learned of his death. Straight away, the majority of them took to their heels. They struck camp and scattered in all directions. They were terrified that somehow they might be held accountable for Harry's demise and that the wrath of Macumazahn might be visited upon them – although, despite their terror, they retained the presence of mind to take the wagons, horses, oxen and other appurtenances of the caravan with them. The bearer alone remained. He was made of sterner stuff and showed his moral fibre by trying to find out more about the death, albeit without success. He was met with only stony silence from the denizens of Silasville, as well as the odd gruff rebuke and even a threat or two. He had, in fact, been on the point of leaving when

I appeared, and was gone by the time I rode out with Harry's body. I did not see him again.

"'Given the timings,' said Macumazahn, 'whatever struck Harry down whilst he was in Silasville cannot have been any disease. No disease scourges a man so utterly that he lies dead within twenty-four hours.'"

"Such is the conclusion I was coming to," said Holmes. "Were there any marks upon the body suggestive of violence?"

"Macumazahn asked much the same thing," said Umslopogaas. "Regrettably, I cannot say either yes or no. I did not look any too closely at the body. It had begun to moulder, as I told you. The skin had discoloured, becoming mottled like the back of a frog, and there were the first signs of bloating. A certain slight malodorousness, too. I am sorry if these descriptions unsettle you, sirs."

"They do not," I said. "I have encountered death in its many forms, as has Holmes. We are inured."

"Harry did not look to have died peacefully, that much is for sure. Even at rest, a body displays evidence of any torment it may have suffered in its final throes. His posture was that of someone who has been wracked by contortions."

"That does not rule out violence," said Holmes, "but it does seem to suggest some other agency."

"Macumazahn, for his part, was unconvinced that Harry's death was of innocent origin. The day after the conversation I have just recounted, he announced that he was leaving for London to delve into the matter further. Sir Henry and Captain Good offered to accompany him, but he turned them down. Their error was to let Macumazahn think he had a choice in the decision. I simply walked out of the house with him. I climbed into his carriage with him. I entered the train station with him. He could see by then that he was not going to get rid of me, and so he set aside any objections and consented to having my presence by his side.

"We were borne south by the train, and here in the capital we have resided for eight days and nights now. In that time Macumazahn has sallied forth on numerous occasions, decreeing that I should stay put in this covert camp of ours and 'hold the fort'. His searchings have led him far and wide across the city and seen him rummage around in certain quarters where he believes useful information might lurk. I liken it to the practice of disturbing the jungle undergrowth so as to cause alarm and see what emerges.

"By such a process was he brought into the purlieu of a man called Inigo Niemand. Any more than that, however, I am forbidden to divulge." Umslopogaas's shoulders sloped apologetically. "Macumazahn has confided in me but has told me in the strictest possible terms not to share those confidences. Mayhap I have already been more forthcoming than I should."

No amount of coaxing and cajoling on Holmes's part could tease anything further from the Zulu. He remained resolutely tight-lipped.

Conceding defeat, we took our leave, but not before Holmes had made it clear to Umslopogaas that he and Quatermain had not seen the last of us.

"I look forward to renewing our acquaintance," was Umslopogaas's equable reply. "Goodnight to you both, good sirs."

CHAPTER EIGHTEEN

THE SKELETON KEY THAT
UNLOCKS MANY A DOOR

On our way back to Baker Street I remarked to Holmes, "At least we know now why Quatermain is involved in this affair."

"And why he is pursuing it so vigorously," said Holmes. "Obsessively, even. He has a personal stake. He believes something occurred at Silasville which impinged directly – lethally – upon his son."

"Is he misguided in that belief?"

"On the scant evidence available at present, I cannot make a definitive determination. However, the balance of probabilities suggests he is not."

Upon arriving home, Holmes skipped up the seventeen steps of the staircase to our rooms and immediately resorted to his library, busying himself amongst his reference books, almanacs and scrapbooks of newspaper cuttings. I, knowing I was surplus to requirements, repaired to bed.

At breakfast the next morning, which I came down to rather late, I found my friend in a smirking, self-satisfied mood. He looked like a cat that is being petted. I do not think he had slept a wink.

"I have sent a telegram to Lestrade of the Yard," said he, "letting him know what transpired last night in Shoreditch. I have told him where Daniel Greensmith's body may be found, although I strongly suspect it will not be there any more."

"Starkey will surely have disposed of it by now – had it dumped in the river, most likely."

"True, alas. I have mentioned Starkey's name to Lestrade in connection with the death, anyway. We shall see what eventuates. Nothing, I suspect. Starkey will have a cast-iron alibi, no doubt, and the police will not be able to place him anywhere near the scene at the time. But it seemed the least courtesy I could offer poor old Greensmith. As for Greensmith's dying word…"

"Fanthorpe," I said, smearing a slice of toast with Patum Peperium, not too thickly because a gentleman does not relish excessive amounts of anchovy paste. "What of it?"

"I now know who Fanthorpe is. Or rather, who and what. Really I should have made the connection instantly upon hearing the name. Sometimes I wonder if the attic of my brain has become too crammed with extraneous lumber and is in need of a good clearing out. How does one go about forgetting facts for which one no longer has any use? How? A blow to the region of the cerebellum concerned with memory perhaps, to shake loose the accreted excess like tapping mud off a boot? A phrenologist might know."

"And who, or what, is Fanthorpe?"

"Finish eating," said Holmes, lighting a cigarette, "and then you shall find out."

Less than an hour later we were in the lower reaches of Mayfair. There, in a terraced street leading off from St James's Square, we presented ourselves at the door of one of the many imposing business premises to be found in that district. A brass plaque beside the bell-pull read: FANTHORPE OVERSEAS VENTURES.

A bespectacled, sallow-skinned clerk let us in, and after Holmes had presented his card and requested a meeting with the board of directors, we were bidden to wait. We seated ourselves in plush, leather-upholstered wingback chairs that seemed designed to impress with their opulence, as did the rest of the decorations in the reception area. The gilt-framed paintings on the walls, for example, were all Old Masters, although whether genuine or reproduction I am not qualified to say. They looked authentic enough to me.

"Do you really think the board of a company as august as this one will be willing to speak to the likes of us?" I said to Holmes, when the clerk had left us alone for some ten minutes.

"If not, I have a contingency plan, but one I would prefer not to resort to unless absolutely necessary."

Further minutes passed, during which time I occupied myself reading the latest edition of *The Times*, which had been left on a side table, neatly folded, for the convenience of visitors. A headline on the fourth page caught my eye.

WOLVES ESCAPE FROM MENAGERIE

The story detailed how a pack of wolves had absconded during the night from their enclosure on a private estate near Chelmsford. The landowner, a baronet, was an amateur zoologist and something of a maverick, who also kept other animals such as wombats, llamas, an orang-utan and even a Javan rhino on his property. The wolves had burrowed under the fence, and the baronet had vowed to enlist the aid of the local hunt, of which he was a member, in tracking down and recapturing them. Livestock farmers in the area were not, it must be said, terribly reassured by his promises.

Showing the article to Holmes, I remarked that it sounded like a job for our newfound ally Quatermain. "I should put him in touch with this baronet fellow," I said. "He'd have the wolves rounded up and back home in no time."

Holmes did not seem in the mood for my little joke. Instead, he rose and sauntered over to the front desk. There he began leafing through the appointments diary that lay open on the desktop.

"I don't think you should be doing that," I averred.

"Is it my fault the clerk has deserted his post and the diary is unattended?" came the reply.

"But what are you hoping to find?"

"Can a fellow not indulge his curiosity? Just keep an ear out in case the clerk comes back. A throat-clearing will do as a warning."

Three tense minutes followed while Holmes perused the diary and I listened for footfalls. Then my companion returned to the wingback chair beside me, looking vaguely thoughtful.

A further five minutes elapsed before the clerk finally did return. The length of time we had been left cooling our heels told us just how unimportant we were in the scheme of things, at least as far as those who ran Fanthorpe Overseas Ventures were concerned.

"The directors are busy today," the clerk said, resuming his seat at the desk.

"All day?" said Holmes.

"All day. Perhaps you might care to try again tomorrow."

"At what hour?"

The clerk smiled unctuously. "Name a time."

"Ten o'clock."

"I'm afraid not."

"Eleven."

"I'm afraid not."

"Twelve."

The clerk shook his head.

"You are not even checking." Holmes jabbed a forefinger in the direction of the appointments diary.

"I don't have to."

"I see. Well then, you leave me no other recourse. Would you do me the inestimable honour of going back to the directors and saying one word to them?"

The clerk wrung his hands in a parody of servility. He could have given Uriah Heep lessons in obsequiousness. "One word, sir?"

"Yes. They will change their minds when they hear it, I guarantee you."

"They will? Just one single word? I should be most curious to learn what it is."

Holmes leaned closer to him and murmured something which I only just caught and which made as little an immediate impression upon me as it did upon the clerk.

"Mycroft."

"That is it?" said the clerk, raising an eyebrow. "'Mycroft'?"

"Run along and see what effect it has. You may be surprised."

The clerk disappeared again, and in his absence I queried Holmes about "Mycroft". What did it signify? Was it a place? A code? Something akin to the Freemason's secret handshake?

"It is an 'open sesame', Watson. It is the skeleton key that unlocks many a door, especially here in such close proximity to Westminster and the corridors of power."

I pressed him to elucidate, but he would not. My regular readers will of course apprehend the reference. For me, though, the mystery of "Mycroft" would not be resolved until some four years later, when Holmes finally, formally revealed to me the existence of his older brother during the affair of Melas, the Greek interpreter.

The clerk returned to the reception area with considerably

greater alacrity than before, and in short order was escorting Holmes and me up to the first floor. The magical spell of the word "Mycroft" had wrought a marked change in his attitude. Now he was no longer fawning to us in a condescending, sarcastic fashion, but as if he meant it.

"This way please," said he as he opened a pair of double-doors.

Beyond lay a boardroom the size and splendour of which cannot be overstated. From the hanging tapestries to the oak panelling to the alabaster statuary in alcoves, it was poised at the tipping-point between grandeur and grandiosity. A vast mahogany table dominated the space, and at one end sat three men who were close in age to one another, all in their early forties or thereabouts, and so similar in physical appearance that they had to be related somehow. All shared the same sandy hair, the same puffy, dimpled cheeks and the same slightly going-to-seed build.

"The brothers Fanthorpe," said Holmes as the clerk closed the doors behind us. "Kind of you to grant us an audience. We are much obliged."

"We felt we had no choice," said the central Fanthorpe, who looked to be the oldest. "Certain insinuations of influence cannot be disregarded."

"You may have five minutes of our time," said the brother to his right, "and not a second more."

"Then let us not waste another moment bandying about pleasantries," said Holmes. "Fanthorpe Overseas Ventures is one of the world's largest and most successful exploiters of mineral rights. You have mining interests around the globe, but a good sixty per cent of your business is concentrated in southern Africa."

"Yes," said the third brother. "So?"

"Silasville," said Holmes. "Christened after your late father, I believe, Silas Fanthorpe, founder of this illustrious enterprise which the three of you inherited."

"You have done your homework," said Fanthorpe Major. "What about Silasville?"

"The gold mine there has proved a spectacularly lucrative source of revenue. Your company has been excavating the site for over two decades, and the seam has yet to be exhausted."

"Is there a point to all this stating of fact?" said the brother on the right. "Or have you come merely to lecture us upon a subject in which we are already eminently conversant?"

"You are Samuel Fanthorpe, am I right? The middle brother, one year the junior of Sebastian, one year the senior of Stanley."

As though at a roll-call, each brother reacted to the sound of his name with a small, perhaps unconscious gesture of acknowledgement.

"I enquire about Silasville," Holmes continued, "purely in order to establish whether its reputation as a place of hideously draconian working practices is warranted or not."

At that, all three Fanthorpes bristled.

"How dare you, sir!" barked Sebastian, the eldest.

"The impudence!" said Stanley.

"To come to our headquarters and insult us to our faces," grumbled Samuel. "You have a nerve."

"What I have," said Holmes, "is a handful of newspaper articles, culled over a half-dozen years, all of which indicate that at Silasville your workforce, which is composed almost wholly of native Africans, has been subjected to systematic harsh treatment. The miners are paid a pittance and made to work long hours in conditions that are at best precarious, at worst lethal. The ground in the locale is made up of notoriously unstable strata, and this has resulted in a number of cave-ins, with attendant loss of life. In addition, the—"

"May I stop you there, Mr... Holmes, is it?" said Sebastian

Fanthorpe. "Before you go on with this rant of yours, understand that mining is far from a risk-free proposition. In our business, loss of life is a fact of life. Men go underground, hacking away at the bare rock, entirely at the mercy of whatever geological faults and anomalies may lie in wait for them. A fissure here, a sinkhole there, and disaster strikes. It is as tragic as it is unavoidable."

"Then there are the pitfalls associated with the use of dynamite in enclosed spaces," said Stanley.

"Not to mention the danger from unexpected flooding," said Samuel, "and from pockets of methane gas which may be ignited by the merest spark. You must know this."

"Think of the coal mines in these very isles," said Sebastian, "the product of which our nation depends upon to power its factories and transport, to heat its homes. Accidents happen at those all the time. Just the year before last there was a vast methane explosion at the Trimdon Grange colliery up in County Durham. Sixty-nine miners were killed."

"Not all died in the explosion itself," Stanley added. "Some were asphyxiated by afterdamp, the mixture of toxic gases that is given off by such a conflagration."

"Not a man went down that mine unaware that an incident of this nature might well occur," said Samuel. "Would you not have them do so? Would you deny thousands of British miners the opportunity to make a living and keep the heart of the empire beating, simply because there is a chance some of them might die?"

The three Fanthorpes looked at one another as if in smug agreement. They had, they thought, presented a convincing rebuttal to Holmes's accusations.

"I am not talking about mining in general," said Holmes. "I am talking about Silasville in particular, where the death toll is conspicuously higher than average. Then there is the manner in which labour disputes are handled – or, I should say, *mis*handled. It is not unknown for individual miners to be cudgelled with a knobkerrie or whipped with a *sjambok* when they express discontent. On one occasion what amounted to a riot was put down by the mine overseers using rifles. Eight miners were shot dead. That is a matter of record. You cannot deny it."

"Nor will we," said Samuel. "Silasville has been problematic, we accept that. There have been shortcomings on both sides, workforce and management alike, although more egregiously with the former than the latter. We have taken steps to address the issue."

His brother Stanley chimed in, likewise adopting a passable impression of a conciliatory tone. "The use of small arms in a disciplinary capacity was perhaps ill-advised. The site foreman would not have authorised it, however, had he not felt that his and his fellow overseers' lives were in genuine jeopardy. They were facing a mob, outnumbered ten to one. They had to redress the balance somehow."

"Besides," said Sebastian, "the events you mention all took place some while ago. For the past eighteen months Silasville has been free of trouble. The workers have been behaving in exemplary fashion, docile as cattle. Not one voice has been raised in complaint. What does that tell you, Mr Holmes?"

"It tells me that you have found some other means of subjugating them," replied my friend, "something subtler than brute force."

As one, the three brothers heaved irritable sighs.

"There is no reasoning with some people," said Sebastian Fanthorpe. "They will believe only what they choose to believe."

"That other fellow was just the same," said Samuel. "The one who stormed in last week and caused a fuss. Quarterstaff, was it?"

"Quatermain," said Stanley. "Dratted old fool. He barged

in here just like you, Mr Holmes, full of bluster, pointing the finger, levying all sorts of allegations. Something about his son. He became quite heated. He said if we were 'real men' we would own up to what we had done. The trouble was, we had no idea what it was we were supposed to be guilty of."

"Clearly we had committed some manner of offence," said Sebastian, "but we couldn't for the life of us think what."

"Still can't," said Samuel. "It didn't help that Quatermain was barely coherent. He came across as quite unhinged, in fact. His son had died of a disease at Silasville, he said, yet it could not have been a disease. How is one to make sense of that? Very cryptic. A disease that is not a disease. Like a riddle, almost."

A contemptuous little titter passed amongst the three Fanthorpes. I found it somewhat unnerving, the way they displayed emotion like that, in unison, and the way they spoke too, playing pass-the-parcel with their comments, one to the next. They put me in mind of the Graeae of Ancient Greek myth, those three crone-like sisters who shared a single tooth and eye, which they took turns using.

"He would not be placated," said Stanley. "Nor would he leave the premises when asked to. He declared he would not budge until he had had satisfaction. In the end we had to send for the police."

"That did the trick," said Sebastian. "Quatermain was gone like a shot, before any constable arrived. Proof, if it were needed, that he was a scoundrel. Who but a scoundrel flees at the merest mention of the law?"

"I should hope, Mr Holmes, that we shan't have to do likewise for you," said Samuel. He glanced over at a mahogany longcase clock with an ornately filigreed dial. "Well, your five minutes are up. Will you leave quietly?"

Holmes gave each brother an appraising look, then nodded.

"Good day, gentlemen," said he, and made for the door, beckoning me to follow.

Outside, in the street, Holmes was in ebullient form.

"What a fascinating threesome!" he said. "Cocooned by wealth, they seem incapable of feeling the slightest affinity towards their fellow men. Human lives are just statistics to them, numbers on a sheet of paper. As long as the profit margin remains fat, naught else matters."

"Did their protestations of innocence ring true to you, Holmes?"

"Was it innocence or ignorance? The two are often hard to distinguish from each other. Similarly ignorance and wilful blindness. It strikes me that the brothers Fanthorpe would rather not know what goes on at a place like Silasville. As long as the gold keeps coming out of the ground, they do not care *how* it keeps coming out of the ground. The day-to-day administration is left to the likes of site foreman Marius van Hoek, Umslopogaas's boorish Boer. The Fanthorpes are happy to delegate the dirty work to underlings. That way their hands stay clean."

"And their consciences."

"Assuming they have any, which is debatable."

"I still cannot see what you hoped to accomplish by confronting them," I said, "besides earning their enmity. You seemed to know a considerable amount about their mining operations already, Silasville in particular, beforehand. Did you glean anything further from talking to them?"

"Not a great deal. Provocation, however, can sometimes precipitate retaliation, and retaliation can be illuminating."

"You mean they might lash out at us somehow, in response to our visit?"

"They might, if they consider us sufficiently threatening. Equally, they might not. But if they do, it could be taken as a mark of culpability – the act of men with something to hide. Then there was the appointments diary I sneaked a look at. That, too, afforded some interesting information."

"Namely?"

In place of an answer, Holmes yawned. "How about a coffee, old friend? I don't know about you but after the trying night we have had, and the attendant lack of sleep, I could do with a pick-me-up. There is a coffeehouse just round the corner, I believe."

I knew I was not going to get anything more out of him than that, at least for the time being, so I accompanied him to the coffeehouse. Thence I embarked upon my rounds, while Holmes repaired to Baker Street, where, he said, he had some thinking to do.

CHAPTER NINETEEN

BAT AMONGST THE PIGEONS

A soft, muffled fluttering awoke me. I must have been sleeping lightly, or perhaps it was that the sound was an uncommon one, something I was not accustomed to hearing late at night.

I lay in bed, ears pricked, wondering if it would recur.

It did. Its origin was somewhere in the room, but it took me a moment to determine where exactly. It emanated from the fireplace.

The third time it came, the sound was quite insistent. It was quite obviously caused by a bird's wings.

I lit the lamp and clambered out from under the covers with something of a sigh. This was hardly a novelty. We had had birds become stuck in the chimney flue before. The creature – a pigeon, most likely – had carelessly toppled down through the chimneypot and was now trapped. I would have to free it, otherwise the flustered thing would flail around for hours until it died of suffocation or fright.

I thrust up the window sash, in time to hear the clock of St Marylebone Church strike three. Then I went down on hands and knees beside the hearth. The fire had long since gone out. I reached up inside the firebox to grasp the handle of the damper, which was open only a couple of inches. As soon as the bird emerged, I would shoo it towards the open window. With luck, I would be able to return the pigeon to its rightful place outdoors without it leaving too much of a sooty mess behind.

As soon as I swung the damper fully open, out the bird flew, straight into my face. I reeled back, half blinded by soot, coughing and spluttering. An oath or two escaped my lips.

When I regained my poise, I saw that the bird was indeed a pigeon and that, far from making for the window and freedom, the damned thing had instead settled atop one bedpost. From there it eyed me beadily, every so often spreading its wings and flapping them, which sent a shower of black dust onto the bedclothes.

I waved my hand at the bird. "Be gone with you!" I hissed. "Go and pester someone else!"

Any normal pigeon would have taken the hint. They are not, as a rule, bold creatures, and in London they have learned to steer clear of humans, even as they weave around amongst us, living on our litter and debris.

This member of the species, however, seemed to regard my actions not as intimidation but as invitation. It continued to stare at me, utterly untroubled.

Cursing under my breath, I set about trying to evict the pigeon with a will. I was hampered by the need to move slowly and tread delicately so as not to disturb the other two residents of the house. I lunged for the bird with a kind of stealthy exaggeration, waving my arms and uttering a throaty snarl.

The pigeon took the hint and flew off from the bedpost. Alas, it went no further than my chest of drawers. Thence, after another bout of intimidation from me, it made for my dressing table mirror, after which it revisited the bedpost. Throughout this process its steady orange gaze remained fixed on me, giving an impression of both insouciance and contempt.

The soot stains the bird was leaving everywhere were bad enough, but I feared that if I could not get rid of it soon, the inevitable might occur and some item of furniture or clothing would be besmirched with droppings. The thought lent urgency to my task, yet still the pigeon eluded me. Every time I got near, it flapped across the room to a fresh perch. The only place it seemed not to want to go was the gaping window. Its natural habitat apparently held no attraction.

So far, this episode would seem to constitute a farcical interlude, no more than that: Dr Watson attempting to oust an intrusive fowl from his room at three in the morning, and failing.

Then things took a turn for the strange. A second pigeon gained ingress to the room via the fireplace. It joined its comrade roosting upon my bedstead.

Berating myself for not having closed the damper – not that I could have foreseen that another bird might be so foolish as to follow the first down the chimney – I flapped my arms aggressively at the pair of them. The second pigeon was no less imperturbable than its comrade. Both of them took off and alighted side by side atop the bookcase.

When a third pigeon flew in and stationed itself beside the other two, that was when I felt a distinct stirring of unease. Together the three birds regarded me from the bookcase, all lined up in a row. They seemed to me speculative, as though like Poe's raven they were judging me and found me wanting. Not a single purr or coo escaped them. Now and then one of them would preen or run a beak through its soot-begrimed plumage, but otherwise they seemed content just to sit in silence and stare.

"Right, you feathered vermin," I said, low-voiced. "That's it."

I closed the damper, in case yet more pigeons chose to

invade. Then I fetched up the cricket bat which was leaning behind the door. Although a rugby man through and through, I have been known to enjoy a spell at the crease. Like my fellow physician W.G. Grace, I am an all-rounder, although of course I cannot claim to be anywhere near as proficient at either batting or bowling.

"I will have no qualms about bashing you flat," I told the trio of pigeons, raising the bat. "The exit is over there." I gestured to the window. "Now is the time to use it."

The birds remained infuriatingly imperturbable.

"Fair enough. You cannot say you weren't warned."

I swung for them, and the pigeons scattered in different directions to various vantage points. I beleaguered them with the cricket bat, whisking it this way and that, doing my utmost to avoid damaging anything inanimate. My hope was that, even if I did not make contact, my frantic flailing would convince the pigeons to seek sanctuary outdoors, away from the madman in his pyjamas with the whirling slab of willow.

At last the birds seemed to get the message. They grouped themselves upon the windowsill. Determined to make the most of the opportunity thus presented, I drew the bat back for a sweep shot, as though a bowler had just delivered a slow ball square on the leg side that I was going to knock for six. I planned to take out all three pigeons at a stroke.

That was when I saw it. Outside the window, looming from the darkness, were dozens more pigeons. A flock of them. A *swarm* of them. They were hurtling towards me, a great cloud of plump grey bodies and whirring wings.

I acted on reflex. In a flurry of horror and incomprehension, I leapt for the window and slammed it shut.

Onwards, before my incredulous eyes, the birds came. The three already in the room had retreated to the wardrobe as

I brought down the sash. The multitude outside dived for the window at full speed. One after another they hurled themselves at the panes. Impact after thudding impact resounded through the frame. Glass cracked. Cracks multiplied. Glass broke. Fragments sprayed in, even as I stumbled backwards.

Then, through the hollow, shard-fringed gaps between the mullions and transoms, pigeons insinuated themselves. Squirming, struggling, sometimes cutting themselves in their eagerness, they spilled into the bedroom in their droves. I was surrounded all at once by an airborne horde, buffeted by wings, scraped by talons. I wielded the cricket bat one-handed like a swordsman, not aiming, caring little what I hit as long as I hit something. Repeatedly I felt the thump of wood striking flesh and often heard the crunch of tiny bones fracturing. Dead pigeons fell to the floor, yet plenty more remained alive and aloft.

In some distant corner of my mind I wondered whether I was actually still asleep and dreaming. Such was the sheer phantasmagorical absurdity of this pigeon incursion.

Regardless, I swung and swung again with the bat until I perceived that I was beginning to whittle down the pigeons' numbers. The room was littered with their corpses while increasingly few remained active.

The realisation galvanised me. My strength had been flagging, but now I found new reserves of stamina and pitted myself against the invading birds with ever greater vigour. Whereas before I had had no trouble hitting one since there were so many of them, now I had to take specific aim. It required accuracy to bring each down. I had got my eye in by then, however. With almost machine-like precision I walloped pigeons in mid-air and had the satisfaction of seeing them slam sideways against the wall, stone dead. Others caught only a glancing blow, spiralling down to flutter and hop uselessly on the floor, perhaps with a wing or leg broken, or else just stunned. Polishing them off was the simplest of tasks.

Soon a mere handful of the creatures remained, and these I dispatched methodically and mercilessly until at long last the weird battle of man versus beast was over. Panting hard, I leaned upon the handle of the bat and surveyed the aftermath. Feathers filled the air, a swirling grey blizzard, and I stood ankle-deep in a sea of dead fauna. I estimated the tally to be nothing short of two hundred birds. The sight of them was repugnant, as was the smell, which consisted of the pigeons' natural musty odour overlaid with the tang of spilled blood and burst entrails.

I myself had sustained a few superficial scratches but was otherwise unhurt. As I struggled to bring my laboured breathing under control and gather my wits, there came a knock at the door, swiftly followed by the entrance of Sherlock Holmes.

"Watson. By the living Jingo! Are you all right?"

"I have been better. And you? I see you have had tribulations of your own."

Holmes looked as harassed and dishevelled as I must have. His pyjamas were shredded in several places and he was bleeding from a number of cuts that looked suspiciously like tiny bite marks.

"I am alive, by the grace of God," said he. "So it was pigeons for you, eh?"

"You were attacked by something else?"

"Rats. A plethora of rats. They came pouring in under the bedroom door. All were slick with water, and the damp trail they left indicates that their point of access was the bathroom."

"Up through the pipes, you mean."

"It is the clear inference. You armed yourself with a cricket bat. Very enterprising. My choice of weapon was the nearest heavy object to hand: a boot. I beat the rats with the heel of it from the safety of my bed, which became my fortress. They laid siege and some of them got past my defences, clawing their way up the bed frame and onto the mattress. Hence these minor injuries I have sustained. I was gnawed, but I was the victor in the end. I exterminated every last one of the vile things."

"What... What has happened here?" I said. "How come we have both been the victim of assault by wild creatures? Can every single animal in London have gone mad?"

"Before anything else, let us make sure Mrs Hudson is well. Since you and I have been molested, perhaps she has too. I have not heard any untoward noises from her room, but it would be best to check."

A polite tap at Mrs Hudson's bedroom door yielded no result. Holmes rapped louder, calling out our landlady's name, until at last he was rewarded with a bleary-sounding, "Yes? What is it?"

"Mrs Hudson, I apologise for disturbing you," Holmes said through the door. "I take it you have been sound asleep."

"Up till now, yes."

"And you have been – how shall I put this? – in no way incommoded."

"Other than by a certain tenant waking me, I have not. I have lately taken to stuffing my ears with cotton wool before I go to bed, in order to ensure an uninterrupted night's sleep. So often do you receive visitors at unsociable hours, Mr Holmes, sometimes ones incapable of continent behaviour, that I have felt the need for such measures. The last straw was the hullabaloo the other night." She meant our fight with Allan Quatermain.

"Cotton wool," said Holmes approvingly. "You are the most pragmatic of women, Mrs Hudson, as well as the most forgiving."

"Why are you at my door anyway? What has occasioned this disruption?"

"Nothing, my dear lady. Nothing you need concern yourself

about. Return to your slumbers."

We left Mrs Hudson grumbling to herself and went back to our rooms. There was no sleep for either of us the rest of that night. I busied myself gathering up the dead animals in coal sacks and swabbing clean the patches of soot and bird blood in my room and the clots of rat innards in Holmes's. Holmes, meanwhile, found occupation at his chemistry bench, where he dissected one specimen of each of the two kinds of creature.

"Ah, yes," he said at the conclusion of his gruesome study. "The stomach contents tell a story. Chemical analysis reveals that both this rat and this pigeon have been fed grain adulterated with some form of alkaloid. It's a fairly safe bet that the same is true of their brethren."

"Alkaloid," I said. "You mean a drug."

"I cannot determine the precise sort but it appears to be plant-derived and has distinct psychotropic properties. The dosage, for beasts so small, is high – high enough to warrant the unusually aggressive behaviour they exhibited. Neither rats nor pigeons are wont to attack humans unless provoked."

"In other words, somebody set loose drug-addled vermin on us."

"That would seem to be the case."

"Good grief."

"You, of course, played into our assailant's hands by opening your window."

"I had to. How else was I to get the birds out?"

"But our foe predicted the move," said Holmes. "The first three pigeons he introduced down through the chimney were precursors. Once the window was open, he could release the rest of the flock, who would make straight to join their fellows."

"I managed to close the window in time, but they came on regardless. They were relentless."

"As were the rats. Once they had infiltrated the house by means of the plumbing, they went with single-minded determination to find the nearest potential victim. The fact of my bedroom being nearer the bathroom than yours decreed that that victim should be me. Count yourself lucky, Watson. Had our domestic geography been different, you might have had two sets of animal adversary to contend with."

It was some small blessing, I thought.

Come the morning Holmes sent for his gang of street Arabs, the Baker Street irregulars, and paid them a princely sum to take the sacks full of rodent and avian corpses for disposal.

"Under no circumstances," he admonished, "are you to think of selling the pigeons for food. Am I making myself quite clear? I know your ways. They and the rats are to be tossed into the Thames, or better yet, incinerated."

Naturally those young ragamuffins were curious about the combined infestation of rat and pigeon, and Holmes blamed it on the cut-and-cover excavations that were currently under way nearby for the building of the new Circle Line underground railway. The creatures' various nests had been disturbed by the works and they had been seeking new refuges. 221B Baker Street had just so happened to lie in the path of two simultaneous mass exoduses.

When the irregulars were gone, and while we were waiting for a glazier to come and repair my window, I asked Holmes if he had any inkling who might be behind the attack.

"Put it this way, Watson. I do not think it a coincidence that we were targeted thus just hours after our meeting with the Fanthorpe brothers."

"I feared you might say that. You mean we are getting too close to the truth for comfort."

"I mean precisely that. We have been given notice. Someone would like us to know that they regard us as meddlers and are unhappy about it."

"The Fanthorpes, presumably. You predicted the possibility of retaliation."

"If not the Fanthorpes, then a person or persons in their employ. The rats and pigeons were a threat, Watson. Whoever made it, however, has failed to apprehend one thing about me. I do not take kindly to threats. I consider them provocations. In fact, I would go further than that and call them declarations of war."

CHAPTER TWENTY

ANOTHER KIND OF JUNGLE, ANOTHER KIND OF WILDLIFE

Holmes resolved that we should call upon Quatermain at his camp in Victoria Park. "We have greater insight now into the secrets he has been withholding from us," he said. "We have lit a few candles to dispel the darkness. It is high time he came clean and illuminated the shadowy corners remaining."

Upon opening the front door to leave, however, whom should we find standing upon the step directly outside but Quatermain himself. His hand was raised as though he had been just about to grasp the knocker.

"Speak of the Devil," said Holmes. "Allan Quatermain. The very man we were off to see. Bless you, you have saved us a cab fare."

"Holmes," said Quatermain. "May we talk?"

"I insist upon it. But not here. There is a glazier upstairs making merry with chisel and putty. Our privacy is not assured. Why don't we go for a stroll and talk as we walk? The sun is shining, and it feels as though this may be one of the last few clement days of the year. There is that sense of irrevocable decline in the air."

As we strode off along the pavement three abreast, I enquired after the state of Quatermain's arm.

"It is fast improving, Doctor, and I thank you for your professional ministrations. Here is my card with my Yorkshire address. If you would be so good as to send your bill there…"

"Good heavens, I should not dream of it! You saved our lives at Starkey's warehouse. Treating you was the least I could do in return."

"You are too kind. Umslopogaas has been singing your praises every chance he gets, you know. You have made quite an impression upon him."

"As has he upon me. He is a sterling fellow. Quite the soliloquist, too."

"Yes," said Quatermain, sounding a touch rueful. "I understand he has been indiscreet and shared certain information which he perhaps ought to have kept to himself. It is to discuss that topic that I came to see the both of you."

"Rather than indiscreet," said Holmes, "I think Umslopogaas felt that he was being a responsible friend. He wished us to understand what has motivated you to journey to London and embroil yourself in these curious proceedings. Your seemingly erratic and uncoordinated activities now make more sense."

"Erratic? Uncoordinated? Well, possibly. You must at least be able to see that there has been method in my madness."

"And more than a dash of madness in your method. You are, if you don't mind my saying so, Quatermain, no detective. There is a signal lack of logical consistency in your modus operandi. Your plan, assuming you even have one, seems to be to either lie in wait or else ruffle feathers in the hope that one or the other will somehow, as if by magic, cause the truth to reveal itself. I have found the patient, forensic accumulation of knowledge a far more reliable system."

I refrained from commenting that "ruffling feathers" characterised what Holmes had done at Fanthorpe Overseas Ventures the previous day. He would no doubt have viewed the exercise as just one weapon in his arsenal of strategies, whereas Quatermain appeared to have few others.

"I do not profess to be an intellectual, Holmes," Quatermain said. "I am what I am, and I do what I do."

"Yet that which works when hunting upon the plains of Africa does not necessarily work in an urban context."

"A city is just another kind of jungle, and people just another kind of wildlife."

"A fair analogy," said Holmes, "but not entirely accurate. You overlook the greater level of sophistication typically found in human actions. People may be driven by the same base impulses as animals – to eat, to nest, to procreate, to ascend in the social hierarchy – but they dress them up in sometimes very elaborate guises, to such an extent that they do not necessarily recognise them for what they are. The banker who enriches himself from interest rates and speculation sees figures mounting in his ledgers and the material possessions his wealth enables him to buy, but may not fully appreciate how these things cement his position at the top of the pecking order, how they make him lead dog in the pack. The same holds, at the opposite end of the scale, for the cracksman who steals jewellery from the safe at the banker's house. Uppermost in his mind is not feeding himself or his family, even though that will be the by-product of the deed. What he is thinking about is outwitting the manufacturers of the safe and not getting caught in the act – the perverse thrill of larceny. We do not always consciously acknowledge that which compels us, and this makes us less predictable and easy to read than the game creatures you are wont to pursue."

"You might be surprised how wily some of those game

creatures are," said Quatermain. "I take your point all the same. There is a whole different dynamic at work here in so-called 'civilisation', and it is one in which I am obviously not as well versed as a man like yourself. I am humble enough to acknowledge as much. What say we forget whatever disharmony has arisen between us and try to cooperate from here on? Bygones?"

"Agreed." Holmes clasped Quatermain's proffered hand. "Bygones. I believe we may achieve far more by putting our heads together than by butting them."

"Hear, hear," I said, with feeling.

"In that spirit," Holmes continued, "perhaps we can begin right now with you telling us how you fared during your visit to the Fanthorpe headquarters."

"Oh, you know about that?" said Quatermain. "Well, it was a singularly unfruitful exercise. Those three brothers were as obdurate as can be."

"I found them similar."

"You've been to see them yourself?"

"Fanthorpe's mining interests link our two suspicious deaths, those of Inigo Niemand and of your son Harry. My sincerest condolences on the latter."

"Mine too," I said. "Frightful shame, Quatermain. I feel for you."

Briefly Quatermain's face darkened, and I could tell that he was touched by our commiseration even as grief, that unending wellspring of pain, brimmed up within him once more. My sympathy was heartfelt and had a very specific source. My elder brother had been dead for nearly a decade, and still the ache of loss throbbed, at times catching me unawares with its intensity. He had never been the most dependable or affectionate of individuals, yet he had been my brother, my last living kin, and I missed him sorely.

"As for Niemand," said Holmes, "I suspect you are aware that Inigo Niemand is not his true name. He is in fact called Bradford Wade."

Quatermain nodded sagely.

I myself was taken aback. "How do you know that, Holmes?"

"You will recall, Watson, how yesterday in the lobby of the Fanthorpe offices I took it upon myself to inspect the appointments diary upon the clerk's desk. Amongst the entries dating back to early last week was one in the name Bradford Wade. Now tell me, what were the initials embroidered upon Inigo Niemand's handkerchiefs?"

"'B.W.,'" I said.

"Excellent!"

"But there is no way you could be certain that the Bradford Wade who had a meeting with the Fanthorpes is the 'B.W.' of Niemand's monogram. There must be any number of people with those initials in London. Hundreds of them. Thousands, even."

"Quite," said Holmes, with that regal superciliousness which was perhaps his most taxing personality trait. "However, after you and I parted ways outside the coffeehouse, I took myself to Chancery Lane. To Serjeants' Inn Hall, to be precise, better known as Companies House. There I availed myself of the register of companies and perused the list of principal employees currently under contract to Fanthorpe Overseas Ventures. Amongst them was a Mr Bradford Wade, whose job title was given as 'itinerant site inspector'. Thus did an association which might be dismissed as flimsy harden into something firmer."

"How so?"

"An 'itinerant site inspector' working for Fanthorpe would surely be a man who travelled abroad, visiting the company's various mines and reporting back to the directors. Such a man would undoubtedly acquire a tan if he had lately been in the tropics or equatorial regions, where the vast majority of the Fanthorpe mines are located. The evidence pointing towards Inigo Niemand and Bradford Wade being one and the same person was starting to mount, especially if you take into account the African tribal fetish we saw at Niemand's flat."

"The fetish which he could have picked up during a stopover on his way home from India."

"Yes, but then there is his choice of pseudonymous surname."

"Niemand, the German for 'nobody'. How is that relevant?"

"It happens to have the same meaning in Afrikaans as well. Afrikaans is, after all, a dialect of Dutch, which in turn is related to German. The word *niemand* is common to all three languages. So it is perfectly possible that Wade would have gained a cursory working knowledge of Afrikaans if he had spent time in South Africa. Based upon this connection and the fetish, I asked myself, what if Wade was never in India at all? What if that was a ruse and he had instead been in South Africa? From there is hardly a leap to make the conjecture that his most recent mine inspection was carried out in that country, perhaps even at Silasville."

"It is conceivable, I suppose."

"None of this would have occurred to me were it not for the fact that Inigo Niemand, with his self-abnegating surname and his handkerchiefs sporting their 'B.W.' monogram, was almost certainly living in hiding under an assumed identity. What earthly reason would a man have for doing that if he were not frightened for his life? And if Niemand was Wade, as I thought, it would be reasonable to infer that he had stumbled across something significant on his latest fact-finding mission abroad, something which had prompted him to hasten back to London and deliver a report to his superiors in person, much as Umslopogaas did with the news of Harry Quatermain's sad demise. The same something was so terrible, so potentially injurious to Wade's own welfare, that he saw no alternative but to confine himself in a benighted quarter of west London, giving his landlady a false name and lying to her that he had been working for the Imperial Legislative Council in India and had returned to England in poor health. Am I wrong in any respect so far, Quatermain?"

"Not a one," came the reply.

"Now, in light of Umslopogaas's story about Harry, one might readily infer that Bradford Wade could have learned of that young man's unaccounted-for death and discovered the truth about its circumstances. Thus have I been weaving a web of connections, and I hereby call upon you, Quatermain, to corroborate its substance."

We had by this time reached Hyde Park, whose network of pathways seemed as good a venue as any for us to continue conducting our ambulatory discourse.

"Niemand was Wade, yes," said Quatermain, "and I met him by happenstance outside the Fanthorpe building after I made my somewhat ignominious departure from the boardroom. He was entering by the front door as I was leaving, and I'm embarrassed to say that the encounter was physical. To wit, I barged into him when storming out and knocked him flat on his back. Quite by accident, of course. I was in high dudgeon and not looking where I was going.

"I helped him to his feet, naturally, full of apology. He picked up the briefcase he had dropped, brushed himself down and gave me a glare.

"I excused myself, muttering something about having just had to deal with some of the most unhelpful idiots the world had to offer, and Wade – although I did not yet know him by name – replied that if I was referring to the directors of Fanthorpe Overseas Ventures, it was an opinion I would be better off keeping to myself. He said this in such a way that it could have been taken as a company man asserting his loyalty to his employers, but I noted a distinct edge to the words.

"That aroused my curiosity. Some inner prompting – I don't know what it was – told me that here was a fellow who might be of advantage to me. My enquiries up until then had proved bootless. Could this stranger, who radiated a manifest anxiety, present the breakthrough I was looking for?

"I bided my time, waiting for Wade to emerge again from the building. An hour later he did, and he appeared hardly more comfortable than he had when going in. On the contrary, his demeanour was now that of someone preoccupied, deeply worried.

"I refrained from buttonholing him until he had gone some distance down the street. At the back of my mind lurked the thought that I was reading too much into his behaviour. This man had nothing to do with Silasville or Harry or any of it. He was merely some Fanthorpe functionary, fretful over some professional matter entirely unrelated to my business.

"Nevertheless a feeling in my gut was telling me otherwise. I imagine, Holmes, that you do not pay much heed to instinct. It is all brain, brain, brain with you."

"You imagine wrong, Quatermain. Instinct is a powerful force. It is the unconscious mind's way of nudging one in the right direction. However, it has no value if divorced from rigorous observation and testing."

"Well, at any rate, I obeyed mine. I approached the fellow from behind and tapped his shoulder. He was so startled, he practically jumped out of his skin.

"'You!' he cried. 'Who are you? What do you want?'

"'Calm down,' I said. 'I am not here to hurt you.'

"'You knocked me down before. Do you mean to do it again?'

"'Not unless the situation warrants it.'

"I spoke in jest, but the humour, grim as it was, was lost on him. 'Do you work for Fanthorpe?' he said, backing away, his lip quivering. 'Are you some kind of enforcer?'

"'I have no connection with Fanthorpe whatsoever,' I said. 'I am an interested party, that is all.'

"'Interested party? And what is that supposed to mean?'

"'You tell me. Why are you so scared?'

"'Scared? I am not scared.' His wide, bloodshot eyes and strangulated voice rather gave the lie to that statement.

"'You could have fooled me,' I said. 'You are as jumpy as a scalded cat.'

"'If I am, then it is none of your concern.'

"'I should like to think that it is.'

"'Think what you will, sir,' said Wade, turning to go. 'I want nothing to do with you, and if you are wise you will have nothing to do with me.'

"I could not let it go at that. I grabbed him by the collar and swung him round.

"'Listen, and listen well,' I said, looking him square in the eye. 'I am a man in mourning. I have lately lost a son, my only child. I am convinced that Fanthorpe Overseas Ventures is in some way responsible for his death. At the very least, the Fanthorpe brothers may well know more about it than they are letting on. I have no idea who you are or what your role at the company is, but I am asking you – no, begging you – if you have any insight into its operations, if there is any conceivable way you can be of assistance, oblige me. I would not be importuning you like this, were I not at the end of my tether.'

"He blinked at me, then said, 'Yes. Yes, you are at the end of your tether. I can see that.' He shot a glance right and left, debated with himself, and at last, with a sigh, bade me accompany him to a pub.

"We found ourselves a quiet nook in the pub where we would not be overheard. Wade, having ordered himself a whisky, downed it at a gulp. It was the first of several he drank in swift succession.

"'You realise that, by taking you into my confidence, I may be placing you in jeopardy,' he said.

"I shrugged. 'I fear no man.'

"'It is not necessarily a man that is the danger here.'

"'No?'

"'No,' said Wade. 'You told me your son has died. What was his name? Was it by any chance Harry Quatermain?'

"'It was,' I said.

"'I thought as much. And you, therefore, must be Allan Quatermain, famous across all Africa as Hunter Quatermain.'

"'None other. And you?'

"'Bradford Wade is my name, but I am presently going by the alias of Inigo Niemand to all who do not know me. It affords a certain level of protection.'

"'Protection against what?'

"'Reprisals. Those who would silence me. Those who might wish me dead. I also have this.'

"Opening his briefcase, he took out a fetish. It is probably the same one to which you referred a moment ago, Holmes."

"A wooden doll carved in the shape of an African warrior brandishing a spear?" said Holmes.

Quatermain nodded. "It is a charm designed to ward off evil. In theory, he who bears it should be immune to the depredations of ghosts, demons and any number of other malign supernatural influences. Whether or not Wade fully believed that it would fulfil its intended purpose, the mere fact that he was carrying such a fetish was telling.

"'I purchased it from a witch-doctor outside Piquetberg,' he said to me. 'I know that, as a Christian born and bred, I should have no truck with this sort of pagan superstition. Yet if even half of what I reckon to be true *is* true, I would be mad not to take every precaution available, up to and including a talisman like this.'

"And just what are you hoping the fetish will guard you from?' I asked.

"'Black magic, Mr Quatermain,' Wade replied. 'Specifically, a pernicious evil known as the Devil's Dust.'"

CHAPTER TWENTY-ONE

THE DEVIL'S DUST

Our footsteps had led us to the banks of the Serpentine. Around us, the park bustled. A pair of nannies pushed perambulators side by side, gossiping. A young boy in knickerbockers and a sailor hat scampered across the greensward, attempting to get a kite with a beribboned tail to fly while his mother looked on dotingly. A courting couple occupied a bench, oblivious to anything but the sweet nothings each whispered in the other's ear. In the river itself, men in bathing costumes splashed about, enjoying what was possibly the last swim of the season with the water at an agreeable temperature.

It all presented a delightful prospect: Londoners at their leisure.

Yet Quatermain's words seemed to cast a sinister pall over the scene, and my nape-hairs prickled as though wafted by a chilly gust of wind.

"The Devil's Dust?" I said, affecting scorn. "Preposterous name! What on earth is it supposed to signify?"

"Death," said Quatermain simply. "That is what it signifies.

Horrible, painful death. The Devil's Dust is a sorcerous concoction that leaves the victim choking, vomiting, wracked with agony. The innards bleed. The skin reddens. The face swells. Its only redeeming feature is that the end comes with relative swiftness."

"The symptoms you describe are applicable in the case of Bradford Wade's demise," said Holmes. "Tell me, would 'Devil's Dust' by any chance translate into one of the African languages as this?" From his pocket he withdrew the scrap of paper he had found in Wade's flat and gave it to Quatermain to read.

Quatermain's wrinkled brow furrowed into a scowl. "Who wrote this?"

"Wade, as he lay dying. I surmised that he might have been trying to write something longer but succumbed before he was able to."

"You are right. *Uthuli* is Zulu for 'dust', and the 'L' could indeed be the first letter of *lukaDeveli*, meaning 'of the Devil'."

"Then the import behind the words becomes apparent," I said.

"Indeed," said Holmes. "Wade was not attempting to identify his killer, which we touted as one possible theory. Rather he was attempting to identify the method by which he had been killed."

"According to Wade," said a grim-visaged Quatermain, "*Uthuli lukaDeveli* – the Devil's Dust – was how Harry came to be killed too. Wade told me that he arrived in Silasville to conduct a regular site inspection two days before Harry showed up. He had not visited the place before, having been employed by Fanthorpe for a little under a year, but he knew of Silasville's reputation. It was notorious as one of the worst-run, most unruly mines on the entire continent. He saw no sign of that himself, however. Everything seemed perfectly orderly to him."

"The Fanthorpe brothers assured us that a new leaf had been turned over at Silasville," said Holmes. "It had put its dark times behind it."

"That was the impression Wade had too, at least to begin with. The site foreman, a Boer called Marius van Hoek, boasted to him that there had been no untoward incidents at the mine for eighteen months – none worth reporting, at any rate. Productivity was up, Van Hoek said, and while there had been the odd accident, even a death or two, the rate was not above the statistical mean. Wade's own researches confirmed it.

"'What I did notice, though, Mr Quatermain,' Wade said, 'was a distinct unwillingness amongst the miners to talk to me. Each I approached affected to be too busy to spare me the time. One lot were sitting round a fire after nightfall, eating supper, seemingly idle, but as soon as I turned up, without a word they all set down their dishes, stood and left, dispersing in different directions. It did not take me long to figure out that the picture at Silasville was not as rosy as Van Hoek had painted. Something was awry. The workers were cowed, reluctant even to look me in the eye, let alone be interviewed. What had them so browbeaten was hard to determine. I cannot say that relations between them and the management were cordial, but neither was there any obvious antagonism directed one way or the other. With the miners it was more a case of obedience – the cringing, craven obedience of a dog that has been beaten so frequently by its master that all the fight has gone out of it and it knows nothing except how to behave.'

"Then," Quatermain continued, "who should come ambling along into this uneasy milieu but my boy Harry, all fresh-faced optimism, with his retinue of waggoners and riders and bearers. He set up camp outside the town and ventured in alone. Wade learned of his presence when he overheard a couple of the miners speaking excitedly about 'the son of Macumazahn'. The majority of them were Zulus, while the rest spoke Fanagolo – a pidgin of Zulu favoured by miners – so that they could all communicate with one another. Wade was not fluent in the Zulu tongue but had picked up enough to get the gist. He knew, too, who Macumazahn was. My fame is widespread across Africa. Wade was curious to meet Harry, but that was not to be, for Harry was in Silasville for only a few hours before he abruptly vanished."

"Vanished?" said Holmes.

"I cannot specify how, or where he got to, for the simple reason that Wade himself did not know. All he knew was that everyone had been discussing Harry Quatermain, son of Macumazahn, and then all of a sudden everyone was not. A veil of silence had fallen over the town. Harry was nowhere to be seen. Nobody was even mentioning him. It was as if he had never been there."

"How singular."

"Then, the following morning…"

Quatermain paused. It was clearly a struggle for him to say what he said next.

"The following morning, Harry's corpse was found lying in the street. Left there like… like *litter*. Like a piece of wax-paper wrapping someone has thoughtlessly discarded. That was when Wade heard the first fretful mutterings amongst the workers. The state his body was in was one they seemed to know only too well. '*Uthuli lukaDeveli*,' they said to one another in hushed tones, rolling their eyes and wringing their hands. '*Uthuli lukaDeveli*.' There were marks upon Harry, signs, clear indicators of a specific cause of death. Blood. Vomit. Puffed-up face. Redness of the skin."

"The Devil's Dust had been used," I said.

"By cautious eavesdropping Wade was able to glean that *Uthuli lukaDeveli* was some form of black magic, and he would of course gladly have pooh-poohed the whole idea as nonsense, the kind of native mumbo-jumbo that no white man should ever take seriously."

"And rightly so," said Holmes. "There is no such thing as magic."

"Really?" Quatermain's eyes took on an obscure, ruminative cast. "Let me tell you, Holmes. I have seen things, many strange and inexplicable things, in my long lifetime. I have seen an infant slain by a kiss. I have seen an orchid eight feet in diameter that was worshipped as a god. I have seen a man haunted by the ghost of a foe slain in battle, so tormented by this shade that he had become a shell of who he used to be, practically a ghost himself. I have seen the image of a monstrous creature, half man, half ape, conjured up from the embers of a fire by a wizard. I have met the queen of a lost race dwelling in catacombs beside a ruined ancient city, a woman blessed – or perhaps cursed – with not only unearthly beauty but immortality. All these experiences have led me to the inescapable conclusion that there is more to life than simply that which we can touch and hear, see and smell. There are mysteries that cannot be rationalised away. There are people gifted with powers beyond our mortal ken. And there is, yes, magic."

"Well, certainly there is," Holmes said, "if one attends the splendid shows put on by Maskelyne and Cooke at the Egyptian Hall."

"Holmes…" I said, shaking my head in despair at his flippancy.

"I am not talking about stage conjuring, Holmes," said Quatermain, "and you know that full well. I am talking about witchcraft. The dark arts. The ability to exert an influence upon others from afar, to use potions, powders and spells for eldritch ends, to divine the future in visions and portents, and much more besides."

"I have long held the view that if a phenomenon may not

be empirically proven, it is almost certainly a false reading," said Holmes. "Moreover, it will yield its truths to scientific analysis once sufficient time and attention have been brought to bear."

"We shall just have to agree to differ on the subject. Perhaps, when you are older and have travelled more, you will come to appreciate how wild and weird the world can be. For now, it will have to suffice that at Silasville something uncanny was at play, at least as far as the miners were concerned. As far as Wade was concerned, too. The mumbling terror he saw around him was deep-rooted. It stemmed from bitter experience. The miners had seen others perish from the effects of the Devil's Dust before, that much was apparent. Harry was just the latest in a series of victims. As one of the miners said within Wade's earshot, 'He has caused offence and was struck down by *Uthuli lukaDeveli*. A white man! Not one of us, one of *them*. Who is safe now? Who dares raise his head and speak his mind if even a white man may be attacked?'"

"The Devil's Dust, then, whatever it might be, sorcery or not, was being used as a kind of disciplinary instrument," said Holmes.

"Wade drew the same inference. The Devil's Dust was responsible for the 'perfectly orderly' atmosphere he noticed when he first arrived. It would only have required the deaths of one or two troublemakers from the Dust to set the example. After that, you would have no problem making the workforce toe the line. The threat of *Uthuli lukaDeveli*, the mere fact of its existence, would be enough."

"Domination by fear. A much more efficient regime than beatings and shootings. Much less of a drain on manpower and resources. Wade, I presume, went straight to Marius van Hoek to demand elucidation. As a diligent site inspector he could do no less."

"You are correct in your presumption," said Quatermain,

"and it was a decision he would quickly come to regret. Van Hoek's response was as blunt as it was hostile. He told Wade he should forget anything he had seen or heard. If he knew what was good for him, he should leave Silasville forthwith and tell their paymasters in London precisely nothing about the incident.

"'I wish this had not happened,' Van Hoek said, and Wade sensed that he meant it. The Boer was chagrined and also, it would seem, vexed. 'However,' he went on, 'what's done cannot be undone. It can only be disregarded. Do you understand, Mr Wade?'

"Wade understood only too well, and he cleared out of Silasville that same day. I do not blame him for that."

"Neither do I," said I. "It was not cowardice, only common sense."

"Yet his sense of duty – of simple moral decency – would not allow him to ignore what he had witnessed. He went to the nearest port with a view to securing a berth aboard the first available packet steamer to England and conveying his findings about Silasville directly to the Fanthorpe brothers. Along the way he bought that fetish of his, just in case. He said he felt a deep, ineluctable dread the entire voyage, not aided by a vicious storm in the Bay of Biscay. 'It was as if doom was dogging my footsteps, Mr Quatermain,' he said. 'As if, even though I had fled Silasville, the dire spectre of death I had stumbled upon there were pursuing me. I hardly slept or ate. I was jumping at shadows. During the storm I was convinced the ship was about to go down, and I believed that somehow whoever was behind your son's death had whipped up this tempest by necromantic means, with the express intent of drowning me. It sounds absurd, but it felt quite logical at the time.'

"He looked around the pub where we were sitting. It was as pleasant and mundane a drinking establishment as you could hope to find, but I could tell that Wade was incapable of perceiving it as such. To him, menace lurked in the varnished wooden countertops, the etched window glass, the ceramic handles of the beer pumps, even the placid, beefy features of the publican.

"'I cannot shake the impression,' he went on, 'that I am still in danger, here in London. Hence I have taken lodgings where nobody knows me, and I refuse to show my face outdoors for long. I have even adopted a false name. As Niemand, I am nobody, and that suits me for now. If people are looking for somebody, then they are not looking for nobody.'

"He seemed obliquely pleased with this little bit of wordplay, but he was by then on his fourth or fifth whisky.

"He proceeded to tell me that it had taken him several days to pluck up the nerve to face the Fanthorpe brothers and inform them about Harry Quatermain and the Devil's Dust. He might have found his courage sooner had he not had all those interminably long weeks of sea voyage during which there was little to do but stew in his cabin.

"'I can see that I have allowed my worst, most primitive fears to get the better of me,' he said. 'But if you could only have seen those miners, Mr Quatermain… How utterly terrified they were. Their terror has infected me, like some sort of plague.'

"In the event, setting out the facts before the Fanthorpes did little to allay Wade's concerns. He had been hoping for reassurance from them. He had expected them to hear him out, tell him he had done the right thing, and promise that the appropriate measures would be implemented.

"'But they could not have cared less,' he said. 'They showed nothing but disdain. They called me hysterical. Sebastian likened me a breathless old biddy clutching her chest with an attack of the vapours. He said I had been hired to supply frank, impartial reports, not to spout claptrap about magical spells and inexplicable deaths. Samuel Fanthorpe suggested that I was perhaps not up to the job and dropped heavy hints about my contract being put under review. Stanley, meanwhile, said that he and his brothers had already been told about Harry Quatermain via a cable from Van Hoek. The young man, Stanley said, had died of the smallpox that was raging through the region. Such was the determination of Silasville's resident medic, and who were they to dispute that? Who, for that matter, was I?'

"'They were attempting to bully you into submission,' I said.

"'And doing it fairly well. You may be a man of means, Mr Quatermain, with your fortune in diamonds, but I am not. Both parents dead, no siblings, no real family, certainly no inheritance. I am making my own way in the world, and I can ill afford to lose what income I have. My one main qualification is my degree in the geological sciences, and that is hardly a passport to riches. In short, I desperately need to keep the job I have.'

"Wade sighed heavily, and I felt that it was time to give him a good talking-to. Here, if ever there was one, was a man in need of having his sinews stiffened.

"'You are braver than you think, Mr Wade,' I said. 'Look at what you have done. You have confronted three very powerful men. The encounter may not have gone the way you wished, but you at least gave it your best shot. You have stood up for what you think is right, at the risk of your livelihood. Take a moment to celebrate the achievement.'

"A glimmer of pride entered his eyes.

"'Furthermore,' I said, 'you have furnished me with some valuable intelligence. I have a clearer idea than before of the circumstances of Harry's death. For that I shall be eternally grateful. Henceforth, I shall carry the baton. You return to wherever it is you have sequestered yourself and leave the rest to me. I am a seasoned old campaigner, a veteran of countless battles. I am prepared to take up arms on your behalf – and Harry's.'

"Really, the look of relief that came over Wade then was a sight to behold. His shoulders sank as his woes lifted. He looked about a stone lighter.

"Not long after that, we parted ways, or so Wade thought."

"But you followed him home," said Holmes, "covertly, as seems your habit."

"Of course," said Quatermain. "He was still too much in the grip of paranoia to trust me with his address, but following him thither, unsuspected, was child's play. I then set up watch over the place."

"Let me intuit why. You were using Wade as bait."

"Not exactly. Instinct was telling me – instinct again! – that the Fanthorpes might not be content with simply threatening Wade with getting the sack. If they feared a scandal or scrutiny of their company's business practices, should Wade decide to go to the authorities with what he knew about Silasville and Harry, they might take things further."

"Wade might come a cropper," I said.

"So you were standing sentinel over him," said Holmes, "trying to keep him from harm. At the same time, though, you must have been hoping that something might happen, that the Fanthorpes or someone in their employ might make a move against him. Then, as a father thirsting for satisfaction over the death of his son, you would have an attack to thwart and an enemy to put a face to."

"Proof," said Quatermain. "That was what I was after. Proof that Harry had been murdered. And an attempt on Wade's life would provide it. I lurked outside that house in Notting Hill day after day, changing position, overlooking it from several different vantages, front and rear. On the rare occasions Wade ventured out, I went with him, keeping him in sight at all times while remaining unseen by him."

"A veritable guardian angel."

"What I did not realise, until Daniel Greensmith turned up at his door, was that Wade had decided to get in touch with the press. He must have wired Greensmith on one of his outings to the post office and invited him over. Obviously my little rallying talk at the pub had been more effective than I thought. When I spied Greensmith approaching the house I feared he was an assassin of some kind, until it became clear that he was there by arrangement. I eavesdropped at the front window and discovered that he was a journalist and Wade wished to publicise the events at Silasville."

"You eavesdropped at the front window?" said Holmes. "I saw no footprints to indicate that."

"Ha! Holmes, I do not leave footprints if I do not want to. I could walk across wet concrete and you would not know I had been there."

"Remarkable."

"No, simply bushcraft. Any Zulu, Bantu, Xhosa, Kikuyu or Hottentot worth his salt could do likewise. It is nothing special."

As airily as he dismissed his accomplishment, Quatermain could not help but come across a touch smug. I had an inkling that, although he and Holmes had buried the hatchet, there would ever remain a rivalry between them, each vying to get one up on the other.

"Wade's decision to blow the whistle on Fanthorpe presented a problem, however," he said. "Merely revealing what he knew about Silasville to readers of *The Times* might not achieve the desired result. It might be considered mere hearsay, especially the part about the Devil's Dust. That would play right into the Fanthorpes' hands. They could use it to destroy any credibility Wade's account might have. 'Here is a man blathering on about African superstition,' they might say. 'How can anyone take him seriously?'"

"You felt Wade had made an error of judgement," said Holmes, "so you took steps. You persuaded Greensmith not to pursue the story."

"Not much persuasion was necessary, in the event. Greensmith already had half a mind not to follow it up. He, hardnosed reporter that he was, found many aspects of it, particularly the Devil's Dust, difficult to swallow. He told me that while there was always a certain pleasure in landing a solid blow upon establishment figures like the Fanthorpes, in this instance he doubted there was enough weight behind the punch to make it worth his while. In fact, it might rebound on him. Wade's testimony was compelling but lacked substance. It was one step up from hearsay. 'The question a man in my line of work must constantly ask himself,' Greensmith said, 'is, "Will this stand up in a court of law?" Because, if not, then taking on men as powerful as the Fanthorpes is a fool's errand and a fast track to the poorhouse. Unless one possesses watertight proof of malfeasance, their kind are more or less untouchable.'"

"But even though you thought you had removed Greensmith from the equation," said Holmes, "you continued to keep tabs on him."

"That was after Wade was dead," said Quatermain. "If the Fanthorpes knew of Greensmith's association with him, he might be next on the list – a loose end that needed to be tied up. Such was my thinking."

"Hence you followed him during his wanderings through the East End."

"Yes, him in that damn-fool disguise of his. It wasn't even as if he was interested in Wade and Fanthorpe any longer. That was a blind alley as far as he was concerned. He was trying to ferret out a fresh story, something he successfully could turn into news. Still, I feared the Fanthorpes might send someone after him – someone ready, perhaps, to use *Uthuli lukaDeveli* again, this time on a nosey journalist."

"Not wishing to be indelicate," I said, "but if you had been keeping watch over Wade, how did he come to be killed? I don't for one moment denigrate your abilities. I am simply surprised that Wade's killer managed to get past you."

"As am I, Doctor," Quatermain said with feeling. "Yet it is not so surprising when you consider that I was conducting a lone vigil. Nobody can stay at his post indefinitely. One must eat, sleep, answer the call of nature…"

"Could you not have recruited Umslopogaas to stand in for you during your absences?"

"I thought about it, but a black man may not linger in any London neighbourhood for long without arousing suspicion amongst the locals and perhaps, too, the police, whereas I would easily be able to blend in. The long and the short of it was that I was not present when Wade's killer struck, or if I was, somehow he slipped past me."

"If he was some sort of sorcerer," said Holmes, "as is implied by the likelihood that the Devil's Dust was used on Wade, then it is possible the fellow turned himself invisible, or flew, or perhaps transformed himself into an animal."

"You are being facetious, Holmes," Quatermain said gruffly, "but there may yet be a grain of truth in what you say."

By now we had crossed West Carriage Drive and were in Kensington Gardens, just to the north of the Albert Memorial. Tall trees surrounded us, gently divesting themselves of what remained of their golden foliage. Today this area of parkland was less frequented than its counterpart on the other side of the road.

"Witchcraft should never be underestimated," Quatermain continued. "Its practitioners are amongst the cleverest and most cunning of men. They are capable of feats of— *Down!*"

He shouted the last word, at the same time seizing Holmes and me roughly by the necks and pushing us flat to the grass.

Just beside us, there was the crisp snapping sound of a small object colliding with a tree trunk at high velocity. Bark splinters showered us, while the *crack* of a gun report rolled forth from not far distant.

We had been shot at, and, if not for Quatermain's extraordinary, almost prescient reflexes, the bullet might have found a home in one of our heads.

And there were more where it had come from.

CHAPTER TWENTY-TWO

UNDER FIRE

I had been under sniper fire before, not least at Maiwand where I received my bullet wound. I knew well the strange blank incredulity that comes over one in such a predicament, with its accompanying undertones of panic and helplessness. A fellow man wishes to kill you and is prepared to do so from afar, at one remove. To him, as he squints down his gunsight, you are not a human being, just a target, a bullseye. He does not hate you. He simply needs you eliminated and is going about the task in a clinical, dispassionate manner, for if he allowed himself to feel any sense of affinity with you he would never be able to pull the trigger.

I had no doubt that our unseen sniper in Kensington Gardens regarded the three of us with no less indifference than had the Ghazi who fired his Jezail at me. As if it needed confirming, a second bullet struck the turf a few inches in front of us, kicking up a small plume of dirt.

"Move!" Quatermain urged. "He is finding his range, and we are doomed if we just lie here."

We scrambled for cover on hands and knees as a third bullet whined over our heads. A fourth pierced a low-hanging branch of the tree, a stately fat oak, behind which we took refuge.

By then I had my Webley out, thanking the Lord that I had seen fit to bring the revolver with me. This was not the result of foresight on my part. I had not anticipated any attack. However, after recent events, from Quatermain's nocturnal shenanigans to Starkey to the pigeons, it seemed sensible to go about armed.

Although unsure precisely where the shots were coming from, I leaned round the side of the tree. The coast was clear, no innocent bystanders in sight. I returned fire in what I was almost certain was the right direction, emptying the Webley's cylinder.

"Don't waste your ammunition, Watson," said Quatermain. "He is too far away for your pistol. Can you not tell by the interval of time between bullet impact and gun report? He is shooting from at least a hundred yards' distance."

"Well, he now knows we are capable of retaliating," I retorted. "It may make him think twice."

A cessation in the shooting appeared to bear out my hypothesis. I dared to poke my nose out – and almost had it blown off. The round struck the tree a hand's-breadth from my face.

"Then again, perhaps not," I said, a little breathlessly.

"Quatermain," said Holmes, "gunplay is more your province than mine. What do you propose?"

"If our assailant is operating solo, as seems to be the case, then one option is to sit tight. The oak is broad enough to shield us. He may decide he has been thwarted in his objective and retreat."

"I do not think it likely, and you sound as though you do not either."

"No. Were I he, I would even now be edging round to get a better angle. The fellow is a hunter, after all, and it is what a hunter would do."

"How can you know he is a hunter?" I asked.

"That's a Mauser rifle he is firing," said Quatermain, "one which has been adapted to take .50-calibre rounds. The report is quite distinctive – a shortened barrel makes its own particularly resonant *boom* – and bullets of that size inflict the level of devastation one can see from the gouge in the bark just by your head. Such a Mauser is favoured by safari sportsmen who are after big game."

"And game does not come much bigger than human beings," Holmes observed dryly. "Our best tactic, then, is to flee before he repositions himself."

"Indeed," said Quatermain. "We should scatter, too, rather than run bunched together in a group, each of us thus lessening his chances of being hit. It is what antelope herds do. But unlike antelope, we will not merely be bolting. We will circle round. You go clockwise, Holmes, you anticlockwise, Doctor. That way the both of you may close in on the fellow from two sides."

"Agreed," said Holmes.

"What about you, Quatermain?" I said. "Which way shall you go?"

"Up."

So saying, Quatermain sprang to the nearest bough of the oak, hauling himself up until he was squatting upon it. He then climbed nimbly into the middle reaches of the tree and sidestepped outward along a branch just sturdy enough to support his weight. A leap, and he was clinging to an outstretched branch of the tree adjacent. He swung monkey-like around the trunk, making for the next tree along. In short order I lost sight of him.

"Ah," said Holmes. "So we shall be flanking our foe in three dimensions, not just two. Ready, Watson?"

My pistol was reloaded. I nodded. "Ready."

Off he and I went on the divergent courses prescribed by Quatermain. I hunched low as I scurried from place of cover to place of cover. At every moment I expected the singeing impact of hot lead, the feeling of being thrown helplessly to the ground, the giddy disorientation of shock – all sensations I could recall only too well from my misadventure in Afghanistan.

Soon I was passing the Round Pond and doubling back towards the southern edge of the park. At the first sign of the sniper, I knew I would have to shoot on sight. Were the roles reversed, he would not extend me the courtesy of hesitating, so I could not either.

The exchange of gunfire had shattered the park's tranquillity. Here and there, panicked folk scurried, some of them yelling in their alarm. There was the shrill peeping of whistles, too, as policemen began to converge on the area from the adjacent streets. Given the number of attempts there had been on our queen's life, it was hardly surprising that gun reports not far from Buckingham Palace would bring members of Her Majesty's Constabulary out in force.

However, the policemen seemed unable to pinpoint precisely where the shots had been fired. The one pair of constables I saw were, indeed, running *away from* rather than *to* the relevant spot. I nearly waved at them to attract their attention, until I realised that they might mistake me, with my revolver, for the sniper. Masking my gun hand beneath the flap of my coat, I carried on.

Then I spied him. Or at any rate I spied a figure skulking in a patch of shrubbery. He was engaged in some furtive practice, rustling around amidst the dappled shadows. I tiptoed nearer, pistol raised. Was it the sniper?

Now within fifteen feet of the fellow, I silently thumbed back the revolver's hammer. I still could not get an unimpeded view of him, but who would be lurking in shrubbery when everyone else was fleeing for their lives? Who but the cause of the hue and cry himself?

I determined that, as soon as I saw his rifle and my suspicions were confirmed, I would loose off a round at the blackguard. I would not give him any kind of verbal warning. He, after all, had been quite content to assassinate us without the least advertisement.

I was within ten feet of him, and poised to fire, when something heavy descended on me from above.

No, not something. Some*one*. Allan Quatermain. He plummeted from overhead, batting my gun arm down and bringing me to my knees with the force of his landing.

"Are you insane, man?" he thundered. "Look!"

He gesticulated in the direction of the shrubbery. The man within, alerted by Quatermain's bellowing, had emerged from his place of concealment.

It was Sherlock Holmes.

"My God!" I ejaculated, my face growing hot with shame. "Holmes, I very nearly… It was that close… Had Quatermain not…"

"It is quite all right, old man," Holmes said. "The fault lies partly with me. I should have heard you creeping up. I was completely absorbed in other matters. Yonder" – he pointed to the shrubbery – "lies the place our sniper was employing as his hide. Here is the proof." He held out a shell casing. "For a .50-calibre round, is that not so, Quatermain?"

Hunter Quatermain inspected the hollow brass cylinder and nodded. He sniffed the open end. "Recently fired."

"One of several left behind," Holmes said, "all alike."

"And the fellow himself?" I said, clambering unsteadily to my feet.

"Gone," said Quatermain. "I was just now at the summit of that ash over there, which afforded me a panoramic view over the vicinity. The sniper is nowhere in sight. He has quit the scene."

"I concur," said Holmes. "Footprints leading out of the shrubbery show that he has made off towards Kensington High Street."

"We must follow with all due haste," I said.

Holmes shrugged his shoulders. "If he has any strategic sense, he will have left a cab waiting for him there. But if you insist..."

The road was busy with traffic, while crowds milled about on the pavement. Many of these people had been drawn by the gunfire, and they were jabbering noisily to one another, speculating on what it might mean. For us even to hope for a glimpse of our would-be killer was futile.

I huffed with frustration, but Holmes was sanguine. "All is not lost," said he. "In addition to the shell casings, my delving amidst the shrubbery yielded clues about the sniper's physical appearance, his smoking habits, and his footwear, all of them useful and pertinent. More generally speaking, this little escapade has been instructive about our enemy's frame of mind."

"Oh yes?" I said. "How?"

"Our enemy is becoming ever more aggrieved and desperate. To attempt to kill us in broad daylight is a bold stroke. It is clear we are setting alarm bells ringing ever louder, and the more precipitate the action launched against us is, the likelier it will be that the instigator makes a mistake and exposes himself."

"I cannot fault your logic, but neither am I comfortable with it. As the attacks upon us escalate, so do the odds of one being successful. Fatally so. It was bad enough when it was just rats and pigeons. Now it is gunfire. What next? A twelve-pound cannon aimed at our lodgings?"

"Rats and pigeons?" Quatermain queried. "What on earth are you talking about?"

Briefly I related the events of the previous night.

"Hmmm. Wild animals being used as a weapon, targeted

specifically against two individuals… What does that say to you? To me, it smacks of witchcraft."

"To you, Quatermain, everything smacks of witchcraft," said Holmes. "The rats and pigeons were drugged, that is all. They had been driven out of their minds by the ingestion of a powerful psychotropic substance. No further human intercession was necessary beyond simply introducing them into our lodgings and letting their feral natures, unshackled from their accustomed timidity in the presence of humans, do the rest."

"Nevertheless, hear me out, Holmes. The ability to command animals to do your bidding is a common one amongst African witch-doctors. That wizard I mentioned – the one who showed me an image of Heu-heu the man-ape in fire – he was capable of just that sort of sorcery. Zikali was his name. He was my nemesis, that dwarfish old rascal, and proved a formidable antagonist. He was also a shameless trickster and cheat, but I never once had reason to doubt he possessed weird powers. I saw them in action too many times to deny them."

"We are in London now, not Africa, Quatermain."

"Magic is magic, wherever you go."

"But there is no Zikali here, is there?" Holmes insisted. "There are no wizards at all."

"There is no Zikali, that is for sure. I watched him die. It was five years ago, but I remember it as if it were yesterday. I watched the little fiend plunge into a foaming waterfall with a yellow-bellied snake wrapped around him. He was committing suicide after wreaking his final, most terrible act of wickedness, the murder of King Cetawayo. However, he is not the only wizard ever to have walked the earth."

"And another is amongst us now, at large in London?"

"Yes," said Quatermain ominously. "Even if you do not believe it, I do. There can be no other way of accounting for what happened to the two of you last night."

"I am at least prepared to accept that an African witch-doctor works for Fanthorpe Overseas Ventures," said Holmes. "The conclusion seems more than plausible; it seems probable. The use of the Devil's Dust at Silasville would only really be effective as a restraint on the miners' behaviour if it were the handiwork of one of their own kind, someone like your Zikali who, by dint of his 'warlock' status, could command reverence and terror. Would you not agree, Quatermain?"

"I would. I have met few in Africa who are unafraid of magic. As a breed, wizards and witch-doctors routinely evoke in their countrymen an awestruck dread of just the kind Bradford Wade described."

"Then – setting aside for the moment the question of whether magic actually exists – what we have is a witch-doctor on the Fanthorpe payroll meting out summary justice upon the workforce at the mine, doubtless at the management's behest. It is the perfect solution to the labour problems Silasville was experiencing."

"And what if that witch-doctor is now over here, having pursued Wade to England?" Quatermain said. "You must admit it is not impossible."

"Someone is over here deploying the Devil's Dust, that much seems certain. And someone – whether or not it is the same person – despatched hordes of vermin against Watson and me, and has subsequently shot at all three of us, a rather more prosaic form of aggression. I daresay that this someone will not rest until either he has finished the job or we show clear signs of abandoning our investigation. Maybe that was all this attack in Kensington Gardens was meant to do – scare us again. It would explain why the fellow departed with such alacrity instead of staying to bag a kill."

"Or," said Quatermain slowly, "his intent was simply to keep us occupied."

"What do you mean?" I asked.

Quatermain stepped out into the roadway, raising one hand aloft while inserting fingers of the other between his lips in order to emit a very loud, piercingly shrill whistle. A passing hackney cab – a four-seater brougham – drew to an abrupt halt beside him. Had the cabman been slightly slower off the mark and less adroit with the reins, his horses might have trampled Quatermain.

He sent some choice oaths Quatermain's way, but the latter, seemingly oblivious, climbed into the cab and demanded to be taken to Victoria Park.

Holmes leapt in beside him, and I swiftly joined them. The cabman cracked the whip and yelled "Yah!", and off we trotted.

"Victoria Park," said Holmes to Quatermain. "You are concerned about Umslopogaas."

"I feel the need to check on him," came the reply. "It may be nothing, but suppose the man with the Mauser rifle has been tracking me all day. He may then know where I came from. He may be returning thither now to lie in wait, so that he can take another crack at me. In the meantime he may decide to take a crack at Umslopogaas."

Quatermain's mouth was set in a grim line.

"That hoary old Zulu is as close to me as any brother," he said. "I would never forgive myself if something happened to him."

CHAPTER TWENTY-THREE

ROMULUS MINUS REMUS

The traffic, bad on Kensington High Street, worsened around Hyde Park Corner. By the time we were halfway up Park Lane, the brougham was crawling along at a snail's pace.

Quatermain chafed at the delay, drumming his fingers upon his thigh ever harder. Eventually, as we came to a complete standstill, he thumped on the roof of the cab to get the cabman's attention. "What's the hold-up?" he barked.

"Looks like an omnibus up ahead at Marble Arch, guvnor. It's turned over. Can't see if anyone's hurt, but it's a right old mess. Blocking the entire road. I expect we'll be here for quite a while before the wreckage is cleared."

"Quite a while!" Quatermain declared, fuming. "That's not good enough. Don't you know an alternative route?"

"If you look around you, sir, you'll see that the whole road's jammed, that side as well as this. There's others what have had the same idea as you, and they've got themselves all nicely snarled up. Nobody's going anywhere in a hurry."

"We'll see about that."

Quatermain flung himself out of the cab and headed forward. Without a second thought he leapt astride one of the pair of horses.

"Oi!" the cabman cried. "What do you think you're doing?"

"Going somewhere in a hurry," Quatermain replied. Producing a knife, he bent and slashed through the leather traces attaching the horse to the carriage. Another couple of slashes severed the reins. Yet another slash put paid to the pole strap.

By now the cabman was on his feet and shouting. "Devil take you, sir! How dare you! Those things cost money."

"And I will reimburse you," Quatermain said over his shoulder. "I'm good for it. Ask those two."

"I don't care if you're a ruddy millionaire," said the cabman. "You can't just steal a man's livelihood right from under his nose."

He drew back the whip and lashed it at Quatermain, just missing the tip of his ear.

By then, however, Quatermain had freed the horse entirely from its trappings. At the snap of the whip, the beast reared and whinnied, and Quatermain, with his hands clamped around the backband, dug his heels into the creature's flanks, spurring it on.

Next moment, the horse was galloping off down the road, with Quatermain crouching atop. For all that he was riding more or less bareback, he appeared as at ease and in control as if his steed were equipped with the full panoply of bridle, saddle and stirrups. He wove a deft path through narrow openings in the stationary traffic.

"Remus!" the cabman called out, somewhat forlornly. "Remus, come back!"

The horse, if it even heard, paid no heed. The partner it had left behind tossed its head and stamped its hooves in apparent bemusement, as though it could not fathom how the other had escaped while it remained stuck fast.

"Oh, Romulus," the cabman lamented to the remaining horse. "Your brother. He has kidnapped your brother." He rounded on us. "You," he said with venom. "That man is your friend. I hold you answerable for him."

"You should not," said Holmes, alighting from the cab. "Allan Quatermain is a force of nature. We can restrain him no more than we could the tornado or the tsunami."

"Here," I said to the cabman. "A half-crown for your troubles. And this." Along with the money, I handed him the card Quatermain had given me earlier. "Whatever expenses you incur buying new tack, send the bill to that address. You will be repaid. As for your horse, rest assured you will get it back unharmed. Simply write the name and address of the stables you use in this notepad. I shall do the rest."

We walked away, leaving the cabman to gnash his teeth and mutter.

"You should not make promises you cannot keep, Watson," said Holmes.

"I will see to it that Quatermain does the right thing. The man is a liability but, for the time being at least, he is *our* liability."

"Never let it be said that my Watson is not a shining beacon of integrity."

"I try."

It took us some while to find another cab, and the journey to Victoria Park was torturously slow. Locating Quatermain's camp was the work of a further half an hour. This time we did not have a blood trail to follow, and the park looked very different in daylight than it had at night. After some trial and error we found the thicket, which Holmes affirmed was the one we sought because there were fresh hoof marks in the surrounding grass. He called out Quatermain's name while I kept lookout in case any passers-by happened along. There was no answer, and nobody else in sight, so we ventured in.

Of either Quatermain or Umslopogaas within, we found no sign. Another notable absence was Groan-Maker, Umslopogaas's axe.

"They are gone," I said.

"There is nothing quite like stating the obvious," said Holmes. "The question is, under what circumstances did they leave? The lack of Groan-Maker is suggestive. If Umslopogaas had been kidnapped by force, he would not have taken his beloved weapon with him. He would not have had the opportunity."

"Unless he was lured out first, bringing Groan-Maker with him as a precautionary measure, and then was ambushed."

"In which case, there would be signs of a struggle outside, and I have discerned none," said Holmes. "What I do discern, however, is a significant difference in the condition of the camp since last we saw it."

"It looks little changed to me," I said. "A shade untidier, perhaps."

"Look harder. Do you not see one thing which was not there before?"

I peered around, to no avail.

"The ground, Watson," said my friend. "To be specific, the image drawn in that patch of loose soil there."

I followed his pointing finger. There was indeed an image scratched into the floor of the camp, which I reproduce here:

It was crudely delineated, and to judge by the thickness of the lines, either a stick or a fingertip had been used as a stylus.

Beside it lay a smattering of copper pennies, the coins seeming to have been casually discarded.

"What do you make of it?" my friend enquired.

"It resembles a geometry problem," I said. "Or it could be an arcane symbol of some sort, evidence perhaps of the witchcraft Quatermain insists is in play."

"And the pennies?"

"If it is an arcane symbol, might the coins represent an offering? A stimulus for future prosperity? You are no doubt going to tell me I am nowhere near the truth with any of this conjecture."

"At present I cannot claim to know what the image is," said Holmes. "It is notable nonetheless. It is no casual adornment. It has been added here for some purpose, and the coins are part of it. There is also a smaller anomaly, which you may be forgiven for having overlooked."

He bent to examine the ground close by the image. Between thumb and forefinger he picked up a scrap of soil. He held it to his eye for close scrutiny, then sniffed it, before dropping it into one of the small envelopes which he kept in his pocket for collecting samples of this kind.

"What is so interesting about that particular piece of soil?" I asked.

"Nothing," Holmes replied, straightening up, "other than that it doesn't belong. It is from elsewhere. Whence exactly it originates, however, is another matter, one I shall conduct research into back at Baker Street."

"At least we can assume that Umslopogaas departed under his own steam."

"An alternative interpretation of the evidence is that he and Quatermain have trekked off together on some mission."

"We have not."

These words came from without, and were accompanied by

a soft equine snorting. We crawled outside to find Quatermain there, still astride Remus. He had managed to ride up to the camp so stealthily that we had not heard so much as a hoofbeat. His expression was grave.

"Umslopogaas?" I said.

"It is as I feared," said Quatermain. "He is nowhere to be seen. While I was off gallivanting, someone took him."

"Can you know that for sure?" said Holmes. "He could simply be running some errand and will return forthwith."

"You do not think that any more than I do, Holmes. I have quartered the entire park, all eighty-odd hectares of it. If he were anywhere hereabouts, I would have found him. Nor would he have departed without leaving me some indication why and whither – unless he had no choice in the matter."

"Did you not look inside the camp?"

"I did not. I called to him from out here, and when there was no reply, I commenced my search of the park."

"Perhaps you should go in and see for yourself."

"See what?"

"There is a mark upon the ground. It could be some sign from Umslopogaas as to his current whereabouts, a clue which he is confident you, and only you, are able to interpret."

Quatermain dismounted and entered the camp. Re-emerging a few moments later, he said, "You mean that pattern of circles and triangle?"

"Yes. You know its significance?"

"Haven't the foggiest." Quatermain accompanied the remark with a shake of his head.

"It isn't some witch's sign, by any chance?" I offered.

"None that I am familiar with. But that is not to say that Umslopogaas was not taken from the camp by unconventional means."

"What other means might be there be beyond the conventional?"

"For you to ask such a thing, Doctor, after our recent conversation, suggests you have not been paying attention."

"He has been magicked away? Spirited elsewhere by sorcery?"

"I am minded to think so. In which case, maybe the symbol did play a role in that. It may be some occult pictogram as yet unknown to me."

"But to what end?" I said with more than a touch of anguish. "However it was done, what does kidnapping Umslopogaas achieve?"

Quatermain grimaced. "To create a hostage? To curb my involvement in this affair? To torment me? Perhaps all three. It is a move calculated to hobble me, that much is clear. Cripple me, even."

"There, at least, we are in accord, Quatermain," said Holmes. "The method of Umslopogaas's abduction is open to dispute but the purpose is plain. It is a message: 'Back down, Allan Quatermain. Leave things be, or else.' Will you heed it?"

"Don't be absurd, Holmes," the great hunter snapped. "Of course not. Umslopogaas would not wish me to. He would be furious if I allowed his predicament to compromise my actions in any way. He would rather die."

From what I knew of the Zulu, this seemed a fair assessment. Umslopogaas's devotion to Quatermain was unswerving to the point of self-sacrifice. I wondered whether Quatermain knew how lucky he was to have such a loyal, dependable friend.

"Our first priority," Holmes said, "is establishing where Umslopogaas has got to and how to retrieve him."

"I am glad you said that," said Quatermain. "Any ideas?"

"None as yet. You?"

"None either, but I can at least reconstruct his movements up to a certain point. I know that when Umslopogaas stepped out of the thicket, his tread was wary. The way his feet have crushed the grass stems and the close distance between his footprints all imply as much. He went some dozen or so paces that way, northward. Thereafter he began to run, with that long-legged, easy, loping stride which enables a Zulu to cover huge distances at a stretch while conserving his energy. After a few hundred yards he joined an asphalt pathway, whereupon it becomes impossible to know what became of him. Even I cannot track spoor on a bituminous surface. Skills like mine are rendered impotent by certain features of the modern world."

"How far could he have travelled, running at such a pace?"

"Assuming it has been one hour, eight or nine miles. Perhaps three times that if he was drawn away from the camp not long after I left to come and see you."

"Twenty-odd miles," I said, both impressed and glum.

"Without stopping," Quatermain said. "It would be nothing to him. The distressing truth is that Umslopogaas could be well outside the limits of Greater London by now."

"It makes sense to me to restrict the search to London itself, for the time being," said Holmes. "It puts a practical limit on the scope of the task. Only once we have ascertained beyond all doubt that Umslopogaas is not in the city should we consider expanding the radius. I shall apply myself to the problem for the rest of the day. What about you, Quatermain? What are your plans?"

"With respect to your methods, Mr Holmes, I am going to look for Umslopogaas in my own way."

"Applying your tracking skills, no doubt."

"Not as such." Quatermain's manner was evasive.

"If not that, then what?"

"That is my affair."

"You are not prepared to elaborate?" said Holmes. "We may be thinking along the same lines, after all, and it would be better to apportion out our resources rather than each find himself doubling the other."

"I very much doubt you will be doing what I will be."

"As you wish. Perhaps, then, come the evening, we can meet up and compare notes."

"I am not against that idea."

A rendezvous was set for eight o'clock at Baker Street, and Holmes and I made our goodbyes, although not before I had handed Quatermain the details of Remus's owner and had exacted from him a reassurance that the horse would be returned where it belonged, namely Shipley's Yard, near Waterloo Station. His somewhat cavalier attitude towards property and propriety might be all very well in the more lawless corners of Africa, but in civilisation there were certain strictures one abided by, and even Allan Quatermain was not exempt from them.

CHAPTER TWENTY-FOUR

THE ANGLER'S TALE

Back at Baker Street, Sherlock Holmes summoned and then despatched the Baker Street irregulars, sending them off to all points of the compass to scrounge up sightings of a man matching the Zulu's description.

While waiting for them to return, Holmes sent two cables. One was to Inspector Lestrade on the subject of Umslopogaas. It yielded nothing of any consequence. The Met official furnished a reply, the terse wording of which conveyed depths of exasperation:

```
Unless African gentleman runs
amok with axe no crime committed.
Will instruct officers to keep eye
out nonetheless. Also alert for
possibility of wild hippopotami on
the loose.
```

"Ah, Lestrade," Holmes said, addressing him as if he were

present. "Would that you put half as much effort into your work as you do into these sardonic dismissals of yours. England would be a far safer place. Still, I am sure you felt it worthwhile spending an additional sixpence above the basic shilling for those last few extra words. 'Wild hippopotami on the loose' indeed!"

As to the other telegram, Holmes did not vouchsafe to me the identity of the recipient and I knew better than to ask. When he was being secretive, it would be easier to get a Trappist monk to open up and tell all than he.

For about an hour afterward he sat at his chemistry bench, using his microscope to examine the specimen of soil he had taken from the camp. Just as he was packing away the instrument, the first of the irregulars came back.

The lad was rueful. "Nothing, Mr Holmes," said he. "Couldn't find a single soul what has seen a Zulu with an axe."

One after another the other irregulars traipsed in. All reported a similar lack of success – all save Wiggins, their putative leader. He brought with him a man who had a story to tell.

At first our guest was hesitant, turning his hat round and round in his hands by the brim.

"Go on," Wiggins encouraged him. "Mr Holmes won't bite."

"I'm told there might be money in this for me," the man said.

"I assure you, you will be recompensed for your trouble," said Holmes. "Speak."

The fellow, it transpired, was a keen angler in his spare time, and he told us that, while fishing on the Lea earlier in the day, he had spied a tall black man coming along the bank opposite.

"Where exactly on the river was this?" Holmes asked.

"The stretch where it meanders through Hackney Marshes," the angler replied. "Plenty of trout there, in season. Moment I caught sight of the bloke, I ducked down in the reeds. He just didn't look the sort you'd want to get on the wrong side of, if you know what I mean. Big, lanky individual like that, and carrying an axe to match. Fair gave me the collywobbles."

"I can well imagine. How fast was he going?"

"Sort of a loping speed. Not quite walking, not quite running. Somewhere in between. Startled as I was," the angler continued, "I was all the more startled when I saw there was somebody with him. Another of his race."

Holmes cocked his head. "Describe this second person."

"I didn't get a clear view through the reeds, only the merest of glimpses, but I can tell you it was a child, sir. A boy, keeping pace with the man. Judging by his height, he could not have been more than five or six years of age. But that wasn't the queerest thing. The queerest thing was that he was singing."

"Singing?"

"Yes, sir. This funny little repetitive song, in a high-pitched voice. At that distance I could only just hear it, but it sounded strange. Like a lullaby, only none I'm familiar with. I didn't recognise the tune, nor the language. The other bloke seemed to like it, mind. He was smiling and his eyes were sort of glazed, if you know what I mean. He was going along with the boy, meek as a lamb. It's a sight I won't forget, and no mistake. Those two, man and boy, in the middle of Hackney Marshes. I thought there must be a circus nearby or something."

Wiggins and the angler left, each richer by a shilling which I, of course, provided.

"That certainly must have been Umslopogaas," I remarked.

"Quite," said Holmes. "And if our angler's testimony is reliable – and I have no reason to think otherwise – it places the Zulu at the north-eastern outskirts of the city sometime around mid-afternoon. Frankly it is surprising there have not been a multitude of similar reports. Umslopogaas and Groan-Maker in tandem would make for an unforgettable sight. Seemingly he has been avoiding the main thoroughfares and keeping to backwaters and byways."

"And what of the African boy with him? Who do you think that might be?"

"I confess I have no idea."

"Quatermain did suggest that a witch-doctor could be over in England."

"Can one be a witch-doctor at the tender age of five or six? It is beyond my scope of expertise, but I doubt it."

"What do you make of Umslopogaas's 'glazed' eyes, then?" I said. "It suggests to me some kind of hypnotic state."

"He may well have been in a trance, but let us not go further, as Hunter Quatermain might, and call him spellbound."

"What if the trance was induced somehow by the child's song?"

"Really, this level of speculation benefits no one, Watson. At the very least we should wait until eight o'clock, when Quatermain is due. He may be able to shed more light upon the matter."

CHAPTER TWENTY-FIVE

A VISION OF HIGHWAYMEN

The clock chimed the appointed hour with no sign of Quatermain. It was closer on nine when he finally showed up, and immediately it was obvious that something was awry. It was not just his tardiness. A shambling gait and pinkened eyes denoted some form of intoxication, as did his seeming inability to answer a simple question straightforwardly.

"Quatermain, have you been drinking?" I said.

"Have I been drinking? No, I have not, Doctor. Not drinking. But have I been thinking? Oh yes. That I most definitely have. Thinking, and seeing, and imagining."

"I am nonplussed. What do you mean?"

"Mean?" came the distracted reply. "I mean what I mean. What do *you* mean?"

"This is a disgrace. Look at the state of you, man. How can you resort to alcohol at a time like this, when your friend is missing, perhaps in peril of his life, and counting on you to come to his rescue?"

"Rescue. Fescue. Fresco. Best go. Ho! Where was I again? It is all a bit of a haze."

"Good grief!" I turned to Holmes. "Whatever shall we do? He is quite useless to us. He is babbling like an idiot. I thought better of him than this."

My friend evinced surprising equanimity. "Observe his pupils, Watson," said he. "Look how dilated they are. I don't believe Quatermain is drunk at all. I believe he has been partaking once again of *Taduki*."

At the sound of the drug's name, Quatermain pricked up his ears.

"*Taduki!*" he said. "Yes! Sweet, strange, terrible *Taduki*. It takes me places. It allows me to travel while standing still. It opens doors and crosses boundaries and parts the mists of time. In its embrace I have been transported to past lives, other eras. I have been myself as I do not remember I was, in yesterdays I have never known. Within me have been awoken ancestral memories, so that I seem to inhabit the skin of one or other of my ancient forebears. I have been Shabaka, a nobleman descended from the Ethiopian king of Egypt of that name, half a millennium before Christ. I have been Wi, a caveman in Ice Age times. And now…"

"Now?" Holmes prompted.

Quatermain collapsed into a chair. "I have travelled again, but this time not nearly so far back in history. I rode the vapours of *Taduki* with the specific intent of finding Umslopogaas. I hoped that the herb would grant me a vision of his current location."

"And did it?" I asked.

"Perhaps yes, perhaps no. I am unsure. As the *Taduki* took effect, I found myself once more perched upon the ladder of my existence, whose every rung is a separate life. I know, I know, Holmes! It is all just so much mystical whimsy to you. Bear with me."

Holmes said nothing, but by lighting his clay pipe he seemed to be indicating that he would for now be giving Quatermain the benefit of the doubt, if disputatiously.

"I descended the ladder," Quatermain continued, "in that peculiar way which feels like floating and falling at once and certainly is no bodily action. The ladder is suspended, you see, between the Rock of Being and the gates of Eternal Calm. In a realm like that, the physical laws that govern our world no longer apply. There is no inertia or momentum. Even the very notion of 'up' or 'down' becomes irrelevant.

"Then I was watching a man, a bold desperado on horseback. He wore a tricorn hat, frock coat and leather britches, and a neckerchief was drawn up around the lower portion of his face to form a mask. I knew that my spirit had formerly dwelled within this form, some century and a half ago. I knew his name to be Tom Chalmers, but that he was known, too, as Raider Tom and was a notorious highwayman.

"No more was I watching him. Now, through some ghostlike gliding motion, I had become as one with him. I looked out through his gimlet eyes as he surveyed the road beside which he loitered. It was a broad, earthen track that curved through dense woodland, and by the light of a half-moon it gleamed with silvery promise, at least as far as Raider Tom was concerned.

"Raider Tom had been plying his infamous trade along this stretch of highway in Essex, just to the east of London, for nigh on a decade. An associate of Dick Turpin had he been, and on many an eve had the pair of them roistered together in taverns before sallying forth to hold up coaches and relieve those aboard of their gold and other valuables. Turpin was now dead, hanged in York upon the gallows at Knavesmire, but Tom Chalmers carried on the practice, undeterred by the grisly fate of his friend and fellow highwayman. He knew of no other way of making money. Highway robbery was his living and would surely one day be his dying, as it had been Turpin's. Tom was resigned to that. Sooner or later his luck would run out and he would be caught, tried and executed. Until then, however, he would continue to plough his crooked furrow."

"You speak of this Raider Tom as though he were someone else," I said. "Yet was he not you, or rather you he?"

Quatermain offered a wry smile. "It is a queer paradox, Doctor. Under the influence of *Taduki*, one inhabits one's past incarnation but feels remote from him at the same time. I could refer to Tom in the first person, but it seems more appropriate to use the third."

"I see."

Quatermain picked up where he had left off before my interruption. "Tom's mare, Grey Jenny, stamped uneasily beneath him, her ears twitching. He knew this to be a sign that a carriage was approaching. Jenny's hearing was acute, far sharper than his. She detected, long before he did, the drum of hooves and clatter of wheels. Her excitement began to mount, as did Tom's.

"Round the bend it came, a stagecoach drawn by a team of four. Nor was this just any stagecoach but a mail carrier, and Tom licked his lips at the prospect. He licked them not only from eagerness but to moisten them, for they had all of a sudden gone dry. The coach's red and gold livery promised loot galore, there being every chance that it was ferrying chests of currency between branches of a bank. There were likely to be passengers also, with wallets and purses fat with travelling money. However, in counterpoint to that, there would be a guard riding up top with the driver – a guard armed with pistol and blunderbuss and ever on the lookout for felons such as Tom.

"Raider Tom damped down the flutterings of fear. The game, he thought, was more than worth the candle."

Quatermain rose and went to the drinks cabinet, where, uninvited, he helped himself to a brandy, which he soused with soda water from the gasogene.

Whistle wetted, he resumed his seat and his narrative. I was finding the tale oddly enthralling, for all that the authenticity of its provenance was, to say the least, dubious.

"Tom burst out onto the road as the mail coach thundered towards him. Flintlock in either hand, he raked Grey Jenny's belly with his rowels so that she rose onto her hindlegs, her forelegs waving. It was pure theatre, and horse seemed as conscious of this as rider was.

"Then came the time-honoured cry: 'Stand and deliver!'

"The mail coach shuddered to a halt, the body of it rocking back upon its leaf springs. Tom levelled one flintlock at the driver's head. With the other he gestured towards the guard ensconced in the jump seat at the rear.

"'Do not raise that blunderbuss, sir,' said he. 'Not unless you value your colleague's life. Toss it thither onto the verge. There's a good fellow. The pistol likewise. That's it. There is no need for anyone to die tonight, not if we all remain calm and behave. You know the drill. Anything that's worth having, hoist it out and deposit it by the roadside. Passengers?'

"The driver nodded.

"'How many?'

"'Four.'

"'Tell them to lift the blinds, open the door, and drop out their cash, jewels, watches, the lot. Let's do it nice and slowly. Then we can all be on our way.'

"The driver relayed Tom's instructions. There was a pause before the blinds were raised. That delay should have told Tom that all was not as it ought to be. Frightened passengers were, as a rule, only too quick to comply with his demands. Some even seemed to derive a perverse thrill from being robbed by a highwayman and couldn't wait to do as he told them. It was almost a badge of honour, and it would provide them with an exhilarating anecdote with which to regale friends around the dinner table at a later date.

"As it transpired, the four passengers in this mail coach were not mere quailing civilians. They were, to a man, Post Office employees, and they were, to a man, armed.

"The trap was sprung. The passengers leapt out, guns blazing. The guard, too, sprang down from his perch and fired. Over and above the percussive roar of gunpowder detonating, Tom heard gruff, defiant yells: 'Got you now, Chalmers!' and 'You've had this coming a long time, you villain!'

"Raider Tom got off two good shots with his flintlocks, both balls finding their mark. The two nearest of his opponents fell, never to rise again. The remaining three were still on their feet, however, and Tom had no time to reload. They ran towards him, bringing him within easy range of their pieces.

"So far Tom was unscathed. A blunderbuss was terribly inaccurate at distance. Up close, by contrast, accuracy was hardly a necessity. The spread of buckshot was such that the weapon had only to be aimed in the general direction of its target to hit it.

"Tom turned Grey Jenny around and made for the woods. Standing his ground would be futile. Flight was the only option. If fortunate, he might live to rob another day.

"He was not fortunate. Pain seared his back, so shockingly agonising that he never even heard the blast from the gun. He slumped across Grey Jenny's neck, feeling as though he had been sundered in twain.

"The next several minutes were a blur. Tom was dimly aware of Grey Jenny charging through the woods, with him barely clinging on. When sense returned, he was conscious of the pain – it felt as though his lower back were on fire – and also of the warm wetness spreading down his buttocks and thighs, a flood of blood. He knew that he had been dealt a mortal wound.

Nothing could save him. Tears stung his eyes, remorse at a life that had been full of turmoil and incident but not, in the final reckoning, well spent. There was little doubt in Tom's mind that he was destined for an unpleasant afterlife somewhere very hot. He could only hope that his Maker, in His infinite mercy, might find a way to forgive him for his many sins eventually.

"Grey Jenny slowed to a canter, then a trot, and finally walked. She had outrun the post office men, and it was as though she knew that danger had passed – and also as though she knew where she was going. Raider Tom was more or less a passenger now. It was the most he could do just to stay upon her back. He let her go whichever way she fancied. It was all much of a muchness to him where they ended up.

"That she took him to a cave should not perhaps have come as a surprise. The cave was well known to both her and Tom, for it was where he had on several occasions found refuge in the company of Dick Turpin, therein to count spoils and celebrate the successful taking of another haul.

"He dismounted, crying out with pain, and staggered into the cave's mouth. He was discovered within that stony maw some three days later by a local woodsman. He was, by then, quite dead."

Quatermain spread out his hands.

"And there, gentlemen," said he, "my *Taduki* vision ended and I came round. Make of it what you will. For my own part, I am convinced it is germane to our present crisis. I do not know how. The specifics are not obvious. If I have learned anything from these regressions into my past lives, though, it is that they are instructive. They do not occur randomly. There is a purpose and a meaning intrinsic to them. Dreams have practical value, visions all the more so."

"Do you," said Holmes, "believe this particular vision of yours showed where we might find Umslopogaas?"

"The cave in the woods? Yes. I even know its whereabouts. Epping Forest."

"Dick Turpin was rumoured to use a cave in Epping Forest as a hideout," I said. "If I recall rightly, it lies somewhere up near Loughton Camp, the Iron Age fort."

"That certainly sounds familiar," said Quatermain. "A name like that flitted through Tom Chalmers's thoughts, even as he was slowly dying. I can only assume, then, that that is where Umslopogaas is now. Why else would my vision have directed me thither?"

"Why else indeed?" Holmes remarked drolly. "It may interest you to learn that Umslopogaas was spotted this afternoon in Hackney Marshes."

"Really? Well then, that lends weight to the possibility that he could now be in Epping Forest. The one location is a mere two or three miles from the other."

"He was seen in the company of a boy of five or six years old, an African like himself."

"A child?"

"According to our eyewitness. Would there be any reason that you can think of why Umslopogaas would ally himself with a child? Does he have a son?"

"None that I know of, and certainly at his age it is unlikely he would have one so young."

"Could the boy possibly be the witch-doctor from Silasville?" I said.

"I very much doubt it," said Quatermain. "Wizardry is a complex art, one which takes years to learn. No one of such tender years could possibly master it, and no one who has not yet achieved manhood would even be considered for initiation into the mysteries of magic."

"The boy appeared to be leading Umslopogaas," Holmes said.

"He may even have hypnotised him," I added.

Quatermain shook his head. "It cannot be. There must be some other explanation. All the same, I am now more convinced than before that Umslopogaas must be at Loughton Camp."

"You intend, I suppose, to travel there," said Holmes.

"I can do naught else."

"And forthwith?"

"Why delay?" said Quatermain. "Might I ask if you and Dr Watson would accompany me? You have both proved yourselves worthy comrades in the field and I should be glad to have you by my side."

"Accompany you on what would appear to be, to any right-thinking person, a wild goose chase?" said Holmes.

"Well, if you are going to be an ass about it…" With a gesture of irritation, Quatermain rose to his feet.

"As a matter of fact, Quatermain, I believe Watson and I shall join you."

I darted Holmes a look. "Really?"

Holmes shrugged his shoulders. "A jaunt out into the countryside. What could be more enlivening?"

CHAPTER TWENTY-SIX

JOURNEY TO EPPING FOREST

Quatermain had a cab waiting outside, and driver and horses alike were familiar. It was the same hackney in which we had travelled that afternoon. The cabman, as he saluted us with forefinger to forelock, looked exceedingly content with his lot, by which I could only infer that Quatermain was rewarding him well above the going rate for his services.

"We met again at the stables, didn't we, Tucker?" Quatermain said to the cabman. "I brought back Remus to be reunited with Romulus, and who should be there but the very fellow hoping for that eventuality. We had words, not all of them ill-tempered, and now we have come to an accommodation that is, I think, mutually beneficial."

"More than that, Mr Quatermain," said Tucker.

"I shall ride up front beside you. The evening breeze should help blow away the last of the cobwebs. Mr Holmes and Dr Watson can occupy the interior."

"Where to, sir?"

"Epping Forest, my good man. Loughton Camp. You know it?"

"Know *of* it. I can get us near enough that signposts can do the rest."

"Excellent. Onward!"

Facing us on the front seat of the cab was a rifle whose barrel was so long and bore so wide that it had to be an elephant gun. Beside it sat a bandolier replete with thick, finger-length double-eight cartridges.

As the cab started off, I nodded at the rifle. "Next to that thing, my Webley looks rather puny."

"You have the pistol on you nonetheless," said Holmes. "That is good. We may need all the firepower we can get."

"You don't honestly think there is anything to this cave nonsense?"

"Let us say I am keeping an open mind."

"You astound me."

"Constantly? Or just at the present moment?"

"We are pursuing not a firm lead but some half-baked fancy arising from a drug-induced hallucination. That is hardly congruous with the Sherlock Holmes I know."

"Youthful exuberance in one as aged as Quatermain should be endorsed, not curtailed."

"Is it that in him you see a fellow-traveller, one who indulges in narcotics just as you do? Is that behind this?"

"You wound me, Watson. As if my occasional predilection for cocaine is in any way comparable to Quatermain's fondness for the altered states brought on by this *Taduki* stuff! As if I would act upon so tenuous a motive!"

He lowered his voice somewhat, even though it seemed impossible that Quatermain, outside, could hear us.

"I do wonder whether Umslopogaas will be in the cave. There is no reason to think so and every reason to think not. Quatermain merely had an hallucination about being a highwayman, and an hallucination is nothing upon which to base a decision. It would be like building a castle upon a cloud. The issue here is not whether Quatermain is right but that he is almost certainly wrong. Proving it is going to be rather satisfying." Holmes gave an enigmatic little smile. "Unless, that is, he is right unwittingly."

"Unwittingly?"

"It may be that he has known all along where Umslopogaas is. He has been in possession of some insight, hidden even to himself, which the *Taduki* has unveiled. The drug has brought a memory to the surface, much as a seven per cent solution of cocaine sometimes spurs my mind into making connections hitherto unperceived."

"A memory perhaps of a conversation he and Umslopogaas had about a certain cave in Epping Forest," I said. "Could it be that Quatermain mentioned it to Umslopogaas once? Could it even be that he read a story about Dick Turpin's cave and it has lodged somewhere in the lower reaches of his mind, below the threshold of conscious thought?"

"Not quite. I am thinking more of the symbol in their little den in Victoria Park."

"A circle within a triangle within a circle. You have fathomed its import?"

"Think of a highwayman, Watson. Think what a highwayman typically would wear on his head."

"A tricorn hat."

"Quatermain even mentioned such a hat when recounting his vision of a past life as Tom Chalmers. And does a tricorn, when viewed from above, not resemble a circle within a triangle?"

"In its most simplified form, yes."

"So then," Holmes continued, "a tricorn hat positioned inside a larger circle might be taken to denote a highwayman who has taken refuge in…"

"In the mouth of a cave," I said. "Gracious me, yes."

"And then consider the pennies which accompanied the symbol. What might they represent?"

"Stolen loot."

"An extra element to cement the symbol's full meaning."

"So Umslopogaas did leave a clue after all."

"Umslopogaas or someone else – perhaps the strange child he was seen with."

"And Quatermain made the connection with Dick Turpin's cave by means of smoking *Taduki*."

"The drug provided the solution in the guise of a waking dream," said Holmes. "Quatermain knew the answer all along, without knowing he knew it. The *Taduki* dredged it up from the nether reaches of his mind. And of course, alongside the symbol, there was a further clue that Loughton Camp was Umslopogaas's destination."

"The speck of anomalous soil?"

"Just so. In certain areas in and around London the earth is a particular mix of sand and clay known as the Bagshot Beds. The sand is fine-grained with a high quartz content, while the clay is the whitish kind called 'pipe-clay'. I was able to identify the sample I gathered as coming from the Lower Bagshot Beds, a specific geological stratum that is found on the western edge of Essex, not least around Epping."

"Then that explains why you agreed to go along with Quatermain on this expedition. It has nothing to do with his *Taduki* vision and everything to do with the clues left at Victoria Park."

"Hard evidence," said Holmes with a nod. "However, though it shames me to admit this, it took Quatermain and his drug to make sense of it all. Without his contribution, I do not know if I would have divined the meaning of the symbol – certainly not so soon. Through a confluence of Quatermain's approach to the mystery and mine, we arrived at an answer I could accept. The one shored up the other."

"The question remains, why would Umslopogaas go to Loughton Camp? Why has he allowed this unknown boy to lead him there, if that is what happened?"

"Umslopogaas may be acting against his will. The boy may have some hold over him."

"Compelling him by blackmail, perhaps."

"Or some other, more exotic means. Drugs, for example."

"His 'glazed' look."

"That in conjunction with the song the boy was singing," said Holmes. "Together it is possible they might have a mesmeric effect, sapping Umslopogaas's willpower and making him the boy's thrall."

"It is an outlandish supposition."

"But remains within the bounds of plausibility, just."

"While you are in an expansive mood, Holmes," I said, "is there any chance you might tell me now about the data you gleaned in Kensington Gardens, concerning the sniper? I have held off from asking you about it."

"But you can contain your curiosity no longer. Very well. Now is as good a time as any. The discoveries I made in the sniper's hide weave yet tighter the tapestry of this case. The shell casings, you know about. Another of my discoveries was a boot print in the soil. A highly distinctive one."

"It matched the print you found in Mrs Biddulph's yard?"

"Bravo, Watson!" Holmes said brightly. "In both instances I noted a Y-shaped crack in the heel, not unlike a lightning bolt. The two prints cannot but have been left by the same sole. The shoe sizes were identical, as were the tread patterns, but it is that singular crack that puts the matter beyond doubt. He who shot at us is also he who lurked outside Wade's flat."

"And who presumably administered the Devil's Dust to Wade."

"That we cannot state with any certainty, but the *prima facie* evidence, as the lawyers would have it, is compelling. The third discovery I made in the shrubbery was a hair caught in the fork of a twig. It was short, coarse and freshly shed."

"How do you know it was freshly shed?"

"I could tell from the glossiness of it, particularly its root bulb which was still coated with sebum, a secretion that tends to dry out quite quickly. The hair can only have come from the sniper. Its main distinguishing characteristic, however, was its hue. It was red."

"The Fanthorpes," I said. "Their hair is reddish."

"Hardly. Sandy is not red. The red I am talking about is a deep fiery shade of the colour. My fourth and final find was the butt of a cigarette. It had been freshly smoked and the brand was distinctive. Herman and Canard."

"I have never heard of them."

"They are a South African manufacturer. They use Turkish tobacco, which is very popular in that country, but it is rare to find their product beyond that nation's borders. This implies the smoker of the cigarette, our sniper, must be a South African. Now then, Watson, who are we aware of that has fiery red hair and hails from that part of the world?"

"Let me see. I have it! The Boer. Van Hoek. The foreman at the Silasville site. Umslopogaas said his beard was that type of red. 'Red as fire."

"Again, Watson, you excel. We shall make a detective of you yet."

"Our assailant, then, is none other than Marius van Hoek," I said, piecing it together. "He came to England in pursuit of Wade, in order to prevent Wade sharing with anyone his discoveries at the mine regarding Harry Quatermain's death. Since then, he has tried to eliminate us too, or at least intimidate us."

"Such is my thinking."

"But has Van Hoek been acting of his own accord or at the instigation of another?"

"You mean someone of superior rank, such as the Fanthorpes? It seems feasible that if Van Hoek wired the brothers about Harry Quatermain and mentioned Wade in the process, they would have instructed him to track Wade down with all due haste and ensure his silence. Failing to catch up with him before he left Africa, Van Hoek would have seen no alternative but to board the next available passenger steamer and finish the job over here."

"I picture them in a procession of three ships, all northbound from Africa and following much the same route: Wade, then Umslopogaas, then Van Hoek, one after another, each separated by no more than a few days' sailing. It would almost be comical if it were not so serious."

"As soon he arrived in England, Van Hoek would have gone to Wade's last known address, which the Fanthorpes would have supplied him. Wade, however, had taken the wise precaution of staying elsewhere, away from his known haunts. His plan to keep a low profile served him well, up until the point when he finally went to see the Fanthorpes. That was his great misstep, albeit one he could not help making."

"By then Van Hoek was in England," I said. "He was there at the Fanthorpe headquarters, with his employers' connivance, lying in wait for Wade, primed, ready to pounce."

"It was more than likely that Wade would show his face at Fanthorpe Overseas Ventures eventually," said Holmes. "Van Hoek only had to bide his time. As soon as Wade's meeting with the brothers was over, he simply followed him home in order to learn where he was living. Then he could kill him at leisure, when an opportune moment arose."

"But hold on, Holmes. Quatermain, too, followed Wade back to Mrs Biddulph's, after they talked at the pub. So Van Hoek was dogging Wade's footsteps at the same time as our friend there." I gestured at Quatermain's lower legs, which we could see through the brougham's front window.

"You seem to consider that remarkable."

"Do not you? Quatermain is a hard man to catch unawares. Would his acute senses not have alerted him to Van Hoek's presence?"

"You would have to ask the man himself about it, but my feeling is that the Boer is a master of stealth and bushcraft, as versed in the ways of stalking game as Quatermain is. Did Quatermain detect Van Hoek's proximity to us in Kensington Gardens before he opened fire? He did not, not until the very last instant, when it was almost too late. In Van Hoek we have a hunter who, if not Quatermain's equal, would appear to run him a close second."

I shook my head. "How did Van Hoek poison Wade with the Devil's Dust?"

"He must have broken into the flat while Wade was off on one of his infrequent forays into the outside world. It would not have been difficult to gain ingress through the window at the rear. A knife tip inserted between the sashes could have been used to lever the catch open."

"There was evidence of that? Scrape marks upon the paintwork?"

"No, but then you may recall me rattling the window. That test determined that both sashes were very loose in the frame, and by drawing them apart, the gap between them could be made fairly wide, a good half-inch or so. Manipulation of the catch with a knife, performed with sufficient dexterity, could have been done so as not to leave a trace. The catch could have been closed afterwards by the same method, sliding the knife the opposite way, and Wade would have had no idea at all that anyone had entered and left. Then the Devil's Dust was simply waiting for him, a booby trap poised to be sprung."

"Where? Where did Van Hoek put the Dust?"

"I have an inkling, and to that end I have been in touch with Mrs Biddulph."

"The second telegram you sent this afternoon. It was to her."

"Precisely. I have asked the lady to set aside, with the utmost caution, a certain pair of domestic items, which I plan to collect and examine at the first opportunity. I should perhaps have fathomed sooner the means by which the Dust was introduced into Wade's body. It is quite elementary, when one thinks about it, but then the cruellest methods of murder are often the simplest."

"It wasn't the mutton stew, then. Or was it?"

"It was and it was not," Holmes said cryptically. "To me the more intriguing matter is the nature of the Devil's Dust itself. What is it? Of what is it composed?"

These sounded like rhetorical questions, but I hazarded an answer anyway. "Some concoction of toxic roots and berries, I should suppose. Is that not how witch-doctors work? Their potions derive their properties from the chemicals inherent in organic matter, principally plants."

"Yet the Devil's Dust mimics the effects of a substance that does not occur in nature, and by 'mimics the effects of' I mean 'is utterly indistinguishable from.'"

"And what substance is that?"

"Arsenic trioxide, Watson. Internal bleeding, reddened skin, swelling of the flesh; all are classic signs of acute arsenic trioxide poisoning. A fatal dose would not need to be a significant quantity. A quarter of a teaspoon would do the trick. That would be enough to end the life of even a healthy adult male such as Bradford Wade. I should be able to confirm this theory once I get my hands on the items which Mrs Biddulph is keeping for me. You know, of course, where arsenic trioxide is commonly found?"

"It is an ingredient in a number of patented medicines," I said, "mostly those used to treat syphilis. It is also to be found in Fowler's Solution, which is both a tonic and a treatment for malaria and cholera." An idea struck me. "What about the doctor at Silasville? The one whom Umslopogaas portrayed as a corrupt, indolent quack?"

"What about him?"

"He would have access to medicines of the kind I've just described. He might have somehow been able to filter out the arsenic trioxide from them, distilling it down to lethal concentrations. Then he could have handed that to the mine's resident witch-doctor in powder form to use as he saw fit. The witch-doctor gave the powder a sinister name – *Uthuli lukaDeveli* – and swiftly it became a source of terror amongst the miners."

"There is a more straightforward way of getting hold of arsenic trioxide than the one you posit," said Holmes. "The compound is a by-product of the smelting of certain metals, mainly copper and gold when they are, as is often the case, mined from areas rich in sulphide mineral deposits. Now, with Fanthorpe Overseas Ventures being involved in large-scale mining operations, to obtain sizeable amounts of arsenic trioxide would be easy for a high-level employee of the company."

"Such as Van Hoek."

"All he would have to do was visit the nearest ore-processing plant, of which Fanthorpe has several in Africa, including one just outside Johannesburg. He could avail himself of as much of the deadly residue as he desired. Hey presto, a dust that can be passed off as a sorcerous powder."

"How grotesque," I said. "A Fanthorpe mine's leavings being deployed against the company's workforce."

"Grotesque, but also fiendishly efficient. One has to admire that level of resourcefulness, while at the same time deploring it."

"And Harry Quatermain?"

"What of him?"

"His death by Devil's Dust was the catalyst for all this, but why did he have to die?"

"It could be that he, like Wade, found out about the nefarious goings-on at Silasville," said Holmes. "He appears to have been an intrepid and inquisitive young man, and it is not beyond the realms of possibility that those same qualities got him into trouble. Van Hoek resolved that he had to be disposed of, and so he was. He resolved, too, that he himself was the only man for the job, not one of his underlings. Yet there is one aspect of the scenario I have just outlined that does not sit well with me."

"Namely?"

"Van Hoek seemed aggrieved by the killing of Harry, if Wade's account is anything to go by. 'I wish this had not happened.' Those were his words, spoken bitterly."

"It might have been an attack of remorse."

"It might, but this is a man who seems to have little compunction about committing murder. It is almost as though he was being swept along by a tide of events over which he had no control, as though he had become a victim of *force majeure*."

"There may, then, be more to Harry's death than we realise?"

"I am of a mind to think so," said Holmes. "Perhaps the role of 'son of Macumazahn' was a double-edged sword. While it conferred a certain cachet, it could also have brought opprobrium. I cannot believe that Quatermain senior has rampaged across Africa all these years and not acquired a fair few enemies along the way. One amongst that rogues' gallery might have wished to strike back at him."

"By murdering his son?" I shuddered. "What a horrible notion."

"I offer it simply as speculation. There are doubtless many other reasons why Harry might have been killed. Africa is not known as the Dark Continent for nothing. As on the American Frontier, new and old civilisations are clashing, and that foments savagery in the hearts of those on both sides of the conflict. In Africa, where there are fortunes to be made and territory to be conquered, it seems that anything goes. I wonder if that is why friend Quatermain feels so at home there. There is a streak of primordialism within him, a wildness that finds the modern world restrictive. Have you noticed how he gravitates towards London's green spaces? Regent's Park, Victoria Park, Hyde Park…"

"Now that you mention it, yes."

"The urban environment just does not suit him. He instinctively seeks out trees, grass, open skies. As life becomes ever more mechanised and industrialised, and cities and populations grow, one has to ask oneself how a man such as he will survive. He is an endangered species, his habitat shrinking. I almost pity him. Perhaps, when he is gone, we shall never see his like again."

The thought, oddly sobering, hung over us for the rest of that drive through the city and out into the night-clad countryside beyond.

CHAPTER TWENTY-SEVEN

EYES

A full moon, a cloudless sky, a freckling of stars, and a soft breeze rustling the tree branches: that was the prospect as we climbed out of the brougham after some three hours of travel. My spine felt tender after having been jounced and jolted around for so long, particularly during the latter portion of the journey once we had exchanged paved roads for rutted tracks. I stretched and bent to ease out my stiffness, while Quatermain fetched his elephant gun and bandolier from the cab.

"Stay put, Tucker," he said to the cabman. "Keep the carriage lamps burning. I cannot say how long we shall be, but I expect to find you here when we return."

"For what you're paying me, sir, I'm happy to sit tight from now until doomsday."

Turning to Holmes, Quatermain said, "Now then, this cave. Where does it lie?"

Before we left Baker Street, Holmes had consulted a map of the area. Now he glanced around, taking the lie of the land, and said, "Unless I am much mistaken, Loughton Camp is situated upon that ridge of high ground over there, and the cave lies a short distance to the north of it. Therefore, once past the hill fort, all we have to do is keep an eye on the Pole Star – there – and we will be going in the right direction. You are aware, are you not, that we may be walking into a trap?"

"What makes you say that?"

Briefly, Holmes enumerated the various deductions he had shared with me during the course of the journey.

"Then the symbol at Victoria Park was not left by Umslopogaas," Quatermain said.

"It is hard to know how he could have managed it," said Holmes. "The evidence points to him having been lured out of your camp in the thicket. It is unlikely he would have been at liberty to go back in and etch the symbol into the ground, having been informed about his destination in the interim. No, someone else is responsible."

"Whoever did the luring."

"Yes, which would suggest that we were meant to find and interpret the symbol."

"Dammit. Why did you not mention this earlier?"

"Would it have changed your mind about coming here?"

Quatermain gave this question the briefest consideration. "No. Do you think Van Hoek is his abductor?"

"Or the African boy, who may or may not be an accomplice of Van Hoek's."

"And let me get this straight," said Quatermain. "Van Hoek killed Wade using *Uthuli lukaDeveli*, in order to cover up what Wade knew about Harry's death, and may also have killed Harry the same way."

"I have yet to establish the latter beyond reasonable doubt."

"But there's a chance he did."

"There is."

Quatermain slotted cartridges into both breeches of his gun and snapped the weapon shut.

"Then I am going to the cave, come what may. Trap or no trap, if Van Hoek is there, he is a dead man."

Quatermain marched off without another word. We fell in behind him, matching our pace to his rapid, forthright stride. Holmes and I were both carrying dark-lanterns to illuminate our way, but for Quatermain it seemed that the light of stars and moon alone afforded sufficient visibility.

We passed through beech woods along broad, smooth paths that may well have been ancient roads. We circumvented the earthworks of the hill fort, the remains of which consisted of a few curving banks and ditches. The incline was gentle, but the downward slope beyond the ridge was steeper and the leaf litter treacherous underfoot, with the result that I lost my footing and slithered down more than once.

Every so often Quatermain would pause, go down on bended knee and examine a patch of ground. I can only assume he was looking for spoor. Whether he found any, he gave no indication. He simply straightened up and carried on walking. The elephant gun was slung over his shoulder but it was clear he was ready to use it at a moment's notice.

All at once, he raised a hand and hissed at us to halt.

Then, in a voice only just audible, he said, "We are not alone."

It was not so much the words themselves that sent a chill through me, as their tone. Quatermain sounded perturbed, and that in itself was perturbing. The great hunter, veteran of lion attacks and Zulu wars and heaven knows what else, possessed nerves of steel – and yet here he was, unnerved.

"Dim the lights," he said, and Holmes and I closed the shutters of our lanterns to the merest chink.

Darkness settled over us. The trees whispered with their

brittle leaves. Now and then a bough creaked like someone moaning in pain.

Quatermain dropped to a crouch, unshouldering his gun and thumbing back both hammers. I scanned keenly the dim woodland all around us. There was movement perceptible in the spaces between the tree trunks, but I could not tell if it was anything other than branches waving and fallen leaves skittering.

Quatermain traversed from side to side with the gun barrels, pausing every so often as if something had caught his attention. His forefinger curled around the trigger.

He sounded almost resigned as he said, "Ah. We are most definitely outnumbered. This is not a situation we can simply shoot our way out of, I fear. You may as well reopen the lanterns, gentlemen."

The light we shed upon the scene revealed the import of Quatermain's remarks.

There were eyes.

Ahead, behind, and to either side, eyes glared at us yellowly out of the darkness. I counted at least a dozen pairs, all at hip height.

Not human eyes. Animals'.

Then I heard a low, menacing growl.

"Was that a dog?" I murmured to Holmes.

"Worse, I fear, than any hound," came the reply. "One can just make out the shape of a muzzle over there. It is tapered in a distinctive fashion and the fur is pale. Watson, these are wolves."

CHAPTER TWENTY-EIGHT

SHEPHERDED BY WOLVES

"Wolves," I breathed.

I knew there were wolf packs still roaming Britain, but their numbers were dwindling and I had not heard of any this far south. There had been sightings in the Scottish Highlands as recently as last year, but none in England since the turn of the sixteenth century. It startled me to find these wilderness creatures so near to the sprawl of London, and I wondered if perhaps the wolves were a single family that had survived for generations in Epping Forest, keeping hidden. But that, surely, was impossible.

Then, all at once, I recalled the article I had lately read in *The Times* about the wolves that had escaped from a menagerie near Chelmsford, a mere fifteen miles or so from Epping. These wolves around us must surely be the same creatures.

I drew my revolver. With its five rounds, and the two in Quatermain's gun, we might account for the majority of the wolf pack in one fell swoop. That, however, was assuming neither of us missed and that we were able to empty our guns before any of the wolves reached us. None of the beasts was more than a dozen yards away, and I had no doubt they could cover the distance in a matter of seconds. However rapidly we shot, the wolves would be faster.

"What should we do?" I murmured.

"Whatever they want us to," Quatermain replied. "They are the masters here. We must comply with their wishes."

"They're animals. They don't have—"

Even as I spoke, some of the wolves ahead of us moved. They parted ranks, creating a break in the encircling barrier they had formed.

At the same time, the wolves behind us padded forward.

"That is it, then," said Quatermain. "We are being given an escort."

And so it was. The wolf pack, as though possessed of a single, unifying consciousness, ushered us through the forest in the direction of their choosing. They maintained a horseshoe shape around us so that we could neither retreat nor dash off to either side. We could only keep going straight ahead.

"Quatermain," I whispered, after we had gone perhaps half a mile with our lupine entourage, "would not a few well-placed gunshots cause the beasts to scatter? We might then be able to make a run for it."

"I do not think that will work, Watson. The wolves' natural instincts have been overridden. They will not behave as they normally might."

"Ah. Much like the rats and the pigeons who laid siege to us at Baker Street."

"This is not dissimilar. Someone is influencing the wolves' behaviour."

"Someone has trained them, you mean?"

"You do not hear that faint piping sound?"

"No."

"Nor you, Mr Holmes?"

"I wish I could say I did," said Holmes.

"Perhaps it is above the threshold of audibility for both of you. I myself can only just detect it. It is intermittent, and broken up into patterns of long and short bursts, not unlike Morse code. The wolves are responding to it as though receiving orders."

"Like a dog whistle," I said. "But who is blowing it? Marius van Hoek, I suppose."

"Could be. Could be."

"You seem to think otherwise, Quatermain," said Holmes.

"It is just that…" Quatermain mused for a moment. "This talk of an African child leading Umslopogaas along the river bank. And now these wolves, taking commands, obedient as anything. It makes me wonder… No. No, that is a futile line of thinking. There is no earthly way it can be he."

"Speak up. If you have something to share with us, something that may be to our advantage, now would be the time."

But Hunter Quatermain would not be drawn to elaborate.

"No," said he. "Just an old man's foolish fancy. Pay it no heed."

"Holmes," I said, trying another tack, "you seem content to go along with this – this death march."

"Content? No. Curious to see where it ends? Yes. We do not even know that it is a 'death march', as you put it. We are sheep being shepherded. Shepherded by wolves. There is, if nothing else, a certain irony about that."

"Everyone knows what happens to sheep eventually."

"Chin up, Watson. If we are threatened with being put to the slaughter, that is when you may mount a spirited resistance, with my blessing. Until then, curtail your violent tendencies. We have come this far. Let us see how the rest plays out."

Presently we entered a large, bowl-shaped clearing. At one

end lay a rocky bluff at the base of which there was a roughly triangular fissure. This aperture, at its apex, was a little taller than a man and looked deep.

"There it is," said Quatermain with amazement and a certain pride. "The very cave. The one I saw. It is as real as it was when I was Tom Chalmers."

"That's far enough! Stop where you are!"

The command was issued from the cave mouth by a voice with a strong Afrikaans accent.

We halted, while our escort of wolves dispersed to the edges of the clearing, leaving us isolated in the middle.

From out of the cave stepped a burly, redheaded fellow with a raised rifle. He trained the gun on Quatermain.

"That *blerrie* great cannon you have there," he said. "Put it on the ground. Nice and gentle."

Quatermain set down the elephant gun.

"Now kick it towards me."

Quatermain nudged the weapon with his toe.

"Again. Further this time. Out of your reach."

Quatermain put more force into the action, and the elephant gun skidded several yards, coming to a rest closer to the Boer than to him.

"If you've a knife on you, do the same."

Quatermain slid out his hunting knife from its sheath at his ankle and tossed it to one side.

"Any other weapons?"

Quatermain shook his head.

"All right. Now you."

The rifle did not leave Quatermain, but it was I who was being addressed.

"That pistol of yours. Ditch it. Don't get any funny ideas. Mr Quatermain's brains would splatter all over you if I blew them out. I don't think you would enjoy that."

I parted company with my Webley, using a bed of leaves to cushion its landing.

"Marius van Hoek, I presume," said Holmes in an affable tone. "We meet face-to-face at last. You have led us quite a merry dance. How are you finding England? Not what you're used to, I'm sure."

"It's the polite chitchat you people are so fond of," said Marius van Hoek, a mirthless grin splitting the red curtain of his beard. "That's what really gets on my nerves, Mr Holmes. No wonder we won the Freedom War and regained our own republic. You Brits and your formalities. Not to mention your army's stupid fussy uniforms. You had the numbers, you had the troops, and you still couldn't defeat a ragtag militia of farmers and cattlemen. The Boer does not stand on ceremony. The Boer does not follow the rules of engagement. The Boer just gets on with the job and does what is necessary. That's the big difference between our races."

"And now that same necessity has driven you to work for an English corporation. How interesting."

Van Hoek gave the merest of shrugs, a twitch of one shoulder. "*Ach*, I go where the money is. Fanthorpe pays well. Besides, it's not good to hold a grudge, especially if you're on the winning side. You have to be generous in victory."

"Where is Umslopogaas?" said Quatermain.

"*Ja*, you see?" said Van Hoek. "Allan Quatermain – the sainted Macumazahn – he doesn't tiptoe around. He gets down to business. That's how we do things in Africa. Straight to the point."

"Answer my question."

"Your Zulu friend is here. He's fine. For now."

"Bring him out. Show him to me."

"I can do that. He has served his purpose, after all. He has got you here, where we want you – where we can finish this whole thing off, once and for all, in isolation, away from prying eyes."

"We?"

"Yes," said Van Hoek. "There's someone else whose acquaintance you might be interested in making. Or, as the case may be, re-acquaintance."

"Your accomplice," said Holmes. "It is he who is controlling these wolves, not you. You are too busy controlling us."

"I am a man of many talents," said Van Hoek, "but I am no practitioner of the hocus-pocus stuff."

"Hocus-pocus? Quatermain has been hearing a shrill whistling which serves to give the wolves their commands. There is hardly any hocus-pocus about that."

"Wolves are not dogs. It takes more than just training to become their master, especially over the span of just a few days. Feed them certain herbs, however, perform certain rituals… See Quatermain's face? He knows this too. He knows there is a deeper art involved here. But that is not my province. I leave that to the experts. Speaking of whom…" Van Hoek directed his next comment over his shoulder, into the cave. "You! They're eager to see that old *impi*. I have them covered. Let's oblige them."

In reply, a cackle sounded from within, shrill and echoing.

I saw Quatermain stiffen, as though an electric shock had passed through him.

"It is," he breathed. "It *is* he after all. But – but that is not possible."

A moment later, Umslopogaas emerged from the cave mouth. He moved stolidly like a somnambulist, his eyes lost and empty. There was none of the animation that usually made his face so lively and engaging. I had seen marionettes more expressive.

Behind him came a smaller figure, a diminutive African. At first I thought him a child, until I saw a mane of long, tangled grey hair and a wizened countenance slyer than any fox's, and realised this was no child but an elderly dwarf. He was clad in what I can only think of as traditional Zulu garb: a calfskin apron, cow tails hanging from his upper arms below his knees, and a headband made of leopard hide. In addition, a necklace strung with lion's teeth and claws hung below his extraordinarily large head down to his sternum.

"Macumazahn," said this outlandish specimen in gloating tones. In his right hand he held Groan-Maker, whose length from hilt to blade tip was not much shorter than his own from toe to crown. Attached to his left wrist was some sort of dried gourd, hanging by a thong, with a series of holes bored into it. "You look surprised. Your jaw is almost at your breastbone."

"Zikali," said Quatermain.

CHAPTER TWENTY-NINE

THE THING-THAT-SHOULD-NEVER-HAVE-BEEN-BORN

"You are dead, Zikali," said Allan Quatermain. "I saw you die."

The dwarf smiled in dismissal, as though death were a minor inconvenience, like an ingrown toenail or a touch of dyspepsia. "You saw me plunge into a waterfall, Macumazahn. That is not dying."

"You never surfaced."

"You never saw me surface. But rivers flow, and currents carry objects, bodies included. Who is to say that downstream, out of your view, I did not rise again from the depths? I am sure that Mr Sherlock Holmes here, with those detective skills he so cherishes, would have ascertained the full facts of the situation before making a pronouncement of fatality."

"It did cross my mind that it might be you marshalling the wolves," said Quatermain. "The feat is well within the scope of your abilities. Then I rejected the idea. 'Zikali is no more,' I said to myself. 'This is the handiwork of some other *nyanga*.'"

From the context, I took it that *nyanga* meant witch-doctor.

"Hee hee! No, Macumazahn. It is I, the wizard of Black Kloof, the one they call the Opener-of-Roads. It is I and no other."

"They call you something else." Quatermain's lip curled. "The Thing-that-should-never-have-been-born. There could not be a more appropriate name for an abomination."

"Come, come," said Zikali. "That is no way to talk. Have we not been amicable at times in the past? Did you not to seek out my counsel some ten years ago during a time in your life when your spirits were at low ebb and you desired proof that the soul survives death?"

"And you sent me to the lost city of Kôr, and to Ayesha, beauteous queen of that place, known as She Who Must Be Obeyed. It was an encounter which nearly proved my undoing, and likewise that of Umslopogaas and my other companion Hans, which I am sure was your intent."

"Had you died, the veil of ignorance would have been lifted and all your questions answered."

"Still, you are no friend of mine, Zikali," said Quatermain, "and you never have been. You are a forger of convenient alliances and a weaver of webs of intrigue, with one eye ever on your own advantage. Had I my gun in my hands right now, I should not hesitate for a second. I would blast that ugly, misbegotten life of yours from the world and not feel an ounce of regret."

Zikali cackled again. There was no humour in his laughter, just maniacal glee, as though his only delights were obscene ones. I had never heard a hyena laugh, but this, I thought, was the sort of sound it would make.

"I have made sure you shall not have that chance, old hunter," Zikali said jubilantly, his grizzled locks shaking. "Look how I have orchestrated it all. How I have led you by the nose to this spot, this moment, this ending. How I have woven one of those webs you just spoke of and ensnared you in its sticky toils."

"If I may interject here, Zikali," said Holmes. "I appreciate that you and Quatermain have much to say to each other, given the troubled, bloody history you clearly share. However, there are a few matters I would care to clear up. It was you, of course, who summoned Umslopogaas out of his and Quatermain's camp and led him to this place."

"True! True! How easy it was to slip a powerful hypnotic drug – a mixture of thorn apple stems and the root of the golden flower – into Umslopogaas's morning meal, so that his mind became lost amongst the white ways of dreams. After that, a simple chant became the beacon by which I led him hither, step by step, as a piper leads a dance."

"Then it was the task of Van Hoek to shoot at us and flee so that we would fear for Umslopogaas's safety and be drawn to seek him."

"At my advising, yes."

"And you kindly furnished us with a clue to aid us – the symbol in the ground."

"I knew that either you, Mr Holmes, or you, Macumazahn, would decipher it, and you did. All of this was my doing! All mine! The fruit of my cunning! Hee hee!" Zikali danced a little caper on the spot.

"Now, no doubt, some dismal fate lies in store for us. Neither Watson, Quatermain nor I will survive the night."

"It is not personal where you and Dr Watson are concerned," said the dwarf. "Please do not think that. I bear no animosity towards either of you. You are inconveniences that must be disposed of; that is all. As is the man who brought you here in his carriage. He cannot be left alive, and will be dealt with later. There must be no witnesses, no one left alive to tell the tale."

"Whereas with Quatermain it *is* personal."

"It could not be more so. Macumazahn has stood against me all his long life and mine."

"Only because you yourself have stood against the Zulu nation," said Quatermain. "You were instrumental in the demise of that proud warrior race, Zikali – your own people – and for what? To satisfy your malevolent lusts. To indulge in your love for manipulating others. To show that somehow, for all your small stature, you are bigger than everyone. How pathetic!"

"I have changed the course of history. How many men can say the same? It is not just you whites who can map out the future of countries and peoples. Someone as stunted and misshapen as I – and I have no illusions about my appearance – has done what whole armies could not. I have exercised power greater than kings and queens. I am the equal of any emperor. Who is small of stature now, Macumazahn?" Zikali puffed up his chest. "Dwarf I may be in body, but my deeds have made me a giant!"

"Zikali," said Holmes, "no one is questioning your superiority. There has been ample demonstration of it, if only through your besting of the three of us. The four of us, counting Umslopogaas. Yet it seems anomalous that one as mighty as you, a witch-doctor of repute, is reduced to working for a mining company. You have, after all, been helping out with labour relations at the Silasville mine, have you not?"

Zikali acknowledged it with a nod and another of those cackles, this one a touch more muted than previous.

"Is that not something of a comedown for a man who has changed the course of history?" said Holmes.

"I am not any the lesser for my new role in life," said Zikali. "I have certain obligations that I must meet. What of it?"

"Obligations to Fanthorpe Overseas Ventures? No. Not that. You are not the type to pledge yourself to any institution. This is a deeper level of debt. Is it by any chance to Mr Van Hoek?"

The dwarf smiled, even as his grip on Groan-Maker tightened.

"That is it, isn't it?" said Holmes. "You are plighted to Van Hoek somehow. You owe him, and in return he owns you."

"Ha!" said Van Hoek. "The fellow has a sharp eye, I'll say that for him. Tell him how I saved you, Zikali. Tell him how for the past five years you have been my right-hand man. It's a good tale."

"What is there to tell?" Zikali said somewhat testily. "Mr Van Hoek pulled me from the river when I was half drowned. With those big fists of his he pounded the water out of my chest and the air back in. I was supposed to be dead. That was the fate I had allotted myself. I had finished my work upon this earth. I had granted the great god of the heavens Umkulu-kulu the sacrifice of multitudinous souls that he craved. It was with joy that I sent myself to my reward. But Umkulu-kulu seemed to have other ideas."

"I thought it was a log at first," said Van Hoek, "a lump of driftwood passing by the spot where I had camped by the river bank. Then I saw that it was a body floating face down, a youngster, or so I assumed. I waded in and retrieved him. You can imagine my surprise when I turned him over and saw *that* face. I almost dropped him in disgust. I would rather have been carrying a baboon. But then something came over me. Perhaps it was compassion."

"It was the will of Umkulu-kulu," said Zikali. "The god breathed upon you, inspiring you to a noble act. You nursed me back to health, and in so doing you put me in the position in which I now find myself, that of your servant." There was a clear distaste on the witch-doctor's face as he said this, but resignation too. He was indentured not just to Van Hoek but to the belief system by which he lived. His god had made a Boer his saviour. Zikali had no choice but to go along with that, however much he resented it.

"We make a good team, Zikali and I," Van Hoek said. "He does whatever I ask, no complaining. That's a fair deal."

"He is your slave, in other words," said Holmes.

Zikali scowled, and I saw his gaze dart briefly to the gourd hanging from his left wrist. The gourd, I could only infer, was the whistle he used to direct the wolves' actions. All he need do was put it to his lips and pipe an instruction – an order to attack – and the animals would respond. It seemed ill-advised of Holmes, therefore, to antagonise him. With Zikali's wolves and Van Hoek's rifle ranged against us, we were in a very vulnerable position.

Holmes persisted nonetheless. "When Van Hoek came to Silasville, he dragged you along with him. Then, after the miners had become particularly troublesome, he put you to work."

"Why not? They knew I was a *nyanga*. It was a chance to wield my powers once more."

"Your powers, or simply your reputation? The Devil's Dust, after all, is nothing more mysterious than arsenic trioxide. You could claim it was magic, but it is merely poison. There is no sorcery involved in killing a man with poison, and to pretend otherwise is rank charlatanism."

"I am no charlatan!" Zikali hissed. "I dominated the rats and the pigeons I sent to harass you. They are meagre creatures, your British beasts, compared with those of my homeland. None has the majesty of the lion or the might of the elephant. Yet still they are mine to command."

"Precisely. Rats and pigeons. You can control pests and vermin."

"And these wolves." Zikali swept a hand around. "Don't forget them. I turned to my advantage their fortuitous escape from captivity. I sought them and found them, and easily became their master. *They* are hardly vermin."

"Still, that is all the once-supreme Zikali is capable of now, tricks with animals. You are a pale shadow of the wizard you were – if, that is, you were ever that wizardly to begin with."

Zikali cackled, but his eyes were ablaze and the laughter sounded more like cursing. "Hee hee! You seek to hurt my feelings, Mr Holmes, but all you are doing is ensuring that your death will not be swift but, rather, prolonged."

"And then," Holmes continued, as though Zikali had not even spoken, "to compound your pettiness, you killed Harry Quatermain. He turned up at Silasville, the son of your great enemy, and you could not restrain yourself, could you? Small-minded, petulant little devil that you are, you lashed out at an innocent young man, directing at him the hatred you feel for his father."

Quatermain's face went ashen.

"Is this true, Zikali?" he said in a cold voice. "It was you? Not Van Hoek?"

It seemed for a moment as though Zikali might deny it, but the stage was his, the spotlight was upon him, this was his time of triumph, and what had he to gain by lying?

"Of course," he said. "Of course it was I. An opportunity fell into my lap. A gift from the gods, one might call it. A young man named Quatermain, the spitting image of his father. He sauntered into town, and as soon as I learned of his presence I knew what I must do. I waylaid him in one of Silasville's less frequented corners. I blew *Uthuli lukaDeveli* in his face from the palm of my hand. He could not help but inhale it into his lungs, in great quantity, and thus was his life ended. I stood over him as he writhed on the ground. I pictured him as his father, dying at my feet. I hugged myself as I thought of the anguish this loss would cause Macumazahn. It was all too blissful for words."

"You—!"

Quatermain lunged for Zikali.

Two things happened at once. First, Van Hoek fired at Quatermain's feet. Second, Zikali raised Groan-Maker and positioned the axe's blade at Umslopogaas's throat.

Together, these two responses served to halt Quatermain in his tracks.

At the same time one of the wolves let out a snarl, its ears twitching. The gunshot had startled all of the creatures, and they shifted about in their disquiet. Zikali, seeing this, raised the gourd and blew into it. No discernible sound emerged, but the wolves calmed, resuming their attentive postures.

"We shall have none of that, Macumazahn," the dwarf said sneeringly. "You may not value your own life, but Umslopogaas's is another matter."

"I will kill you, Zikali," Quatermain intoned.

"How can you, when you will die before you even get close to me? Bluster away, great white hunter. I hold the power here, and I will prove it once and for all."

He lowered Groan-Maker until its blade was level with Umslopogaas's ribs. The taller Zulu was still insensible. He stood as unmoving as any statue.

"King Chaka was a cruel man," Zikali said. "He held sway over the Zulus through fear and intimidation. His punishment for treachery or desertion was execution by the very worst of tortures, all designed to shore up his tyranny. There is a kind of poetic justice in me inflicting just such a punishment now upon his illegitimate son."

"Zikali, no," said Quatermain imploringly.

"Umslopogaas will feel everything and not be able to react. I shall cut him repeatedly, as King Chaka would his victims, until the blood flows freely from a hundred gashes or more. I shall carve off pieces of him, sliver by sliver. He will wish to scream but he will find he cannot. By the time I am done, your beloved friend will be a tattered scarecrow, with lumps of his own flesh heaped around his feet. Try and stop me, Macumazahn, and you and your allies will die."

CHAPTER THIRTY

IMPASSE NO. 1

"He called you his 'pet', you know," said Holmes.

Zikali paused, the axe hovering at Umslopogaas's chest. He had ripped open the other Zulu's shirt to expose his bare torso. I saw again all those many scars and blenched at the thought of the further mutilations Zikali was about to inflict.

"Who?" the witch-doctor said. "Who called me a pet?"

"Van Hoek. I had it from Umslopogaas himself. When Van Hoek confronted him at Silasville, he threatened to unleash his 'pet' upon him. Meaning, quite clearly, you."

"I never said any such thing," Van Hoek protested. "It's a load of *blerrie* nonsense."

Zikali huffed impatiently. "That's enough from you, Mr Holmes. Another word and Mr Van Hoek will silence you for good. Now watch, Macumazahn. Watch as I slice your friend to ribbons. I want you to see him suffer. I rejoice, knowing that that will be a source of suffering to you, just like your son's death."

Umslopogaas's face was impassive, horribly so. He had no notion of the torment that was to come.

"Why would I make up such a detail?" said Holmes. "If you know anything about me, Zikali, you will know that I pride myself in the accuracy of my observations and my retention of facts. It would seem that to Van Hoek you are little better than a dog. Obedient, useful, something he can trust to do what is required, but no more than that."

"I swear, Mr Holmes, one more word from you…"

"But I have to ask myself," Holmes went on, "who really rules the roost in your partnership. You are effectively telling Van Hoek what to do here. How does that sit with you, Van Hoek? Not comfortably, I should imagine."

"You can just shut your mouth, Holmes," the Boer snapped. "I'll say it again, Zikali, I never called you a pet. That is a fiction."

And it *was* a fiction. Umslopogaas had told us nothing of the sort during his account of his brief sojourn at Silasville. Holmes was bluffing.

What I could not see was how this ploy, if successful, might change anything. Zikali was hell-bent on inflicting death-by-a-thousand-cuts on Umslopogaas, and Van Hoek was holding the rest of us at bay with that rifle of his, which I recognised as a Mauser, doubtless the same Mauser he had used to snipe at us in Kensington Gardens. Tweaking the noses of these two, as Holmes was doing, would not deflect them in any way from their plans. It would surely have the opposite effect, inciting them to greater barbarism.

"Shoot me then, Van Hoek," Holmes said. "That is what Zikali wants you to do. He has made it quite plain. Why are you hesitating? Is it that you will not be ordered about by a lesser creature? I am surprised, frankly, that you let him talk to you like that at all. He has ideas above his station."

"Final warning," the Boer growled.

The Mauser was still trained on Allan Quatermain, but Van

Hoek would only have to swing it a few degrees to bring Holmes into his sights.

"Just do it," Zikali said. "I am keen to get on with dismantling Umslopogaas. I cannot abide all these distractions."

The wolves encircling us seemed to echo the sentiment. They were restive again, sensitive to the tensions between us humans. A couple of them pawed at the ground, while a third swung its head from side to side agitatedly.

That was when it dawned on me what Holmes was really up to. Antagonisation was his goal, but not his only one.

The wolves were under Zikali's supervision, but his hold over them was far from complete. Resentment simmered in their wolfish hearts. Unlike their canine cousins, they could never be fully tamed or domesticated. The wild was too strong in them.

All it would take was for one of them, perhaps the head of the pack, to shake off the conditioning that Zikali had put in place. Then the entire pack might mutiny beyond the witch-doctor's power to check them. At the very least it would cause a distraction and provide an opening we could exploit.

"How humiliating it must be for you, Van Hoek," I said, joining in the needling. "Zikali is half your size and of a race whom your kind despise. And the reverse is true for you, Zikali. It galls you, does it not, to be beholden to one of the white men who have overrun your homeland and plundered its resources. How can you be in cahoots with him? Is he worthy of your allegiance? I think not."

"That's enough!" Van Hoek bellowed. "From both of you. Damn English. Always talking. Always maligning. I shouldn't be surprised if one day we Boers wage another war against you *uitlanders*. You accuse us of looking down our noses at the black man, but you treat us with the same condescension. You think we're backwards, pig-ignorant oafs. That will change, mark my words."

"Van Hoek," said Zikali, "stop haranguing them and just kill them. Not Quatermain, only the other two. Quatermain gets to live to see Umslopogaas die."

"Don't you bark orders at me," the Boer rejoined. "Show some respect. Remember who you are and who I am."

"You," said the witch-doctor, "are not my master, and I am not your slave."

"That's what you think."

The wolves were more jittery than ever. Quatermain seemed to have twigged to Holmes's scheme, too, for I could see him tensing. His legs were braced, his whole body quivering like a greyhound's. When the moment came – if it came – he was poised to act, and act fast.

"I should have left you in that river," Van Hoek said. "It would have made my life far easier."

"It would certainly have saved you from having to deal with the consequences of his vengeful impulses," said Holmes. "All of this is down to Zikali. Had he not killed Harry Quatermain, you would not now be having to clean up his mess. You would still be sitting pretty at Silasville. You would not have had to journey all the way to England and murder Bradford Wade. Wade's death must be preying on your conscience, Van Hoek. Zikali has saddled you with a burden of guilt you will be carrying for the rest of your days. I am sure you have no qualms about killing a black man, but a white man? Even if he is an Englishman…"

"I killed Englishmen in the war. Plenty."

"Wade was different. It was not in the heat of battle. It was a premeditated, cold-blooded act, and you had to do it yourself because Zikali for some reason could not. Zikali was unable to enter Wade's flat in order to administer the Devil's Dust, and I can venture a guess why. The protective fetish Wade bought."

"Now, that much is true," Van Hoek said jeeringly. "I told

Zikali I'd seen it through the window, while I was reconnoitring."

"And it worked. It hindered you, did it not, Zikali? It frightened you off."

"Not in the least," said the witch-doctor, but his tone of voice, and a slight ducking of the head, told a different story.

"You feared whatever power is contained within it. Some wizard you are, to be repelled by such a paltry trinket."

"No!"

Zikali screeched the negative, and at that selfsame instant one of the wolves darted forward, breaking rank. Its target was the witch-doctor.

Zikali let out a wail of alarm. The gourd flew to his lips and he puffed hard into it.

The wolf halted in its tracks, but its fangs were bared and its eyes regarded Zikali with barely mitigated animosity. This, I thought, must be the head of the pack, and it harboured enmity towards this human who had usurped its primacy.

Frantically Zikali blew into the gourd again, and the wolf, with reluctance, backed away, its tail slung low.

At that moment, spying his chance, Quatermain acted. While all attention was on the rogue wolf, he somersaulted across the ground, snatching up his elephant gun from its resting place between him and Van Hoek. As he came up out of the roll, he took aim.

The Boer gaped in astonishment.

The gun thundered.

Van Hoek had a head. Then he did not have a head.

At point-blank range, the double-eight cartridge simply obliterated everything above the neck. Blood sprayed in a fine mist. The Boer's decapitated body teetered, still clutching the Mauser. Then, buckling at the knees, it fell.

Instantly, the wolves turned tail and fled. It seemed they had

had quite enough. The noise and bloodshed within the clearing were all too much for their sensibilities. They were, by nature, wary creatures. They could have attacked us but instead, fully aware now of the harm we humans might cause them, they adopted the more prudent tactic of leaving us be.

Quatermain spun, locking his sights on Zikali.

The witch-doctor, however, had taken refuge behind Umslopogaas. Quatermain's friend now stood between him and his target, and Zikali, reaching up with both arms, was holding Groan-Maker's blade poised at Umslopogaas's neck. A trickle of blood leaked down from the axe's cutting edge.

"A flex of the wrist and I open his vein," he said. "Umslopogaas will not die the death I had planned for him, Macumazahn, but he will most assuredly die!"

CHAPTER THIRTY-ONE

IMPASSE NO. 2

We were again at an impasse. No longer was there Van Hoek with his rifle pinning Holmes, Quatermain and me in position, but Zikali still had the upper hand. He could slash open Umslopogaas's jugular with ease. He need not apply much more pressure to the blade, and Umslopogaas's lifeblood would spray out uncontainably.

"Zikali, I implore you," said Quatermain, "in the name of whatever cordiality we have shared in the past, do not do this. You have hurt me enough. You must know this. Harry's death is like a hole at the very heart of me, one that will never heal. I will carry the ache of it to my grave. Do not add Umslopogaas to your tally of victims, not in my name. Take me instead. I will willingly surrender to you, in return for you letting him go free, unharmed."

"Hee hee! Macumazahn begs. Macumazahn pleads. Once more does the Opener-of-Roads outmanoeuvre 'the man who gets up in the middle of the night.'"

"See? As a gesture of earnest, I am putting down my gun." Quatermain suited the action to the word.

Meanwhile, Holmes had dropped to a crouch. Out of the corner of my eye I saw him stealthily scoop something up from the ground and swiftly rise again. Zikali, peeking at Quatermain around Umslopogaas's hip, failed to notice.

"You may do with me as you wish," said Quatermain to Zikali, raising his hands aloft. "If the price of Umslopogaas's life is mine, it is one I shall gladly pay."

I darted a glance at Holmes. He was holding my revolver casually by his side, shielding it from Zikali's line of sight with his leg. His gaze was fixed upon Umslopogaas.

Looking at Umslopogaas myself, I realised that his eyes were clearer than before. Some semblance of sense had returned to him. Perhaps the hypnotic concoction with which Zikali had dosed him was at last wearing off, or else the report from Van Hoek's rifle and the yet more deafening report from Quatermain's elephant gun had succeeded in stirring him from his stupor. Whether it was the one reason, the other, or a combination of both, Umslopogaas was gradually coming round – and he and Holmes were sharing some exchange of confidences through the eyes alone.

Holmes gave the tiniest of nods. Umslopogaas answered with a barely detectable blink. Between them they had come to an understanding, and I had a horrible feeling I knew what it was.

Sure enough, my suspicions were confirmed when Holmes abruptly raised the revolver and shot Umslopogaas.

The bullet smacked into the meat of Umslopogaas's thigh, knocking his leg out from under him. The Zulu toppled to the ground, exposing a startled Zikali to view.

Holmes loosed off a second shot immediately. This one caught the dwarfish witch-doctor in the shoulder, the force of it spinning him around on the spot. His shrill shriek of pain was ear-piercing.

A third bullet hit him in the rump. Zikali was propelled flat onto his front, Groan-Maker tumbling from his grasp. He writhed in the leaf litter, emitting a series of whimpering mewls, which, coming from anyone but him, would have wrung pity from me.

Somehow he managed to regain his feet. He was bent over, bleeding profusely from his two wounds. His features were contorted with as much rage as pain. His chest heaved.

"A curse upon you!" he cried. "A curse upon you all! I spit upon you, Englishmen! A plague be on your land! May my blood envenom your soil! May Umkulu-kulu bring fire and destruction to all you hold dear! May you never know a moment's peace in your lives! May you perish without offspring, unmourned, unloved, as miserable as paupers!"

"For heaven's sake, Zikali," said Quatermain, retrieving his gun, "will you just simply *die*."

Before he could empty the second barrel at the witch-doctor, however, a sleek shape darted out from the trees.

It was one of the wolves – the same one, I thought, that had launched an abortive attack on Zikali a short while earlier. Now it charged towards the witch-doctor with silent, sinuous grace, clearly bent on finishing what it had started.

At the sight of the wolf, Zikali reached for the gourd at his wrist, only to discover that the hard, globular fruit had cracked open when he fell. As a whistle it was now useless. He had no power to rein in the wolf, although I suspect that even if the whistle had been intact, it would have done him no good. He was wounded and in distress, after all, and there is nothing that arouses a carnivore's appetite more than injured prey. The marauding beast would have paid no heed to his commands.

A look of stark terror came over Zikali's face as this very same realisation struck home. He turned on his heel and hobbled towards the cave. Somehow he believed he might find sanctuary there.

To his credit, he almost gained the cave mouth before the wolf overtook him. It pounced, catching him by the throat in its jaws and bringing him to the ground.

As Zikali was dragged down, the remaining wolves poured into the clearing. They converged on the witch-doctor, and at that point I averted my gaze. Loathsome though Zikali was, I had no desire to watch what followed.

Instead, I listened. The cacophony of crunching and rending and screaming lasted a full minute, and when it stopped and I finally dared look again, it was to see two of the wolves playing tug-of-war with some unidentifiable body part while the rest, their muzzles smeared and clotted with blood, gorged themselves on various wet, ragged hunks of flesh strewn over the ground.

In the interim, Quatermain and Holmes had gathered up Umslopogaas and were holding him erect between them. Umslopogaas, though in pain and barely conscious, had nonetheless retained the presence of mind to collect his beloved Groan-Maker from where Zikali had dropped it.

"Come, Watson," Holmes said. "Let us make good our escape while the wolves are otherwise occupied. They may eat their fill of Zikali and be too heavy-bellied to pursue us. They may, on the other hand, consider one so small merely the *hors d'oeuvres*, whereby we become the main course."

I needed no further urging.

With haste we put the clearing behind us, and I for one was glad to see the back of it. I promised myself there and then that I would never again enter Epping Forest, not for love or money. It is a vow I have kept to this very day.

CHAPTER THIRTY-TWO

THE MAGIC OF SCIENCE AND THE SCIENCE OF MAGIC

Sherlock Holmes looked up from his chemistry bench, where he had been busy for some while.

"It is as I thought," he said. "See?"

He held up a small ceramic bowl, the interior of which was lined with a silvery-black deposit. Quatermain and I had just watched him suspend the bowl upside down over a test tube filled with a greyish solution. He had used a match to ignite the gas which the solution was giving off and had allowed the resultant flame to stain the inside of the bowl.

"The colour and intensity of the residue you are looking at confirms my theory," he explained. "I have subjected a sample of the table salt to the Marsh Test, adding zinc and hydrogen sulphide. When oxidised by fire, the fumes arising from the solution become water vapour and arsine gas. The latter, as it cools, sublimes to leave this distinctive silvery-black stain. There can be no question about it. The salt contains the Devil's Dust, and the Devil's Dust is arsenic trioxide."

The sample came from a salt cellar from Mrs Biddulph's

house. The accompanying pepper pot, the salt cellar's near twin, also contained arsenic trioxide. Holmes estimated that the ratio of condiment to Devil's Dust in each instance was two parts to one.

"At such a concentration, a liberal sprinkling of either the salt or the pepper onto his mutton stew would have been more than enough to kill Bradford Wade. Did you know that the French used to call arsenic *poudre de succession* – inheritance powder? Before James Marsh developed his test it was a favourite of poisoners because it was odourless and tasteless. So I think we may once and for all discount any possibility of wizardly doings on the part of Zikali of Black Kloof. If the Devil's Dust is anything to go by, his magic was mere parlour tricks, full of misdirection and sleight of hand, along with a smattering of pharmacology. More doctor than witch, one might say."

"You are wrong," said Quatermain.

"You still maintain that he was genuinely a sorcerer?"

"All I can tell you is that in Africa I saw Zikali perform what can only be called miracles – him and others of his ilk."

"Yet there is nothing he did while in England that cannot be accounted for in rational, scientific terms."

"What if it is a matter of perspective?" I said. "That which to the scientifically-minded is provable by science is, to the mind of someone who lives a life steeped in magical lore, magic. The typical Englishman believes in material things more than he does in magic, therefore magic does not work for him."

"You mean Zikali was unable to use true witchcraft while in England," Quatermain said, taking up my theme, "because the English aversion towards such phenomena prevented it? Perhaps. In Africa, things are very different, that much is certain. If only Umslopogaas were conscious right now. He would back up my argument strenuously."

The Zulu was at present lying in my bed, still under sedation after the procedure of having an Eley's No. 2 round extricated from his leg. Holmes had placed the shot with extraordinary precision so that the bullet struck neither bone nor artery and lodged in the muscle near the surface. Removing it had been much less tricky than removing the bullet Starkey had fired into Quatermain's arm, and somewhat less excruciating for the patient, though still far from pleasant. I expected Umslopogaas to make a full recovery.

Between leaving the camp on Victoria Park and coming to his senses in the clearing at Epping Forest shortly before he gave Holmes consent to shoot him, Umslopogaas remembered nothing. His run of fifteen-odd miles from the one location to the other was not even a blur; it was a complete blank. His last memory in the park was of eating his breakfast, then beginning to feel lightheaded. He had the vaguest recollection of hearing a voice repeating his name, which enticed him out from the thicket. The voice being familiar, he could not help but investigate its origin. If it was not that of Zikali himself, he had thought, then it was someone doing a very good imitation of the witch-doctor.

"At any rate," said Holmes, "what remains beyond debate is that the murder weapon was this innocuous-looking cruet set, which Mrs Biddulph kept for her tenant's use only. All Van Hoek had to do was unscrew the caps on each of the pots, pour in the Devil's Dust, and let the unfortunate Wade do the rest himself. The real devilry of it was that in Ada Biddulph, Van Hoek had the perfect scapegoat, whether he realised it or not."

"Because she was rumoured to have poisoned her husband," I said.

Holmes nodded. "Naturally the police would leap to the conclusion that she was up to no good again, this time her victim being her lodger. When someone is already under a cloud of suspicion it doesn't take much for a rain of accusation to start to fall. The poor woman might well have gone to the gallows for a crime she did not commit. Her great good luck was to be friends with Mrs Hudson, and Mrs Hudson's great good luck was to have Sherlock Holmes as a lodger."

"Mrs Hudson might dispute the second part of that sentence in general terms, but not in this specific instance."

"Sharp, Watson. For one who has not slept in nearly thirty-six hours, you still have your wits about you."

I yawned heavily. I would have been glad of my bed just then, were Umslopogaas not occupying it.

"I will apprise Lestrade of my findings," Holmes continued, "and steer him towards Dick Turpin's cave, where the mortal remains of our two miscreants await. I shall warn him about the wolves, although I imagine they will be long gone by the time he gets there. There is not much left of Zikali, of course, and I wonder if the wolves might not have visited the same depredations upon Van Hoek. Van Hoek's boot, however, ought to be intact, and that is the clinching piece of evidence, along with the cruets."

"What about the Fanthorpes?" said Quatermain. "They should face justice, should they not? Van Hoek and Zikali have paid the penalty for their crimes, but the Fanthorpes deserve punishment too."

"But for what, Quatermain? That is the problem. It will be difficult, if not nigh impossible, to connect the Fanthorpes to anything Van Hoek and Zikali did. The three brothers sit in their ivory tower in Mayfair, insulated from the day-to-day running of their company. The nitty-gritty affairs, the things that actually go on at their mines in foreign lands, remain at arm's length from them. Even if they did know about any shady activities or cruel practices, they can deny it with plausibility. They are, what is more, wealthy and powerful men. They are firmly entrenched within the nation's elite and have the proverbial friends in high places. I fear that any attempt to prosecute them over this business will be doomed to failure. It is as Daniel Greensmith said: 'Unless one possesses watertight proof of malfeasance, their kind are more or less untouchable.'"

"That is a damnable nuisance," Quatermain said hotly.

"It is a regrettable fact of life," Holmes said coolly. "Believe me, if I felt it was in my power to bring the Fanthorpes down, I would. We will just have to hope that some higher authority holds them to account for any wrongdoing they may have committed – even if that must occur not in this life but the next."

A solemn silence settled over us, as outside a blustery rain began to rattle against the windowpanes. Holmes accordingly lit a fire, and together we three watched its flickering birth and growth.

Eventually we heard the sounds of Umslopogaas stirring, and soon the Zulu limped into the sitting-room. His face was wan but he braved a smile.

"Dr John H. Watson of the University of London and Netley Hospital," said he, hands clasped at his chest as if in prayer. "I owe you my life and the continued use of my leg."

"Hardly," I said. "Any doctor could have done what I did."

"But not nearly as well. Let me thank you, Doctor." He did by means of a tight, back-slapping embrace. "I will tell everyone about your tremendous surgical skills. The name of Dr Watson will resound through all of Africa. You will be famed from Tunis to Port Elizabeth, from Sierra Leone to the Gulf of Aden. The same goes for you, the venerable Mr Sherlock Holmes of Baker Street, whose accuracy with a gun rivals that of Macumazahn himself."

"Steady there, Umslopogaas," said Quatermain mock-sternly. "You can take bongering too far, you know."

Umslopogaas chuckled. "If you gallant gentlemen ever should come to my country, rest assured you shall be received as heroes. Nowhere will you not be made to feel at home. Nowhere will the finest meals not be given you and the loudest songs not sung in your praise. So I swear, upon my life."

"One day we may well hold you to that promise," said Holmes.

After I had checked the dressing on Umslopogaas's wound, Quatermain began making noises about leaving. "We have imposed upon you long enough, gentlemen, and are in danger of outstaying our welcome."

"Not at all," I said, but Quatermain's mind was made up.

"You are well enough to walk, Umslopogaas?" he said.

"I am as fit as a fiddle!"

"Then let us make for King's Cross. I believe we may catch the early evening train to York if we hurry."

Farewells were said, hearty handshakes shared, and off went Hunter Quatermain and his companion out into the squall.

Holmes and I watched them from the window as they headed off down Baker Street, shoulders hunched against the weather. Each carried his preferred weapon, wrapped in a length of canvas supplied by Mrs Hudson. Each walked with a hitch in his stride.

"Odd couple," Holmes mused. "Quite unalike, yet both benefiting from the differences between them, the one making up for that which the other lacks."

"Not so unusual really," I said, but the subtext of the remark seemed lost on my friend.

"Quatermain is quite the contradiction, isn't he?" he said. "He is the British colonialist writ large, thrusting like a dagger into our overseas dominions, taking what he can with barely a glimmer of conscience. Yet one is hard pressed to dislike him and may even find him admirable. He has few illusions about himself. He is devoid of self-doubt. He means well. That said, he is amongst the last of his kind, part of a dying breed. His era is slowly but surely coming to an end, and I wonder what will replace it. An era of intellect and uncertainty, maybe, for the two things invariably go together. A new age of conscience and questioning. It seems as unavoidable as the turn of the seasons."

His sigh was melancholy and a tad wistful.

"But I think, still, that Allan Quatermain – antiquated though he is – has one great adventure left in him yet. His time is not quite through."

AFTERWORD

Holmes was correct in his prediction. Allan Quatermain did have one great adventure left in him. It has been chronicled by the author Henry Rider Haggard under the somewhat uninspired title *Allan Quatermain*. Indeed, Haggard has by now – 1904 – published some nine volumes detailing Quatermain's exploits, based upon notes left by the man himself and upon the recollections of his friend Sir Henry Curtis, and I am sure there are more to come.

Allan Quatermain tells of Quatermain's final trip to Africa. Not long after parting company with us, he set off with Sir Henry and Captain Good in search of a fabled white race living in a remote, unexplored territory beyond Mount Lekakisera called Elgumi.

The book also tells of Quatermain's death on that expedition, from a wound to the lung gained valiantly in pitched battle. Umslopogaas's death is likewise recorded in the book, it, too, the result of battle. I cannot help but think that neither Macumazahn nor the old Zulu warrior would have wished to die any other way.

Certain parts of the narrative of *Allan Quatermain* are at odds with the facts presented here in this book of mine. For instance, Quatermain sticks firmly to the story that the cause of his son Harry's death was smallpox. Perhaps the truth was too painful for him to enshrine in prose.

Similarly, he recounts meeting up with Umslopogaas in an early chapter of *Allan Quatermain* as though the two of them had not seen each other in years; whereas, as the evidence in these pages shows, they had been in England together not long beforehand. Why Quatermain omitted to mention their recent escapades upon these shores – or make any reference to Sherlock Holmes and myself – I do not know. Again, I suspect it is because his son's death cast such a grim pall over the events. He would rather not think about Harry, Bradford Wade, Daniel Greensmith, Starkey, the Devil's Dust or any of it. He would rather draw a discreet veil over the whole proceedings.

One final note. The Fanthorpe brothers did get their comeuppance, after a fashion. All three succumbed to a violent bout of gastroenteritis after luncheon at their headquarters. So severe were the effects of the illness, blamed on spoiled shellfish, that they fell into comas and perished within hours of one another.

The fact that Mrs Biddulph's cruet set was no longer in our rooms after Quatermain departed has, I am sure, no bearing whatsoever on the above.

J.H.W.

ACKNOWLEDGEMENTS

My thanks to Justin Webb for his help translating the title phrase of the novel into the Zulu language, and to Titanic editorial tag-team Ella Chappell and Joanna Harwood and copy-editor Sam Matthews, who between them rigorously vetted my references to Conan Doyle, Haggard, and geographical and historical fact, and who have spared me more than a few blushes.

J.M.H.L.

ABOUT THE AUTHOR

James Lovegrove is the *New York Times* best-selling author of *The Age of Odin*, the third novel in his critically-acclaimed *Pantheon* military SF series. He was short-listed for the Arthur C. Clarke Award in 1998 for his novel *Days* and for the John W. Campbell Memorial Award in 2004 for his novel *Untied Kingdom*. He also reviews fiction for the *Financial Times*. He has written *Sherlock Holmes: The Stuff of Nightmares*, *Sherlock Holmes: Gods of War*, *Sherlock Holmes: The Thinking Engine* and *Sherlock Holmes: The Labyrinth of Death* for Titan Books; his new series, *The Cthulhu Casebooks*, launched in 2016 with *Sherlock Holmes and the Shadwell Shadows*.

SHERLOCK HOLMES
CRY OF THE INNOCENTS
Cavan Scott

It is 1891, and a Catholic priest arrives at 221B Baker Street, only to utter the words "*il corpe*" before suddenly dropping dead.

Though the man's death is attributed to cholera, when news of another dead priest reaches Holmes, he becomes convinced that the men have been poisoned. He and Watson learn that the victims were on a mission from the Vatican to investigate a miracle; it is said that the body of eighteenth-century philanthropist and slave trader Edwyn Warwick has not decomposed. But should the Pope canonise a man who made his fortune through slavery? And when Warwick's body is stolen, it becomes clear that the priests' mission has attracted the attention of a deadly conspiracy…

PRAISE FOR CAVAN SCOTT
"Many memorable moments… excellent."
Starburst

"Utterly charming, comprehensively Sherlockian, and possessed of a wry narrator." **Criminal Element**

"Memorable and enjoyable… One of the best stories I've ever read."
Wondrous Reads

TITANBOOKS.COM

SHERLOCK HOLMES
THE PATCHWORK DEVIL
Cavan Scott

It is 1919, and while the world celebrates the signing of the Treaty of Versailles, Holmes and Watson are called to a grisly discovery.

A severed hand has been found on the bank of the Thames, a hand belonging to a soldier who supposedly died in the trenches two years ago. But the hand is fresh, and shows signs that it was recently amputated. So how has it ended up back in London two years after its owner was killed in France? Warned by Sherlock's brother Mycroft to cease their investigation, and only barely surviving an attack by a superhuman creature, Holmes and Watson begin to suspect a conspiracy at the very heart of the British government…

"Scott poses an intriguing puzzle for an older Holmes and Watson to tackle." ***Publishers Weekly***

"Interesting and exciting in ways that few Holmes stories are these days." ***San Francisco Book Review***

"A thrilling tale for Scott's debut in the Sherlock Holmes world."
Sci-Fi Bulletin

TITANBOOKS.COM

SHERLOCK HOLMES
LABYRINTH OF DEATH
James Lovegrove

It is 1895, and Sherlock Holmes's new client is a high court judge, whose free-spirited daughter has disappeared without a trace.

Holmes and Watson discover that the missing woman – Hannah Woolfson – was herself on the trail of a missing person, her close friend Sophia. Sophia was recruited to a group known as the Elysians, a quasi-religious sect obsessed with Ancient Greek myths and rituals, run by the charismatic Sir Philip Buchanan. Hannah has joined the Elysians under an assumed name, convinced that her friend has been murdered. Holmes agrees that she should continue as his agent within the secretive yet seemingly harmless cult, yet Watson is convinced Hannah is in terrible danger. For Sir Philip has dreams of improving humanity through classical ideals, and at any cost…

"A writer of real authority and one worthy of taking the reader back to the dangerous streets of Victorian London in the company of the Great Detective." **Crime Time**

"Lovegrove does a convincing job of capturing Watson's voice."
Publishers Weekly

TITANBOOKS.COM

SHERLOCK HOLMES
THE THINKING ENGINE
James Lovegrove

It is 1895, and Sherlock Holmes is settling back into life as a consulting detective at 221B Baker Street, when he and Watson learn of strange goings-on amidst the dreaming spires of Oxford.

A Professor Quantock has built a wondrous computational device, which he claims is capable of analytical thought to rival the cleverest men alive. Naturally Sherlock Holmes cannot ignore this challenge. He and Watson travel to Oxford, where a battle of wits ensues between the great detective and his mechanical counterpart as they compete to see which of them can be first to solve a series of crimes, from a bloody murder to a missing athlete. But as man and machine vie for supremacy, it becomes clear that the Thinking Engine has its own agenda...

"The plot, like the device, is ingenious, with a chilling twist... an entertaining, intelligent and pacy read."
The Sherlock Holmes Journal

"Lovegrove knows his Holmes trivia and delivers a great mystery that will fans will enjoy, with plenty of winks and nods to the canon."
Geek Dad

"I think Conan Doyle would have enjoyed reading this story: the concept of an intelligent, self-aware Thinking Engine is brilliance itself." **The Book Bag**
TITANBOOKS.COM

SHERLOCK HOLMES
GODS OF WAR
James Lovegrove

It is 1913, and Dr Watson is visiting Sherlock Holmes at his retirement cottage near Eastbourne when tragedy strikes: the body of a young man, Patrick Mallinson, is found under the cliffs of Beachy Head.

The dead man's father, a wealthy businessman, engages Holmes to prove that his son committed suicide, the result of a failed love affair with an older woman. Yet the woman in question insists that there is more to Patrick's death. She has seen mysterious symbols drawn on his body, and fears that he was under the influence of a malevolent cult. When an attempt is made on Watson's life, it seems that she may be proved right. The threat of war hangs over England, and there is no telling what sinister forces are at work…

"Lovegrove has once again packed his novel with incident and suspense." **Fantasy Book Review**

"An atmospheric mystery which shows just why Lovegrove has become a force to be reckoned with in genre fiction. More, please." *Starburst*

"A very entertaining read with a fast-moving, intriguing plot." **The Consulting Detective**

TITANBOOKS.COM

SHERLOCK HOLMES
THE STUFF OF NIGHTMARES
James Lovegrove

A spate of bombings has hit London, causing untold damage and loss of life. Meanwhile a strangely garbed figure has been spied haunting the rooftops and grimy back alleys of the capital.

Sherlock Holmes believes this strange masked man may hold the key to the attacks. He moves with the extraordinary agility of a latter-day Spring-Heeled Jack. He possesses weaponry and armour of unprecedented sophistication. He is known only by the name Baron Cauchemar, and he appears to be a scourge of crime and villainy. But is he all that he seems? Holmes and his faithful companion Dr Watson are about to embark on one of their strangest and most exhilarating adventures yet.

"[A] tremendously accomplished thriller which leaves the reader in no doubt that they are in the hands of a confident and skilful craftsman."
Starburst

"Dramatic, gripping, exciting and respectful to its source material, I thoroughly enjoyed every surprise and twist as the story unfolded."
Fantasy Book Review

"This is delicious stuff, marrying the standard notions of Holmesiana with the kind of imagination we expect from Lovegrove."
Crime Time

TITANBOOKS.COM

SHERLOCK HOLMES
THE SPIRIT BOX
George Mann

German zeppelins rain down death and destruction on London, and Dr Watson is grieving for his nephew, killed on the fields of France.

A cryptic summons from Mycroft Holmes reunites Watson with his one-time companion, as Sherlock comes out of retirement, tasked with solving three unexplained deaths. A politician has drowned in the Thames after giving a pro-German speech; a soldier suggests surrender before feeding himself to a tiger; and a suffragette renounces women's liberation and throws herself under a train. Are these apparent suicides something more sinister, something to do with the mysterious Spirit Box? Their investigation leads them to Ravensthorpe House, and the curious Seaton Underwood, a man whose spectrographs are said to capture men's souls…

"Arthur Conan Doyle was a master storyteller, and it takes comparable talent to give Holmes a second life… Mann is one of the few to get close to the target." **Daily Mail**

"I would highly recommend this… a fun read." **Fantasy Book Review**

"Our only complaint is that it is over too soon." *Starburst*

"An entertaining read." **Eurocrime**

TITANBOOKS.COM

SHERLOCK HOLMES
THE WILL OF THE DEAD
George Mann

A rich, elderly man has fallen to his death, and his will is nowhere to be found. A tragic accident or something more sinister? The dead man's nephew comes to Baker Street to beg for Sherlock Holmes's help. Without the will he fears he will be left penniless, the entire inheritance passing to his cousin. But just as Holmes and Watson start their investigation, a mysterious new claimant to the estate appears. Does this prove that the old man was murdered?

Meanwhile Inspector Charles Bainbridge is trying to solve the case of the "iron men", mechanical steam-powered giants carrying out daring jewellery robberies. But how do you stop a machine that feels no pain and needs no rest? He too may need to call on the expertise of Sherlock Holmes.

"Mann clearly knows his Holmes, knows what works… the book is all the better for it." **Crime Fiction Lover**

"Mann writes Holmes in an eloquent way, capturing the period of the piece perfectly… this is a must read." **Cult Den**

"An amazing story… Even in the established world of Sherlock Holmes, George Mann is a strong voice and sets himself apart!"
Book Plank

TITANBOOKS.COM

For more fantastic fiction, author events, competitions,
limited editions and more

VISIT OUR WEBSITE
titanbooks.com

LIKE US ON FACEBOOK
facebook.com/titanbooks

FOLLOW US ON TWITTER
@TitanBooks

EMAIL US
readerfeedback@titanemail.com